Snow Wolf
Wolves of Willow Bend

Heather Long

Snow Wolf
Wolves of Willow Bend
By: Heather Long
Edited by: Virginia Nelson
Published by Heather Long
© 2015 Heather Long
ISBN-13: 978-0-9970732-3-2
Cover Art by Scott Carpenter

Snow Wolf

Ranae is the youngest of the Buckleys and the only girl amongst three powerful male siblings. Her restlessness and dominant nature affected her every relationship within Willow Bend, not to mention testing the patience of her Alpha. Apprenticeship to the Hunters fed her desire for a purpose. When her Alpha and eldest brother ask her to undertake a mission to the Yukon territory, she's thrilled at the opportunity to be useful. Clashing with the Alpha was the last thing she expected on the dangerous assignment.

The oldest Alpha in the U.S. packs lives a gray existence. The loss of his mate so many decades before wears away at him until he doesn't give a damn about anything. The problems of the other packs are not his, and he prefers to be left to his isolation. The arrival of the Chief Enforcer annoys him, but it is the wolf traveling with him who wakes the predator in Diesel. The scent of mate clings to her, but she rejects his overtures and challenges him on every level.

War may be coming for the Yukon, but Diesel's battle is very personal…

Series So Far

Wolf At Law
(prequel)
Ryan & Tiffany

Wolf Bite
Mason & Alexis

Caged Wolf
A.J. & Vivian

Wolf Claim
Owen & Gillian

Wolf Next Door
Tyler & Claire

Rogue Wolf
Salvatore & Margo

Bayou Wolf
Lincoln & Serafina

Untamed Wolf
Dylan & Chrystal

Wolf with Benefits
Matt & Shiloh

River Wolf
Brett & Colby

Single Wicked Wolf
Giovanni & Murphy

Desert Wolf
Cassius & Sovvan

U.S. Pack Territories

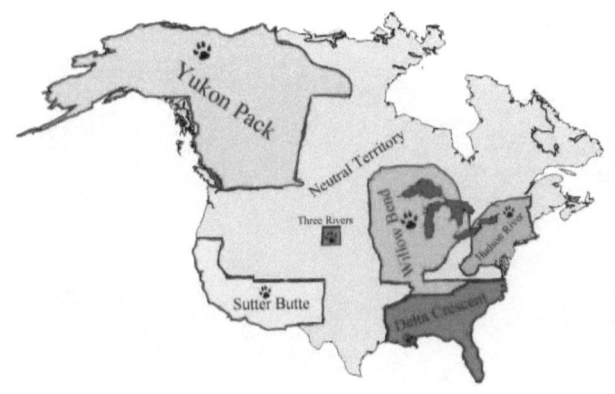

Yukon Wolves

Yukon Wolves

Diesel – Alpha of the Yukon pack.
Cheryl "Fluff" Carter - Sentry, Yukon
Benjamin "Chowder" Strieb – Healer, Yukon – Brother to Grinder
Gerald "Grinder" Strieb – Sentry, Yukon – Brother to Chowder
Montana - Second to the Alpha of the Yukon pack, she looks after most administrative tasks.
Deidre - Elder of the Yukon pack, mother of Amara.
Demon - Yukon youth.
Boone - Sentry of the Yukon
Zipper - Sentry of the Yukon

Wolves of Willow Bend

Ranae Buckley - Hunter to Willow Bend, sister to A.J., Linc, and Tyler. Daughter of Virgil and Claudia.
Tyler Buckley - Mechanic, brother to A.J., Linc and Ranae. Mated to Claire.
Mason Clayborne—Alpha of Willow Bend, mate of Alexis, father of Melissa.
AJ Buckley – Second of Willow Bend, brother to Tyler, Linc and Ranae. Mated to Vivian.

Enforcers

Julian – Chief Enforcer, most senior Enforcer for the U.S.

Sutter Butte Wolves

Trask – Hunter of Sutter Butte.

Hudson River

Luc Danes - Best friend to Brett Dalton, and second to the Alpha of Hudson River.

Delta Crescent Wolves

Serafina Andre-Buckley – Alpha of Delta Crescent, she remains skeptical of sending her Omega into such a dangerous situation. Mated to Linc Buckley

Linc Buckley – Formerly of Willow Bend, the Alpha's mate acts as both her sounding board and best friend.

Etienne Andre – Lieutenant, Delta Crescent – Serafina's brother and her second in command.

Lebeninsk Wolves

Leonid Petrov - Alpha of Lebeninsk.

Chapter One

Ranae maintained her stillness and refused to tap her foot, no matter how long it took her suitcase to appear on the luggage carousel. Her flight had been delayed, and she'd spent the past three hours squeezed into a plane with several hostile passengers, all of whom radiated the desire to be at their destination. The stench of their fury polluted the baggage claim air. Several snapped comments on their phones about the delay, others scrambled to make arrangements for rental vehicles, passenger pickup and more.

Focusing on her breathing, Ranae kept her pulse steady. Frankly, one more bitchy remark from the over-coifed, heavily made-up woman to her left and she might give in to the urge to punch her. No one on the flight had been happy, but the eddies of negativity swirling around them didn't help anyone. Over half the luggage had been unloaded, yet still no sign of her powder blue suitcase. The atrocious color had been her mother's idea—it made spotting her case easy and hopefully discouraged anyone from grabbing her luggage by mistake.

A buzzing in her back pocket provided a distraction from counting her breaths. Easing the phone out, she checked the screen. A.J.'s face stared up at her, with his eyes crossed. He hated the photo. It was why she used it for his contact information

Hitting answer, she put the phone to her ear. "Yes, big brother mine, I'm here. I texted you as soon as we taxied to the gate."

"Good flight?"

"Peachy." She lied through her gritted teeth. "Great passengers. Calm skies. Timely landing." The last was at least partially true. If she'd been sandwiched in there much longer, she might have had to hurt someone.

A.J. laughed. "Good to know. Change of plans. Rent a car and head about an hour away to Paine Airfield. Hanger four. Julian will meet you there."

"Roger that." Relief flowed through her veins. She would have time to herself before having to deal with the Chief Enforcer. The assignment to go to the Yukon thrilled and terrified her in equal parts. Having to work with the biggest, baddest of the Enforcers? Not her idea of a walk in the park. The faith in her demonstrated by Mason's request buoyed her. "Something wrong?"

Her brother could have texted the information.

"Nope. Just wanted to make sure you were really doing okay." After spending several years isolated from pack and family during his internment in prison, A.J. had come home changed, stronger, yet he was still her brother.

Scanning the carousel, she released a chuckle as much to soothe him as to ease her own nerves. "I'm okay. A little stressed, but I think the drive sounds like a good idea."

"Excellent. If you have any questions or concerns, you call me, right?"

"Of course." Though rumor had it the Yukon didn't have a lot in the way of cellular signal. "It'll be fine, big brother. I'm a glorified messenger."

"Yes, and no." Trust A.J. not to sugarcoat it. "Diesel isn't the most stable or friendly. You're going to have to decide whether you need to charm him or piss him off to get a response."

Did he seriously just tell her to piss an Alpha off? "I'm sorry, who are you and what did you do with my brother?" Linc would have told her to be sweet or leave him alone. Ty would have insisted on going with her. A.J.? He didn't seem to have any reservations about her capabilities or encouraging her strengths.

Masculine warmth flooded A.J.'s laughter. "I'm right here, trouble. I know you're not a child anymore. You shouldn't have grown up so fast on me, but since you did—I have faith in you. It's been a hard couple of years, no one knows that better than me. I also watched you get a grip on your temper, throw yourself into your studies, and your mentor has nothing but positive things to say about you. You can do this...but you're the woman on the ground. We have to trust your judgment."

The assignment was important. Russian wolves had attacked two North American packs, either through direct interdiction via a Russian pack member or through insurgents seeking new territory. Based on the briefing A.J. gave her, they didn't know whether they were dealing with rogues, a pack, or something else. In the meanwhile, her other brothers were in the middle of the issue—one in Sutter Butte with his mate and the other in Delta Crescent with his. She was the Buckley on point.

"I won't let you down."

"I know you won't. You got this. Just call in

and let me know how it's going so that Mom doesn't move in and smack me every time the phone rings and it isn't you."

Humor welled up, displacing more of her anxiety. "Tell her to call Ty and bug him about coming home." She hated that he was in Sutter Butte. The pack's bad reputation preceded it…not to mention Claire's history with them. *Don't think about Claire.* She and her sister-in-law had made a sort of peace after Ranae's attack earned her severe punishment from Mason.

"Oh, I like that idea." A door closed in the background, despite the constant hum of humanity around her she even caught A.J.'s soft sigh. "Say hello to Ranae, Vivian."

"Hello, little sister." Game designer and turned wolf, Vivian made A.J. happy. Ranae loved how ridiculously adorable they were.

"How is my niece or nephew to be?" Vivian was in the last trimester of her pregnancy—all big belly and glowing with happiness.

"Active." The nearness of her voice suggested she'd either leaned into A.J. or perhaps her brother had settled in next to her. "I can barely keep up with the one in these developing stages, I can't imagine how your mom handled three."

Ranae snorted. "It was more about corralling them and working them until they had to sleep."

"True."

"Be nice," A.J. said with a soft chuckle, before a kiss echoed over the phone line. "Get the job done, trouble. Call if you need me."

"I promise." No way in hell she'd pull A.J.

from his pregnant mate. Thankfully her blue suitcase chose that exact moment to appear. "I gotta go so I can rent that car. Talk to you soon."

"Soon." The vaguest hint of command reinforced the word, but Ranae smiled as she disconnected the call. Her brothers were overprotective as hell, but A.J. gave her the job in the first place. Grabbing her suitcase, she side-stepped the bitch scowling at the carousel looking for her own bags and followed the signs for car rentals.

A hint of wolf drifted on the air, and she scanned the other passengers. Too many bodies in the close confines made it hard to pinpoint the scent. Another waft of wolf brushed her nostrils, and she pivoted with her phone in hand. *Female*. So, not the Chief Enforcer she'd been scheduled to meet. If another Enforcer had been dispatched to greet her, A.J. would have given her a heads up.

Seattle was outside of claimed territory. Considered neutral, it could be anyone…but with worry about Russians still on her mind, she'd be more comfortable identifying the source. Resuming her path toward the rental car desks, she maintained her watchful awareness. The last thing she wanted was a fight in the middle of a crowded airport, but she couldn't afford an ambush either.

Adjusting her grip on the suitcase, she studied every person who passed her. No other hints of wolf pursued her as she discussed renting the vehicle, handed over her credit card, and then signed the contract and received the keys. Outside the airport, smokers occluded the air, but she didn't detect the other wolf.

I'll mention it to the Julian. They know where all the Lone Wolves are. Better to be certain, especially when she had a job to do. *Look out Yukon, here I come.*

Her hour-long drive took closer to two, but she arrived at Paine Field after devouring a hot sandwich and draining an even hotter cup of coffee. Eating didn't solve problems, but it sure went along way to soothing her ruffled fur after the flight. Her phone remained silent even after she sent a text message to Julian to let him know of the delay. Well, it wasn't like he had to answer her. Theoretically, he wouldn't leave without her either.

At the gate, she presented her identification to the security guard and the information about her flight. After he verified it, he gave her directions to the hangar and noted her license plate and information. It took her five minutes to arrive at hangar six and find a parking spot. Each hangar had a half-dozen dedicated spaces for vehicles. Parked, she stepped out into the sunshine, the air was damp and cool despite the brightness of the day.

Oil, concrete, and mechanical scents perfumed the breeze. Acrid and a little harsh, but a breeze stirred the smells and carried a hint of salt water. She unloaded her suitcase, then slid the strap of her purse crosswise over her torso before cleaning her trash out of the vehicle and locking her keys under the frame in the key coded box.

She paused outside the hangar door and deposited her trash in the bin before entering. Inside, she paused to let her eyes acclimate to the dimness.

The scent of wolf flooded her nostrils. *Male. Powerful. Definitely present.*

Searching the space, she focused on the platinum blond male standing next to a small plane. *Small? It's a fucking toy.* Her gut clenched. She'd seen commuter planes before, but this one seemed ready for amphibious landing and the body would put her practically in the Enforcer's lap.

"Good afternoon, Ranae Buckley. I don't bite." The wolf said by way of greeting.

Yeah, sure he didn't.

Stiffening her spine, she walked across the hangar toward him. Dominance rolled off him in waves, but she kept her chin high. He wasn't her Alpha, and she was there under orders. Still, when his gaze collided with hers as she narrowed the space between them, she couldn't resist darting a glance down.

Dammit.

Thankfully, he didn't smile. Instead, he looked her over. "You should change before we board. We're taking off in fifteen minutes."

What was wrong with what she had on? She glanced down at her jeans, cable knit sweater and boots.

"Layers, little girl. Where we're going it's below freezing more often than it is above. Once we land, we need to hustle to make it to their base camp." He pointed across the hangar. "Bathrooms are that way. Get moving."

Resisting the order, she canted her head. "Good afternoon to you, Julian." Proud of her resolve, she raised her eyebrows. "I'm about to spend several hours inside that tin can, I don't want to get cooked with heat exhaustion. Thanks." She had thermals included in her packing, her mother wouldn't let her leave Willow Bend without going over every single item she packed.

"As you wish." The sardonic note wasn't lost on her. A second wolf strode across the hanger toward them. The male winked at her as he halted before Julian.

"We've got everyone in place around Three Rivers, and Calitri and Sphinx are on their way toward Yukon territory in case you need them. Any other orders?" The newcomer seemed younger than Julian. His words were a sober reminder that the clock ticked down on the upstart pack. Would they kill them all? Chrystal had come from that pack and despite all the bad feelings about Omegas, Ranae actually liked the little wolf. She was so—different from the rest of them.

Though he addressed the Chief Enforcer, he kept glancing at her with a half-smile—*a good looking wolf and he damn well knew it.* She fought to keep a bland expression on her face.

"Yes, stop flirting with Willow Bend's representative." Julian thumped him and the wolf laughed.

"You're no fun."

"No," Julian said flatly. "I'm not."

The younger wolf sighed dramatically and spread his hands wide. "Of course, *sir.*" Without missing a beat, he turned and strode toward her with his hand held out. "I'm…"

"Leaving." Julian's order punched between the

syllables and the wolf retracted his hand. He gave her an apologetic smile before he cut left and strode out the same door she'd entered.

"Well, aren't you a bundle of cheer." She meant it sarcastically, but the taciturn look on his face had her instantly regretting the choice.

"I'm a busy man, Miss Buckley. We have no idea what we're going into. After we determine the situation, if you still feel the need to play, we'll find someone to entertain you."

Joy. She'd dealt with her grumpy and very dominant brothers before. While Julian didn't give her any kind of fraternal vibe, she decided to go with her gut and defer to him while not kissing his ass. "Thanks for the offer. It means a lot." Then she eyed the plane. "Where do I stow my gear?"

"Behind the co-pilot seat. It'll be cramped. You can sit in the back, if you want, but you'll be more comfortable up front."

Yeah, whatever helped him sleep at night. A good stiff wind could throw that plane out of the sky. Keeping the comment to herself, she nodded and carried her bag straight to the plane.

Unlike most of the wolves she knew, he didn't offer to take her bag or give her any assistance. The inside of the plane was even smaller than she imagined. It took a little wiggling to get the case locked into place. Sliding back out, she glanced around the hanger. Save for the other Enforcer, they appeared alone.

"No ground crew?"

"My plane. I am crew." Julian said as he circled the back of the plane. "Mitch filed the flight plan, and

I can open the main bay door to taxi out. Need to hit the head before we leave?"

Considering the coffee she'd drunk earlier, not a bad idea. "Sounds good…" Three steps away, she paused. "Julian, are there any other Lone Wolves or Enforcers in the area?"

"No, Seattle's not popular, at least not currently. Most of the Lone Wolves are farther south. Why?" He pinned her with a look.

"I thought I scented a woman at Seatac when I was leaving." It wasn't a lot to offer. "Didn't actually see who it was, and I didn't recognize the scent."

Julian pulled a phone from his pocket and dialed a number. "Mitch, head to Seatac and run through security cameras for arrivals and departures…" He looked at her.

"I got in a little over two hours ago."

"From four to two hours ago."

"Sure thing, boss…anyone I am looking for in particular?"

"Female wolf. We didn't have anyone scheduled, but that doesn't mean they didn't have a layover. Check it out."

"Will do." Mitch's answer rang clearly before they disconnected their call.

Ranae frowned. "How is he supposed to recognize a wolf from a video feed?" She didn't bother to ask how he'd get access to their security cameras. Enforcers had connections everywhere. They needed them.

"Because he knows how to do his job. Thanks for the information. Bathroom. Go."

Ranae rolled her eyes and spread her hands,

mimicking Mitch's action from earlier. "I'll be sure to powder my nose while I'm in there."

The Enforcer snorted as she walked away.

Damn dominant males.

Then she could have sworn he said, "Damn dominant females."

Though tempted to glance back at him, she fought the urge and pushed open the door to the bathroom. Just for that, she'd take at least ten minutes.

What was he going to do? Leave her?

Six hours later, she and her stomach were both done with the toy plane being tossed by the winds. Julian turned out to be a silent pilot, his focus lasered on the task of flying them north across Alaska. The only words he exchanged were with flight control. They bounced and jerked like she used to when she would try to ride the wind outside the car window with her hand. The thought was hardly comforting.

"We're not in any trouble." The cool tones did little to ease the fist of anxiety gripping her guts. Of course, his scent remained completely unreadable. Hell, if she didn't glance at him periodically, she'd barely know he was present.

How did a wolf hide his scent, even in close quarters?

"Just keep flying." His distraction was the last thing she wanted. They bobbed and weaved enough. Glancing at her wrist, she scowled. Her watch was at home and her cell phone was in her back pocket.

"We're about fifteen minutes from Prudhoe Bay. We'll land, stow the plane then go over land."

How he could tell when the landscape below seemed to be an endless field of white, trees, and more white?

Prudhoe Bay—a small community in far northern Alaska—near to the Arctic Circle. She wanted to shiver thinking about it. A.J. and Dylan briefed her about the Yukon, a sketch of details. They maintained a base camp about two hours east of Prudhoe Bay called Amaruq. Dylan advised her to not be deceived by the mudhole appearance. *"It looks like a half-forgotten fishing village populated by natives who love to not speak English. They're as many wolves as there are natives. Don't be fooled, their humans aren't like ours, they shelter the wolves and revere them to a certain extent. You have to check in in Amaruq, and you'll receive a marker that will let you travel from there to deeper into Yukon Territory."*

"A marker?"

"It could be anything—a scarf, a hat, a piece of jewelry, something colorful. Whatever it is, take it and don't complain." The serious note in Dylan's tone and A.J.'s faint smirk intrigued her.

"What did they make you wear?"

"After I refused the baseball cap?" The corner of Dylan's mouth quirked. *"A lace bonnet."*

She laughed. "So, whatever they give me?"

"Exactly. You wear whatever they give you and you journey overland to Tikaani. Despite what we know, even in the long winter months, the whole pack doesn't shift and roam. Most of them do, but they will have scouts, children, and some of their seniors tucked away in Tikaani. Don't make the mistake of thinking the shifted pack won't know you're there.

They will. There are guest houses on the outskirts.
They're stocked and have heating and other supplies.
Tuck yourself inside, get some food and some sleep
and wait."

"Wait?"

"Wait," Dylan repeated. A.J. nodded.

"For how long?"

"For as long as it takes."

The plane's descent drew her from the memory, and she scanned the desolate looking landscape below. Construction seemed to be ongoing and there was plenty of traffic around the landing strip, despite the isolated locale.

"I thought this was a remote outpost."

"It is for most of the year. The real work begins when everything is hard frozen. It's okay. Makes our journey easier." He didn't have to explain the comment. If the hard frozen land brought in more people, they'd blend.

Twenty minutes later, she stretched her legs and huddled into her jacket. It got damn cold at home, but this took it to a whole new level. It was dark—not a little dark, but middle of the night dark. No sign of the sun anywhere, despite the fact the time said it was mid-afternoon. Thankfully, there were floodlights.

She secured the woolen cap closer over her ears and then tugged her gloves on before reclaiming her case and purse. Julian hadn't wanted her help with securing his plane. The little airport had one building for passengers and a diner, which appeared closed. She hadn't bothered to look for a bathroom.

Maybe she could convince the Enforcer to stop somewhere along the way—if there was an anywhere to stop on the way. Her cheeks were numb and she could barely feel her lips when she caved and slid the neoprene mask on. Her mother had stuffed it into her purse, and she'd told her she hardly needed something they kept in stock for their human packmates.

Well, I'll thank Mom for it later, and it'll make her day. She probably should have texted A.J. to tell him they'd arrived in Prudhoe, but she'd wait till they were in their vehicle. It took another ten minutes before Julian strode in her direction. Bastard didn't even have on a hat. If the cold bothered him, he didn't show it.

He nodded to her once as he bypassed her and continued on. Of course, he expected her to follow.

Then again, he knows where he's going.

She refused to hurry to catch up to him or lengthen her stride. Their path took them around the lonely building and beyond the hangars to a stretch of covered parking. The vehicle waiting for them gave her pause. It looked like a modified jeep. The doors unlocked, but the engine had been running when they arrived.

"Something else they leave for guests?" She couldn't help it; she needed to know.

"No, we keep it here. Saves time on renting a vehicle or finding our own way. We pay a stipend to keep it fueled and no one turns off a vehicle this time of year." It had to be the cold. At these temperatures, fuel lines at home would freeze.

He tossed his bag into the back and held it open with a pointed look at her. The urge to pick up the pace rolled over her and she refused to obey it.

Sliding her case in, she glanced around.

"So, everyone else has to rent one?"

"If they're lucky. Sometimes you just take the old-fashioned way."

And by old-fashioned, he meant shifting and running. A shudder tore through her. *No thank you.* A two-hour drive could be a good half-day run or more on familiar terrain. She didn't even ask whom he expected to drive. He had the keys and the power. Sliding into the passenger seat, she left her gloves and mask in place. The heat blasted from the vents, but the interior seemed as chilly as the outdoors.

One step at a time.

"Anywhere to stop between here and Amaruq?"

"Nope." He slid into the driver's seat and they were off. Her bladder protested, but she stayed silent. They'd make time in the little village—though, damn, what if they used outhouses here?

"The weather going to be a problem?"

"No." He flicked on the lights. Everything around them seemed to be on concrete stilts. The roads weren't flat, but gravel. There was a lot of movement going on, lights everywhere. "We should be there by dinner. We may stay the night, if you're tired."

"You don't want to." It wasn't a question.

"No. It'll be an unpleasant journey, no matter what time we leave."

The sun wouldn't be coming up. "Then we do it your way." It cost her to admit it.

"No arguments?" He spared her a glance.

"Not on this subject. You've been here before. You know the terrain. I'll go with your expert opinion."

"Kind of you."

"Disappointed I'm not arguing?"

"Surprised, actually. I was under the impression you would be difficult."

Good. She didn't want to be predictable, even if difficult was a kind description on the part of her packmates. A part of her wondered who told him as much? Mason? A.J.? No, A.J. wouldn't have called her difficult. *He prefers high strung, as though I'm some kind of instrument.*

Leaning back, she stripped off her gloves and tugged out her phone. She had one bar, so she fired off a message to A.J. before they got out of range of the cell tower. "I don't know where you get your information, Julian. I'm a constant fucking delight."

The Enforcer laughed. It was not an amusing sound. "You might need to be, Miss Buckley." The ominous warning rocked her resolve. "It could help you survive this trip."

"What do you know that I don't?" Dammit, she should never have revealed a weakness.

"Get some sleep, if you can." They were leaving the buildings behind, and the road stretched out into the endless darkness.

"You're really not very comforting." The complaint unfurled from within her, and her wolf wanted to snap.

"Good." The lack of emotion made his tone hard to read. He said nothing else, and she elected to not poke the bear. Maybe this trip hadn't been so much a show of faith in her as a punishment.

Doesn't matter. I do my job, and I do it well

then I take home the information to my Alpha. Maybe dealing with the Chief Enforcer was good practice for when she'd have to talk to the Yukon Alpha. *They're both old curmudgeons, and Julian's kind of a jerk.*

The last thought restored some of her good humor, and she leaned her head back. Sleep sounded good. Or at least the pretense of it. So what if the Enforcer didn't want to talk to her? She really didn't want to talk to him, either.

Every moment the vehicle continued forward, however, her gut clenched. What the hell was waiting for them out there?

Snow Wolf

Chapter Two

The lights danced across the sky. A common enough sight this time of year, yet they still captivated tourists to fly across the sky for the best view. Fortunately, little else disturbed his area of tundra. The pack had angled south, trailing a herd of caribou. They would range along with the herd—in part to hunt and in part to keep an eye out for poachers.

The wild wolf populations had taken a severe dip over the past two years, as outsiders took a special shine to proving their manhood by hunting the last three hundred or so left. With fewer than eighty found during their last count, the whole pack voted to run with them and keep an eye on their wild cousins.

Death—a part of life. Extinction—a fact of death. A howl rolled across the wind. A distant part of his mind identified the wolf—a Sentry—calling out across the darkened landscape. A mile to the south, another wolf answered and then another. It carried on until the wolf song rode the breeze as the pack answered. They were spread out for miles, family groups and mated pairs moving together while the bachelor and Sentry wolves roamed on circuits with at least four Sentries within range of Tikaani at any one time.

Once upon a time, the whole pack would shift during the long dark months. They wouldn't worry about their village or if any one came and went while they roamed. Any mothers with young children would have moved with their infants to the base camp or deeper into human territory, wintering with the tribes who guarded them. The pack would spend their time roaming the tundra, hunting, and behaving as wolves until late February when they'd migrate to Tikaani. Then their young would return home.

Change came slowly to the Yukon, but it came nonetheless. Civilization continued to spread into his territory, larger cities taking up residence while the native population dropped off—either to the attrition of death or to their own young migrating to other parts of the states.

Too few of their Inuit allies remained, so they changed Tikaani, digging deep into the permafrost and sinking concrete struts deeper still, to create an underground compound. When the pack shifted for the long, dark months, the maternals and their young went underground. Sentries took circuits to protect the vulnerable, while other singles took work as far away as Anchorage to keep a constant stream of revenue coming into the pack.

Not that they needed the money, but Diesel recognized the power financial freedom provided his young. They were more likely to return to the pack if they didn't have to worry about how to pay for things.

Change sucked.

A new wolf song picked up where the last one dropped off, but this one carried a note of urgency and aggression. Flicking his ears, Diesel turned his attention from the dance of lights to the west.

Intruders.

Sentries sent up a single call, a vocalization both sharp and mournful, that cut off as soon as it hit the wind. They wouldn't give away their positions by continuing the song. Irritation along with a cold north wind ruffled his fur. Rising from his haunches, Diesel stretched. The Sentries could deal with any genuine threats and if it turned out to be messengers from the other packs... *They can wait.*

One step from turning east and away from Tikaani, he paused. Movement along the tundra beckoned his attention. Dropping his head, he kept his ears tuned to the motion but the wind swirled and danced away, not quite bringing him the scent of the invader.

Yet, he recognized a foreign wolf. None of his would make the mistake of trying to approach him from his flank, nor would any Sentry leave Tikaani to seek him out—not here.

They knew better.

So who dared to venture into his land?

The motion resolved itself into the shape of a wolf, a white shadow moving amongst the snow. Despite their location, no wolves in his pack were as white as he and the only one he knew of who would dare intrude on his time did not even belong to his pack.

Julian.

What the fuck did the Enforcers want?

Aggravated, he let his lip curl away from his teeth as he swung around to confront the interloper. The wolf didn't slow its pace or drop its head as it stalked toward him. Not only were the Enforcers in his territory, their Chief Enforcer thought he could bully his way into seeing Diesel. Personal relationships aside, Julian knew better. Or he should.

Ten steps shy of tearing the Enforcer's fur from

his hide, Diesel paused. The visitor carried a scent that not only didn't belong to him—it didn't belong in the Yukon. The snarl in his throat died unspoken and Diesel rushed the Enforcer. The other wolf had the good sense to halt at his sudden approach. Chin raised, he glared at Julian and the blue-eyed wolf didn't look away. With a low, throaty bark, he jerked his head toward Tikaani.

Diesel ignored the request, testing his nose against the wolf's nearness. The vibrant spice he'd scented in Willow Bend clung to the Enforcer, but it didn't belong to him. Had he brought the elusive beast with him? Circling Julian, Diesel scanned the tundra with all of his senses, but he detected no other wolves nearby. Julian had arrived at Tikaani and slipped by the Sentries including any who'd been set to guard him.

Fluff and Grinder would be annoyed.

They were not alone.

Snapping at the Enforcer, he ordered him toward Tikaani. Only when the other wolf began sidestepping did he stalk after him. Neither gave the other their back. Julian's presence better have a damn good explanation—otherwise, Enforcer or not, Diesel would gut him.

Matching strides, they flew across the tundra toward Tikaani. His wolves called to him as he entered their range, and he answered with a sharp note. Despite the Enforcer's invasion and avoidance of the Sentries on duty, Diesel would not rebuke them. Enforcers were skilled at concealment and hunting their prey, and none more so than their leader. Older than most of the current Alphas, he was more Diesel's contemporary than even those among his pack. The elders gave way each year, more and more letting time and lack of interest carry them away. Diesel remained poised to follow; yet with every season, he found a single reason to stay.

Julian's arrival bearing the all too familiar and provocative scent just above his own beckoned to Diesel in a way he hadn't experienced since his time in Willow Bend. For a brief moment during his visit, he'd held hope that Serafina possessed the alluring markers calling to him, but his pursuit of the Delta Crescent Alpha ended as abruptly as it began.

On the edge of Tikaani, lights blazed at three of the homesteads kept stocked and readied for guests. The others would be warm, and locked, but darkened to hide their access to the underground compounds. Julian peeled away, heading directly to the homestead on the outer ring.

Fluff appeared in Diesel's periphery, her ruffled fur and bared teeth a silent warning as she angled toward the Enforcer. Cutting off her assault with a single shake of his head, Diesel trailed their *guest* to the door of the homestead. Grinder appeared next to the homestead. Like Fluff, outrage radiated off of him. Diesel would either be soothing their bruised egos or punching them both in the head before the night ended.

They knew it.

He knew it.

Rising on his back legs, Julian hit the latch release. Door access allowed even the youngest wolf entrance to the homestead mudrooms. The exterior hatch opened, and Julian stepped into the broad room with Diesel right behind him. The door closed automatically, cutting off the cold wind. Red tiles lit up along the sides as the heat kicked in, warming the room. Without waiting, Diesel shifted. Julian shared the same thought and the men hit their feet within heartbeats of each other.

"What the hell are you doing here?" Politeness was for invited guests or guests who waited their turn. Julian didn't fit in either category.

Grasping a pair of jeans, the Enforcer tugged them on without answering. Only after he reached for a shirt and the temperature monitor read fifty degrees did he glance Diesel. "I didn't arrive alone. When that thermostat hits sixty, that inner door will open. You might want to get dressed."

Ignoring the explanation of how the equipment he helped design worked, Diesel folded his arms. The temperature didn't bother him in the least. "I asked you a question."

"The packs have been trying to reach you for weeks. You're not answering."

"So they sent an Enforcer to check on me? How considerate." *Soft little shits.* He'd gone years without answering.

"No one sends me anywhere." Though his expression didn't change nor his scent, Julian's gaze chilled. "I offered to escort the Willow Bend Hunter when Mason decided to send her to check on you."

Her?

"Hudson River's Alpha was challenged by Russian opponents." Julian buttoned his shirt. "He won."

"Really not a reason to notify me." Alphas

survived challenges all the time. It was only of note when they lost and a new Alpha entered the game.

"Sutter Butte suffered a direct invasion attempt, more than a dozen, heavily armed and trained Russian wolves took out an entire family group, and nearly carried out the successful assassination of Cassius."

Moderately more interesting. "Nearly carried out? Cassius isn't dead?"

"No."

The thermostat ticked over 55 degrees. Julian reclaimed socks and shoes and added them to the stack of insulated clothes he'd likely worn in when he came overland. In the narrow confines of the room, the scent Diesel detected on the tundra didn't seem as obvious. Either Julian had played a game with him, or he'd come into contact with the female while in his wolf form. What Hunter had Willow Bend sent?

"You've come all this way to tell me Cassius and Brett are still alive. Mason as well, apparently, if he sent one of his Hunters. What of Serafina?" She interested him only in as much as he respected her strength. A part of him still mourned the potential he'd sensed before realizing it wasn't her.

"She and her mate are fine, although Delta Crescent lost one of its Omegas to Cassius and one of their Hounds to the Russian invaders."

No dead Alphas. "The Three Rivers upstarts?" During the summit, the others had all searched for reasons to let them live. Only Cassius had been willing to execute them.

"Numbered."

"They are allowing the foreigners access through their territory." It would be an unforgiveable sin. Russian wolf packs were brutal, bloody, and downright barbaric at times. The frequent mentions and Julian's unreadable expression spoke volumes.

"We have yet to find conclusive proof."

Proof. What more proof did they need that allowing a new pack to continue to flourish set a bad precedent? They were burying their dead.

The thermostat hit 58 and Diesel grabbed a pair of loose elastic sweatpants from the stacks left for company. They smelled only of fresh laundering and a hint of lemon he associated with Tiger, one of the housekeepers.

At 60 degrees, the inner door lit up green and the lock disengaged. Pushing it open, Diesel blocked Julian's access long enough to inhale a lungful of the wolf waiting for them. A warm mix of ginger, clove, and orange combined with woody notes reminded him of the snap of a crackling fire and the comfort of a hot and aromatic cider.

The decadence drifted over him. Need to roll around in the scent until it coated him overrode his natural instincts toward wariness. One hand braced on the doorframe to keep Julian out, Diesel tracked his gaze around the room. Standing in front of the fireplace was a tall, athletic woman with long brown hair. She pivoted to face him, and her guarded expression warned him off even as her scent beckoned.

"Stay out." He told Julian before entering and closing the door behind him. A split second before the door locks clicked, the Enforcer laughed.

Folding her arms, the wolf raised her eyebrows. She'd gone predator still, but a faint trembling in her jaw betrayed her struggle to hold his gaze. Lasting longer than most, she glanced at the thick, bearskin rugs insulating the floor for a split second before attempting to lock on his eyes again.

Fascinated, he fought the urge to stalk across the room and stake his claim. He settled with resting his hands on the back of the sofa. The flimsy piece of furniture wouldn't keep him away.

"Alpha." *Admirable.* Her voice didn't quaver once as she inclined her head sharply. "I'm Ranae Buckley, Hunter of Willow Bend, and I am here on behalf of Mason Clayborne to deliver grave news as well as to urge you to contact the other Alphas."

"What does Mason want?" He couldn't care less, but he did want to hear her speak again.

The firelight danced over her in a play of shadows. Her gray-green eyes bled gold as her wolf dared a peek at him. The level of control she maintained over her expression didn't betray her, but her eyes? Yes, they revealed a great deal.

"The packs are concerned about a number of attempts on the part of Russian wolves to undermine and destabilize packs in the North American region. Your locations may be compromised, as they were able to invade Sutter Butte by attacking one family group specifically. Enforcers and packs alike are tallying all wolves within the national borders."

"Didn't they do that after the Three Rivers debacle?" He vaguely recalled statements about missing wolves and census taking.

"They did, at least in the case of Lone Wolves and any wolves reported missing from within the packs proper." She shifted her position, resetting her weight. Discomfort kept her shoulders stiff. While power cascaded from her every word, she leaned heavily on her wolf and kept her posture erect. How young was she? She couldn't have been a Hunter for long, or perhaps this was her first mission outside of Willow Bend borders? Though she didn't aggravate his wolf, her actions and behavior were hardly that of an outsider communicating with an Alpha.

Another flick of her gaze away then back. Determination punctuated every action. "Julian can brief you on those specifics, it's why he came."

"No, that's why he *said* he came." Was it courage or obstinacy keeping her shoulders straight?

Ranae blinked. "I'm sorry?"

Smart enough to note his phrasing, green enough to call him on it. "It's a mistake to believe the Enforcers are ever only doing one thing or on a mission for one reason. Only a fool would expect less from their Chief Enforcer." The most senior of their kind and far too old for these kind of games.

Her lips compressed into a thin line. "You should let him in."

"No." He dismissed the suggestion. "Tell me what else Mason sent you here to say."

"I told you, I'm here to bring you up to date on the attacks, to verify that the Yukon is secure, and to make you aware of the potential threats. I have reports on the number of wolves killed and descriptions of those identified as liaisons with the Russian packs…"

When she would have reached for her bag, Diesel shook his head. "I don't care about those details." Surprise flickered in her gaze. "What did he tell you to say to me? Specifically."

"About you or to you?" An element of challenge roiled in those syllables. His cheek muscle ached, and it took him a moment to realize he'd smiled.

"Both." Though he wanted the latter. Why had Mason sent this wolf with her alluring scent? The longer he stood there, the more certain he grew. He'd scented her in Willow Bend. The draw of it pulled at him, demanded he close the deal, but he needed to be sure. Alphas did not like to have their wolves stolen, but if Diesel had his way—Ranae Buckley would not be leaving the Yukon again.

"He said you were old and set in your ways. That I should be patient with you and to obey the restrictions about waiting to contact you."

Old.

Set in his ways.

For a split-second, amusement flared in her eyes. "He also said I only had to wait two weeks."

"For what?"

"To deliver the message and verify that you still ruled the Yukon."

"If you couldn't in two weeks?"

"Then I was to return to the airstrip in Prudhoe Bay, make my way to Seattle, and from there go back to Willow Bend." The corner of her mouth turned down, and her knuckles went white.

There it is... Uncertainty. "How are you supposed to verify I'm still ruling the Yukon?"

"You're alive aren't you?" Irritation won the battle with uncertainty. "I think we should invite Julian in, complete this briefing, and then we'll be on our way."

Yes. He was very much alive. "Julian can wait." Diesel circled the sofa and stalked toward her. "Do you have any idea how beautiful you are?"

Three strides brought him right in front of her, and only the slap of her hand against his bare chest halted him. "I came to deliver a *message*—verbal— that's it."

Sweet contact of her flesh on his sent a shudder through his wolf, confirming what his nose already detected. "I heard your message…but you're mine."

A flush turned her skin pink and her pupils dilated. "The hell I am."

Riding the high of her nearness, Diesel leaned into the force of her hand on his chest. "I know my mate's scent. I searched for you all over Willow Bend. Why else would Mason send you?" The moment the words left his lips, he reconsidered the phrasing. Her eyes narrowed and her nostrils flared.

"I'm a Hunter of Willow Bend. I am here to deliver a message from *my* Alpha—and I don't care what century you were born in old man, but we don't arrange matings. You don't just get to walk in here, thump your chest and say *mine*." The ferocious light in her eyes sent a quiet thrill through his bloodstream. His wolf roused to the hunt, every color and nuance sharpening under their study.

"No?" He didn't want to miss a moment of her reaction. Her dilated pupils constricted even as her mouth tightened. Anger soured her scent and her nails bit into his muscle as he pressed into the contact. Despite a faint tremble, she didn't shift her grip or attack him. Would she? If he provoked her enough?

The idea intrigued the hell out of him. No Alpha wanted a weak mate.

"No." She withdrew the contact then retreated one step. Crowding closer, he refused to let her abandon him. "Dude…get a grip. I came here to do a job." A muscle in her jaw twitched. "Or maybe you are trying to prove you don't hold the Yukon?"

Challenge wound through every syllable. Canting his head to the side, he raised one eyebrow and waited.

"What? Playing crazy, eccentric keeps the other packs at bay and allows you to dictate the terms of your interactions. You don't want to talk; you walk away or slam a door. You want to shut me down; you declare I'm yours." Folding her arms, Ranae raised her chin and, although the gold circle on around her gray-green irises faded, it didn't diminish completely. "It won't work and I'm really not interested in the games. We have serious issues to discuss with you, Alpha. You can get on board or be left behind to cope on your own should the Russian packs turn their gaze on your territory and your pack."

Amusement curved through him. Passionate determination etched into her expression. "Our pack will be fine."

"*My* pack will be, absolutely. Your pack is debatable." The aggravation in her scent muted beneath the sting of frustration. "Now you're baiting me." Sidestepping him, she tried to put some distance between them. He allowed her three steps before intercepting her again. He wanted her gaze on him, nowhere else. "Seriously, you have a problem."

"No, I have a mate, but continue telling me why

our pack is in danger."

Pausing, her lips tightened and her eyes narrowed. The curl of her fingers into a fist telegraphed her next move. Would she do it? He pressed into her space, and she rewarded his effort with fresh contact in the form of a blow. It caught him square above his heart, and the second with her elbow connected with his jaw. He accepted both blows, but refused to retreat.

"Your training is incomplete." Whatever response she'd been expecting, his comment surprised her. "Otherwise you'd understand that two hits will not take down an enraged male, if you want to escape you have to incapacitate or kill."

"I don't want to fight you."

"Wonderful. I have no desire to fight you, but if you need to beat on me to make yourself feel better, go right ahead. I'm very sturdy."

The corner of her mouth kicked into an involuntary smile, and his breath lodged in his throat, the single glimpse of sweetness a better reward than he could have imagined. "Are you insane?"

"Depends on your definition of sanity." The tangle of her hair contrasted with the wool of her pullover. How soft would the strands be? When she failed to respond, he reached out to test his theory. She slapped his hand away, and the sting intrigued him.

"Stop." Command reverberated through the single syllable. "I came here as a messenger, nothing else. Keep your teeth and your hands to yourself. Am I clear?"

In all things, an Alpha could command. He

could take a life. He could grant it. Wolves who pledged to an Alpha could be sent into the heart of danger and forfeit all that they owned. The heart, however, could not be commanded nor could he take what she would not willingly give.

His wolf bucked at the rejection, but Diesel withdrew three steps to give her space. Clasping his hands behind his back, he studied the beautiful Hunter before him. She would not tumble easily, nor would she accept his direct pledge. Very well, if he had to learn to court, then he would find what enticed her. "Dress," he ordered. "Several layers. We will be leaving the guest quarters."

Expecting obedience, he turned to the entrance and pressed the code to allow Julian entry.

"Are you staying with her or leaving?" Her presence was non-negotiable.

"Since you asked so nicely…" The Chief Enforcer's expression barely shifted, yet a smirk echoed beneath his words. "I'd be happy to stay."

Uninterested in the old wolf's games, Diesel spared his mate another studying look. Ranae gaped at him, and she hadn't moved a muscle.

"Trust me when I say it will be more comfortable if you get dressed, but if you insist on testing my patience, I'll happily take care of stripping you first then dressing you."

The taunt did what the order would not. She moved.

His wolf rose, stretching and raking his claws. Yes, they had the scent of this hunt.

Snow Wolf

Chapter Three

Diesel is an asshole. The thought played on repeat in her brain as she tugged on the layers he'd ordered. After the trip out from Prudhoe Bay, she had no desire to venture into the cold without her thermals and heavy jacket. Wolf or not, she couldn't handle the frigid conditions. *The next time I see A.J., I'm gonna punch him.*

After dragging on her coat, she stuffed her other clothes into the duffel before scouring the room for any other items she might have misplaced. The last thing she expected on her trip was to clash with the Yukon Alpha. Pausing with her hand on a bottle of lotion, she glanced at the closed doorway. Even with a door between them, the crisp scent of snow on fur seemed a permanent addition to her nostrils. Her palm stung from where she struck him and her elbow ached. She'd attacked the Alpha of the Yukon pack. The weight of her actions didn't descend until she stowed the last of her things.

Her job was to deliver a message, and she'd failed the first part by letting him control the narrative. Mason had wanted him alerted to the potential danger, not assaulted. Diesel didn't seem remotely put off by her response, if anything… *He seemed amused.*

The order to pack her things so he could transfer her residence caught her off guard. Was he really crazy? Distant? Or was it more of an act? She and Julian arrived forty-eight hours prior. The Chief

Enforcer went looking after he tired of waiting, a fact she'd been grateful for. Julian might be able to stuff all of his dominance down below the surface, but she'd spent two days cooped up with him. The moment he'd left, she'd been able to breathe. The only concession she'd made to the rules of her stay was to keep the leather cuff on she'd been given when she arrived at the base camp.

Tikaani was much farther inland, and the conditions beyond their guest residence left her blood chilly. Hell, she didn't want to strip down to bare skin in the antechamber in order to shift. Diesel's thin clothing and bare feet hadn't been lost on her.

Sucking in a deep breath, she zipped the duffel closed and snagged her heavy coat before stomping toward the door. *No.* Halting, she closed her eyes and breathed through the aggravation. His bold claims to the side, it didn't matter if he was batcrap crazy and declared her his mate. She didn't have to accept. No one could force a mating. If he were like most overbearing and dominant males, he could have said what he did just to shut her up.

Dylan told her stories of wolves who took calls while in his presence. Diesel left them and didn't return for days at a time, leaving them dangling. Even her waiting two days only to have Julian fetch him said he didn't really care about what she wanted or needed. Checking her phone, she made sure she had enough of a charge and then she set an alarm to go off in thirty minutes. The alarm would sound like a ring. If phone calls deterred him—perhaps it would buy her some time.

Grounding her temper, she considered his

actions. Every single one seemed geared to bait her and elicit a response. She'd failed, epically, by striking him. What she needed was to apply rational thought and logic to the problem, not her dominance. *I'll never really win against an Alpha anyway.*

Honestly, she didn't need to win. She only needed to do her job. Stiffening her spine, she resumed her pace for the front room sans stomping and anger. Diesel and Julian waited for her. The Chief Enforcer remained as inscrutable as ever, but the Yukon Alpha actually smiled at her appearance. The smile warmed his chilly eyes and softened the hard line of his jaw. The simple curve of his lips transformed him from impenetrable to almost approachable—not that she wanted to approach him. Standing near shoulder to shoulder, the men also bore more than a passing resemblance to each other.

"Do you have everything?" His question distracted her from the comparison. A good idea, she didn't need to make mental notes about either of them. The sooner she was done with them, the better. How did the other wolves stand to be so near them? Mason was at least approachable—even when he was pissed off at her.

Adjusting her duffle over her shoulder, she worked to get her mind back on task. "I packed light." She'd also stuffed a knit cap over her head, and she had a hood she could pull up. The neoprene mask offered her more than warmth, so she pulled it on. Diesel's brows climbed at her action, yet the firm line of his mouth remained curved. He extended his hand as though planning to take her bag, but she tightened her grip and glared at him.

Maybe she couldn't hold his gaze, but she wasn't some helpless ninny. His smile deepened for a second, and a ripple passed through her abdomen. He really was quite handsome. Didn't matter. According to their mates, all of her brothers were drop dead gorgeous, too. Every single one of them were a pain in the ass, no matter how much she loved them. A pretty face didn't interest her.

"Shall we?" she asked when the silence between them stretched. A moment of humor appeared in Julian's normally expressionless face. Great, now even the Enforcer laughed at her.

"Of course." The low gravel hum of Diesel's voice rasped against her senses. Despite the harshness of it, the sensation wasn't unpleasant. Ignoring the ridiculous response, she fought her hesitation to approach the door. Both Julian and Diesel stood between her and the destination. No matter her dominance, she didn't dare cross them, and she'd already made the misstep of challenging the Alpha.

Months spent stifling her reckless impulses should have made her choice easier. Instead, she relished the anticipation bubbling in her gut. How far could she push them? When neither man moved, she sighed. Another minute passed and she studied the pair of them from beneath lowered lashes. Nearly equal in height, both men sported that nearly platinum shade of blond hair. Their eyes were similar, but where Diesel's burned with some kind of cold fire, Julian's were glacially opaque. They seemed almost equal in their dominance, and though both were considerably older than her, they seemed like contemporaries.

They were also staring at each other. Measuring? Weighing? Considering the best way to take the other out? None of those were ideal in the current situation. Curling her toes inside her boots, the one motion she could make without alerting either of them to her unease, contained the need to tap her foot.

Either these two were about to lash out in some kind of dominance challenge or they communicated on a level she didn't understand. Annoyed by either possibility, she cleared her throat. "Is there a secret password or handshake? Or are we waiting for someone to beam us up?" Once upon a time, her mother accused her of possessing an abrasive personality. Ranae had scoffed. Had her mother never seen how she dealt with Ranae's brothers? A.J., Tyler, and Linc were triplets—

powerful wolves, each and every one, headstrong, stubborn, and each possessing the trait labeled Alpha potential.

If Ranae was abrasive, it was because she'd learned how to manage stubborn, hard asses from her mother at an early age.

The tension in the room seemed to pop, the relief flooding her limbs a visceral reminder of the tangential danger of her position. Diesel chuckled. The harsh sound almost grating and yet liberating in the same breath. She had to bite the inside of her lip to keep from joining him.

"From the mouths of pups," Julian spoke first.

Diesel's amusement evaporated. "Have a care with your tone."

As though undeterred by the warning, the Chief

Enforcer wore a bland smile. "It isn't my tone you take issue with." The men locked gazes and the temperature in the room plummeted even as the tension rose.

Ranae could leave it alone, or she could do her job. After peeling away the neoprene, she slid two fingers to her lips and let loose with a shrill whistle. Both men jerked, and the weight of their attention slapped against her. "Pissing contests later. I didn't put on all these layers to sit here and watch you two butt heads. We have a job to do, and I shouldn't need to remind *either* of you."

The lines around Diesel's eyes tightened, and his gaze went almost incandescent. "You are correct, Sweet. We should relocate this discussion." With only a glance at the Chief Enforcer, he added, "You are only invited so long as you remember your place."

"I have no place in your pack." Julian's even tones carried not even an ounce of rancor.

Diesel raised his hand. "That's all you have to say. You have no place."

For the first time since she met the Enforcer, Ranae glimpsed a ripple of shock disturb his unreadable composure, and she had to bite back a laugh. Some sound must have escaped, however, because Diesel canted his head toward her and a smile flirted with the corners of his mouth.

"Ranae Buckley." He enunciated every syllable of her name like a caress. "Welcome to the Yukon Pack. Please accept that you are under my protection. If you will join me, I will take you to where my pack is wintering."

Affixing her neoprene mask again, she nodded.

The formal declaration deserved a response. "Thank you—Alpha. Forgive me, I don't know your full name."

"Diesel is fine." His muscles flexed as he released the door to the antechamber. He stepped into the room first, then held the door for her. She had to brush past him to step inside. She tightened her grip on her duffle, but he didn't insult her by trying to take it. No sooner had she entered than Diesel released the door. Julian barely caught it before it slammed him in the face.

Thankful for the mask hiding her smile, she angled her gaze at the floor. One of the worst things she could do to a dominant male included laughing at their posturing. When two were involved, it was better to keep herself out of the line of fire.

"I'm touched by your hospitality." The dry note in Julian's tone echoed a hint of humor.

"Don't get comfortable." Diesel advised him, but his attention remained riveted on her. "The temperature outside is too fierce for anything but our wolf coats or heavier gear." He stretched past her to tug down one of the parkas, then held it up for her to slide her arms into. It was an offer. Not an order.

Interesting. Maybe old dogs learned new tricks faster than young ones. Keeping that thought to herself, she set her duffle down before letting him help her into the parka. He tugged the hood up, then zipped the jacket closed.

"Stay close to me. The darkness can play tricks on the mind." Retrieving her duffle from the floor, he held it out to her. "There are ropes between the other dwellings, but we don't attach the guest quarters."

Nodding once, she murmured, "I understand."

"Are you familiar with snowshoes?"

"Yes." She had to bite off attaching the word sir to it then scowled at her kneejerk response. "Yes, sir. Thank you." Having given the inch already, she didn't complain as he set up the shoes for her to snap her feet into place. They were damn awkward, but she hadn't lied. She could ski, snowshoe, and snowboard for that matter. Willow Bend might not be the Yukon, but a little snow and ice wouldn't deter her.

He nodded, then glanced at Julian. The Enforcer slid on his own parka, but didn't bother to zip it. Once he had his snowshoes on, Diesel hit the pressure button to help drop the temperature in the room. A hiss of air indicated the machinery had gone to work. Diesel's eyes tightened. The technology they used to insulate their dwellings impressed her. From all accounts, the Yukon wolves were a throwback to an entirely different century.

The temperature readout on the thermostat on the wall began to drop steadily.

"Remember, Sweet, stay close to me. Don't let me out of your sight." With those words, Diesel shifted. The speed of his transformation left her momentarily breathless. She'd never seen anyone change with such absolute smoothness. Even the crunch of his bones crackled like ice chipping rather than shattering. The wolf standing before her stood nearly as high as her breastbone. He was huge and perfectly snow white. Unlike the wolves she'd known, his eyes were as blue as his human form.

Or were his human eyes wolf?

She was still turning the question over in her

mind when the outer door hatch released. Julian pushed it open, and Diesel caught her gaze, holding it. Command reflected in the depths of his eyes.

"I said I would follow you." Assurance wasn't in her nature, but to be fair, they were infringing on his territory. The wolf nodded, then plunged out into the darkness and the snow. Trepidation tangled with curiosity in her gut, and left her insides knotted as she followed him into the unknown.

Padding only a step ahead of her, Diesel tested the air with his nose even as he listened for any hint of danger on the wind. No matter the admonishment he'd given Ranae, he didn't range far from the Willow Bend Hunter. Julian could take care of himself, a fact he'd already proven by slipping by the Sentries and hunting Diesel down on the tundra. A low growl carried on the breeze and Diesel silenced Grinder with a look. Fluff stalked behind the other Sentry, her gray coat shimmering with ice crystals.

A glower lit her gold eyes and she looked past him to the two wolves trailing in his wake. Adjusting his position, he blocked his Sentries and issued a low sub-vocal growl to warn them off. Both dropped their gazes obediently, then ranged out to the sides. One thing he'd never worried about with his wolves was obedience. They were all loyal, steadfast and one hundred percent his. Even when he didn't take the time they deserved.

The bump of Ranae's leg into his side sent a frisson of awareness skittering over his nerves. Warm honey tickled his nose against the frost and snow. The overlay stimulated him, and he wanted to snap at anyone too close. The unmistakable draw of mate beckoned to his wolf. A sudden gust of wind and Ranae stumbled. Julian caught her arm, balancing her. Lips peeling back from his teeth, Diesel snarled, but Ranae jerked her arm from the Enforcer.

Her growl pleased him. Leaning into the gust, she plowed forward and Diesel cut between her and Julian. Grinder and Fluff wouldn't offer a threat to his mate. The male ranged closer, offering guidance toward the central building. All the cabins looked alike to outsiders, a deliberate choice on their part. Outsiders would never see more than the ramshackle and rustic cabins in the middle of nowhere. It protected his pack, left others with the impression he lived in another time, another century…and it was an impression he encouraged.

At the central cabin, he arched up to hit both paws against the locking mechanism. The door opened to the antechamber. Just like the guest quarters. It was designed to let them shift out of the dangerous wind and weather. He waited for Ranae to enter, then stepped in behind her to shield her from Julian and the pair of Sentries as they stepped inside, too. Julian closed the outer door and the room automatically began to warm. Not waiting for the temperature to hit fifty, he began his shift. He was standing before his Sentries then he shrugged into a pair of sweats.

The speed of his changes coupled with three back to back, left his skin steaming in the chill. Ranae stared at him from above her neoprene mask, her eyes deep pools of mystery. When she caught his gaze, she glanced away. He didn't want to let her retreat, but his wolf clawed at him. The predator understood the hunt even better than the man. She was with them and he was about to introduce her to his world, his pack...on his terms. Giving in on her terms was a small price to pay. Grinder stood a split-half second before Fluff. She raked a hand through her short, spikey hair.

"Why the hell are we letting them—?" The wolf choked off her own question at his look. Clearing her throat once, she clenched her fists and then released them. "Apologies, Alpha. I did not know we were allowing outsiders into protected territory."

"We aren't." He didn't elaborate further. Fluff nodded then grabbed clothes off the rack. Grinder hadn't questioned his choices, at least not verbally. The Sentry positioned himself so he could intercept Julian if he made any move. Neither of the Sentries approached Ranae. Satisfied they understood, Diesel checked Ranae. She had remained silent during the exchange, yet her eyes remained watchful and assessing.

Smart. Calculating. Diesel approved. Understanding the dynamics within a pack, judging who held power and who did not suggested a powerful dominance. The alarm beeped once when the temperature hit fifty degrees inside the antechamber and the inner door released. Ranae stripped off the neoprene mask and shoved her hood back. Diesel knelt a beat before she could then released her feet from the snowshoes.

Her eyes narrowed a fraction, and his wolves went absolutely still at the position he'd placed

himself in at her feet. His lowered head and her stiff
posture detailed the esteem he held for Ranae. Fluff
and Grinder didn't move, but the tension in the air
ratcheted a fraction higher. A distant part of his mind
acknowledged their unease, but he had no interest in
settling their fears or even answering their questions.

All they needed to know was the deference he
held for Ranae. Rising, he captured Ranae's gaze and
held it as he reached his full height. On his feet, he
began to loosen the ties of her parka. She accepted his
assistance, but he didn't let her composure fool him.
She would not be so easily swayed. "Welcome to
Tikaani, Ranae Buckley. You are my guest and under
my protection." He reiterated the welcome for his
wolves.

"Thank you for the welcome, and I will extend
to you my protection as a Hunter of Willow Bend for
the duration of my stay." The politeness in her voice
held the edge of bite and he spared her a half smile.

"I feel very safe in your capable hands."

Anger flared in her eyes then her gaze seemed
to shutter. Irritation raked over him at the way she
closed herself off. They'd made a connection. Surely,
she'd felt it. The rejection irked him. Well aware of
their audience, however, he set the emotion aside
along with her parka. He had to get them inside and
settled with the pack—well, Ranae at least. Julian
could leave.

Pushing the inner door open, he shepherded
Ranae inside. Doubt rolled off her in waves, but he
didn't try to assuage her concerns. With a glance, he
ordered Grinder to stay on Julian. Fluff folded her
arms, but said nothing as she took a middle position,

segregating the Chief Enforcer. If the change in positions bothered Julian, Diesel didn't give a damn.

Inside the main room of the cabin, Ranae tugged off her knit cap. The strawberry blonde of her hair spilled out like autumn fire. The warm color beckoned to him to run his fingers through the thick strands. Would her wolf share the same sable pelt? No spring pup, he controlled the urge.

"How is this any different from the cabin we were in?" The skeptical note in her voice clawed him.

"Be patient and find out." Not waiting for her response, he strode across the room to the broad, brick wall. The hum of the underground generators vibrated against his ears. The sound added a fresh layer of irritation to rasp against his flesh. Flipping open a switch pad, he entered a code. A high-pitched alarm warned him the security doors opened behind the wall. Once they completed their hydraulic withdrawal, the brick wall itself released.

Gripping the edge, he shoved the wall along the runner. A pull switch inside could open the brick, but raw strength was needed to open it from the outside—a security feature should the village be raided while the strongest roamed. They kept their vulnerable secured below.

Ranae released a little gasp at the corridor and stairs he revealed. Drinking in her surprise, he glanced at her. Even the nuances in her scent changed, a hint of sweetness like melted caramel atop dark chocolate. "As I said earlier...welcome to Tikaani."

Snow Wolf

Chapter Four

The steps descended thirty feet to a well-lit corridor. Machinery hummed beyond the walls. The vibrations shivered through her legs and along her frame. Shock piled atop shock—since when did the Yukon have such technology? Everything she'd been briefed on detailed an almost archaic lifestyle. The damn guest cabin had a refrigerator that dated back to the 1950s, if not further.

Diesel strode one pace a head of her. The corridor narrowed at the top of the steps. Despite the almost painfully white walls, it seemed littered with shadows—or maybe it where the stairs disappeared into the darkness below. Claustrophobia wasn't her issue. Fragments collided in her thoughts. As a pup, she'd been afraid of the dark. Not because she didn't have night vision or because she feared monsters in it…but because her brothers used to prank her and each other. More than once, they'd leapt out of the dark and pounced her.

Adrenaline-fueled terror plagued her through childhood. Her brothers always made it up to her. They never complained when she wanted to sleep in their room, but she hated the weakness. Tough wolves didn't need their brothers to protect them. Dominant wolves didn't need to be told it would be okay. She made herself sleep in the dark, even when she couldn't sleep. Even when she stayed up all night, sweating buckets as she waited for something terrible to happen.

Maybe she made it happen herself.
Intellectually, she knew what utter crap the idea that
her fear proved complicit in A.J.'s incarceration or
Claire's abandonment of Ty. Ranae had nothing to do
with either of those events, yet she'd seen one brother
vanish and another have his heart ripped out. The
dynamic within the family changed. Her parents
weathered the challenges, but her brothers Ty and
Linc had seemed lessened until A.J. returned. Before
that happened, Mason overthrew Toman and the pack
split its time between mourning and celebration—
Mason proved a capable Alpha, but even his focus
had been torn between acclimating the pack and
saving his mate.

One thought pinged off another. The air
clogged in her throat. The narrow corridor seemed to
funnel her toward the stairs and the past. Ranae shook
her head. The damn humming behind the walls, the
narrow corridor… It was all too much.

With the wolves swarming behind her, she
couldn't back off and her shoulder brushed against
the Alpha's. Power flared at the contact. Her wolf
bucked at the shadowy quarters. Her chest tightened.
How far down did it go?

Trapped against Diesel, she struggled against
the twin desires of fight and flight striking at once. A
warm hand closed over hers. Strength flooded her,
settling her beast's urges.

Unease pitted in her gut. She didn't want the
Yukon Alpha's comfort or the contact, no matter her
body's traitorous response.

"This is about fear. Not trust." His sub vocal
words ruffled her fur and stifled her argument. How

the hell did he arouse such contradictory responses within her? "Stay with me, and stop scowling. You'll scare the children." *Children?*

Tending to and protecting the next generation united disparate packs at a most basic level. Willow Bend would protect the children of any other pack without question, even those of Three Rivers, a pack on probation who faced dissolution should the Alphas finally reach a consensus. The reminder, however, jerked her attention back to where they stood. The steps descended into the darkness and her wolf surged beneath her skin. She wanted to rip her arm out of Diesel's grip, but he was right.

It was his pack. They were his to protect. Wildness threaded through her veins. Her wolf surged to the surface and no amount of self-control could prevent her eyes from their shift. The lack of light below betrayed the true darkness awaiting them. All she wanted to do was flee, but Diesel's grip steadied her. The race of her pulse betrayed her—when he slid his fingers to thread with hers she relinquished a small measure of control.

It was far better to accept his assistance than to run screaming up the stairs or worse—burst into tears. Her pride wouldn't survive either. Mirroring his use of the sub vocal, she murmured, "Thank you."

He gave her hand a light squeeze then resumed his descent. With no choice but to join him, she fought the harsh tightness of her lungs. Rasping pants wouldn't do much for her ego or her image. Strength steadied her, buoying her past the initial panic.

Inch by inch, the shadows ebbed into light. Either her night vision only noticed the subtle lighting at the edges of the walls or it illuminated slowly of its own accord as they descended. The surety in Diesel's steps offered her almost as much comfort as the hand he held tight in his grasp.

It felt as though they walked forever, though a distant part of her mind acknowledged it couldn't be more than two flights. At the bottom, a panel of red lights offered the hope their time in the dark drew to a close. Diesel released her hand, but shifted so he could rest his free hand against her back.

The liberty should have annoyed her, but since it kept her from turning into a shaking, blubbering idiot, she said nothing. Pressing his palm to a flat screen she hadn't seen, an entirely new shock went through her system. *He has a palm reader?*

Panel lights going green, the door released with a hiss of hydraulic pressure, then swung inward almost silently. Light flooded out of the opening, a split second after Diesel said, "Close your eyes."

It dazzled her, blinding in its effect, and she squinted her eyes shut too late to avoid the brilliance. Spots danced over her closed eyelids, and her claws sliced out. It took her a moment to regain her equilibrium. When her claws retracted, Diesel gave her a light nudge to step inside.

Thankfully, they entered a much wider area. Once she was able to open her eyes to mere slits, almost daytime brightness had been achieved by the lighting embedded around the walls. It was an empty room, and a second door waited at the end.

"A gating system," she verbalized her thoughts, impressed. "In case someone breeches it." The second door seemed barely visible, and it had no access panel that she could see.

"Exactly." Diesel seemed to watch her intently. Movement had her turning as Julian and the other pair of Yukon wolves trailed them into the room. She'd half-forgotten they weren't alone. Grateful for the distraction, she shook off the layer of intimacy which seemed to have draped around her while Diesel held her hand. The light helped, though she couldn't say she cared for the enclosure.

Once they were all inside, Diesel nodded to one of his wolves. The male put his palm on the access panel and sealed the door behind them. A minute vibration passed through the floor. The gears? Or mechanisms maybe? The feeling rotated through the floor, faint but when she cocked her head, she could almost hear the machinery. It had to be top of the line because it was near silent. Across from her, the lines around Diesel's eyes tightened. Did the sound bother him?

Curiosity welled within her. Everything she knew about the Yukon said primitive, yet nothing of their design suggested the same. How had they hidden this from the representatives who came to see them? Dylan certainly hadn't mentioned it.

When the door opened on the far side, Diesel spread his hand and gestured for her to take lead. Or was he simply allowing her to walk in front of him? Confusion tangled with her curiosity. Nothing about this Alpha matched what she'd been told. Cataloging each new discovery, she experienced a stab of guilt. The emotion didn't belong; she was Mason's wolf. Whatever she learned, she had a right to share, didn't she?

Two steps from the open door, she paused. Someone approached from the opposite side. A trickle of running water masked his soft steps, but her nose warned her it was a man.

"Alpha," the man's voice was soft, gentle and loaded with kindness. His scent carried notes of lavender, chamomile, and more. *Teas.* Whomever he was, he'd been brewing tea. The man standing in the doorway was nearly as tall as Diesel, but he lacked his bulk. The lean muscle could be deceiving, however, because it didn't indicate a lack of strength. "We did not expect you to return so early."

Ranae had to admire his composure as his gaze swept first to her, then to Julian. He didn't ask, he merely extended his hand to his Alpha.

Diesel accepted it, then pulled the man in for a firm hug. Another surprise. Apparently her visit would be populated by them.

"Chowder, this is Ranae Buckley. She is my guest and under my protection." The statement had the other wolf's eyes widening before he could recover. His expression seemed filled with wonder and his grin, when he gave it to her, was wide and full of welcome. "Ranae, this is Chowder, he is our healer and brother to Grinder over there. Chowder, take Ranae to my rooms. She will use those while staying with us."

His room? Now wait a damn minute. Before she could voice her objections, Diesel pinned her with a look. The order—no, the demand—in his blue eyes silenced her. When her lips compressed together, he nodded then glanced at Julian. "Come with me, Enforcer. Grinder, you can come with me. Fluff, return to patrol."

The woman didn't like the order but, like Ranae, she said nothing. Her gaze, when it met Ranae's, didn't hold an ounce of welcome. Her, Ranae could deal with. She recognized scorn and doubt. It was like looking into a mirror. She'd felt much the same way about Claire's return.

Meeting her hostile gaze and holding it, Ranae raised her brows. If she wanted a challenge, Ranae wouldn't back off. As a guest, she couldn't offer one. Stubbornness and pride, her mother called it. For Ranae, it was much more basic. Bullies liked to throw their weight around, and the only way to end it was to meet it with equal force.

"Now, Fluff." The order severed the rising tension between her and the other wolf. The woman with the short, spikey hair ripped her gaze away and Ranae glared at Diesel. Having him end the dominance battle before it truly begun wasn't a win for her. With a hint of a smile, he tapped her nose with one finger. "Behave."

The admonishment stymied the rise of her sympathy toward the Yukon Alpha. Clamping her jaw shut around her response, she took a deep breath. A mistake, because it flooded her with his scent. The elusive lure of snow on fur pulled at her—clean, crisp, and captivating. Not shaking her head, she shifted her grip on her bag and transferred her attention to the healer.

He stared at her in wonder, and it was only then she realized all the wolves were staring at her. Despite his call to Julian to follow him, Diesel hadn't moved. Was he planning to stay there all day until she went with Chowder? What the hell was up with the names? Grasping onto the fresh spill of irritation, she used it to buoy her mood.

"After you," she told the healer. He was safe to have his back to her, and he knew it because he simply smiled and turned to lead the way. Only a mad wolf attacked a healer. It didn't matter what pack he belonged to because, like children, they were to be protected.

Steadfastly ignoring Diesel, she went around him and stalked after the healer. It took her three steps to realize she was stomping her feet and to correct the behavior.

Halfway down the new hall, with its running water along the walls, she caught the distinct echo of a faint chuckle.

Fucker is laughing at me.
Fine. Let him laugh.

She was there to do a job and nothing else. She hoped he enjoyed being locked out of his own rooms.

Diesel stared after Ranae as she stomped away from him. Perhaps it was her relative youth, but he'd really annoyed her with the tap to the nose. Her annoyance, though, brought the welcome return of her attention to him. Dominance play with Fluff aside, his wolf wouldn't lay a hand on his mate, no matter how irritating Fluff found Ranae. He'd deal with their contentious behavior later.

Still, Ranae's heavy footsteps earned a chuckle. When she stilled at the sound for a moment, then continued on quieter steps, he almost laughed aloud. The desire shocked him. When was the last time a belly-ripping laugh tore free from him?

Amused, he glanced at Julian then Grinder. "Let's go." If they didn't, he'd follow his mate to his rooms and try to piss her off more. Her anger tantalized him.

Ranae's scent teased him through the portal way. While Chowder took her to the right and toward the personal rooms, he diverted left. Dealing with Julian was a pain in the ass, but the sooner he got rid of him, the sooner he could focus all of his attention on Ranae.

Ahead, a class full of kids trailed behind their mentors and, one-by-one, they turned to look at him. His heart squeezed at the open affection the little ones showed. Many of them only saw their parents now and again during the winter months. The very young had at least one, if not both, parents wintering below, but by elementary age, the kids learned independence and reliance on their year groups. They slept in dorms, with den mothers looking after them.

It was an excellent exercise in both pack bonding and developing their instincts. Still, despite his own age, he could remember missing his parents when they joined the pack on their winter shift. Seeing the question in their eyes, Diesel held up a fist to stop Grinder and Julian from continuing.

Squatting down, he opened his arms and the kids broke from their formation to race toward him. They swarmed him, then he was under a dog pile of happy kids. Laughter and tickles soon followed.

The maternal leading their line followed at a more sedate pace, and Diesel let out a chuckle as three of the boys clambered onto his back. Their arms wrapped around his neck, and they fought to pull him off balance. Sweeping a girl out of his way by cuddling her, he tumbled to the boys then slipped free. Diving into the game, the kids divided, some coming at him from the right while the others came at him from the left.

Pride burned in him as larger kids blocked the smaller, protecting them. The more submissive among the children laughed as they circled behind their more dominant brethren. Soon he had kids locked onto his legs as more began clamber on to him. Working together, they rocked his balance. However, when he raised his arms in mock surrender, he laughed as only some withdrew. The others continued their effort to take him off his feet.

The tussling continued for another five minutes before Bridge cleared her throat. A light, if effective, reminder he was derailing their day. Nearly as disappointed as the kids, Diesel said, "Enough now." Obedience rippled through the wild bunch, and they hopped down before immediately returning to their lineup—all except for little Anya. She raced over to him and held her arms up. Her parents shouldn't have left the tiny one so soon, but both had needed the winter shift. They'd discussed it with Chowder and then with Diesel before he approved their request.

Scooping the barely four-year-old up into his arms, he indulged her with an affectionate kiss to the cheek. Her grip on his neck tightened and he rubbed his chin to her head. Little ones craved affection and, for once, he found himself with plenty to spare. "Anya can stay with me, Bridge. I will send her along within the hour." His statement was both an order and a request.

Though only in her fifties, Bridge preferred the nursery assignments to all others. She'd been a Sentry in her younger years, but it had never been a good fit. "Very well, Alpha." The acquiescence carried a note of amusement and—dare he say—approval? She waited till the last child, sans Anya, had joined the line before she rose on her tiptoes and pressed a kiss to his jaw.

Cupping her cheek, he held her still a long moment. Like the children, contact with his wolves was also important. His distance had been noticed, but he'd never held himself aloof from their affections. His dwindling spirit and desire to continue had never usurped his far more visceral need to protect what was his.

"How is Lucky?" Bridge's mate earned his name a dozen times over in his lifetime. The wolf had a canny sense of when danger approached. Another Sentry, he also divided his time between the roam with his pack and with his mate at the nursery. Somehow, his instincts always put him in the right place at the right time.

"He's being stubborn. Chowder won't let him roam just yet. The broken leg has healed well, though." The wolf had been gravely injured during a fall from an ice wall...one that should have killed him. But he'd still pulled the younglings out of their predicament, broken leg notwithstanding.

"Good. Tell him I said you were in charge of him, and he'd do well to listen."

Her laughter sparked true merriment. "I do that everyday and he grumbles, but obeys." Another kiss, and she gave a second to Anya. "Be a good girl, okay?"

The little one nodded, snuggling to Diesel's shoulder. She wasn't budging from her claim to his attention. Cuddling her, Diesel left the school children behind and grinned at their studious return to their duties. His pack was strong, every single one of them, down to the delicate little flower in his arms. Chowder thought Anya had the taste of a healer in her scent, and Diesel didn't disagree.

However, she was too young to do more than be looked after and be allowed to grow of her own accord. The underground complex never suited him, except today. He found himself seeing it through new eyes. What would Ranae make of the different chambers they'd carved? Some were designed to be forest, while others were open and terraced. Throughout it, running water created pools—both for moisture and to keep the water clean as it tumbled through the system.

His engineers had constructed a thing of beauty and, though many of the pack spent months below, the rotating light system gave them a taste of natural daylight and darkness so their days didn't drag on them. The stone steps he followed down curved into a less used area. His office belowground offered him a private place for discussions when he joined them. Rare was the appearance he put in there, but they kept it clean and neat and no one else step foot inside except the two women he'd entrusted with its care.

Montana eyed him as he arrived—already forewarned, he suspected—and she had the doors wide open. "Should I send for some cookies, as well?" Her gaze rested on Anya as she asked.

"Cookies sound good, don't they?" In fact, now that she'd mentioned it, his stomach rumbled. "I think sandwiches, too. What say you Anya?"

"Yes, please." Soft, barely a whisper, her voice carried nothing but trust. "Can I stay here to eat?"

"Of course, but I need to talk to these two for a moment. Will you wait with Montana?" He could order her, but preferred to avoid it where the tiniest ones were concerned.

Anya switched her attention to Montana. "Do you have hot chocolate?"

"I think we can find some." His assistant held out her hands, and Anya kissed Diesel's cheek before stretching out to let Montana take her. "I'll send for food for you, Alpha."

"Thank you." He cupped Montana's cheek, and she rubbed against his palm. Affection offered and received, touch to reassure and reconnect. Leaving the women, he strode into his office, Julian on his heels. Though turning his back on the Enforcer wasn't always wise, he didn't doubt the man's intentions. He had a mission in the Yukon, or he wouldn't be here.

Inside, Grinder closed the doors to give them privacy and took up a guard position. Diesel crossed the dark wood floor to the desk he'd carved from an old ice ship. It had been one of the last projects he'd done with his own father, a rare time they'd shared together.

After a passing caress against the scarred wood, he reached into a drawer of the desk and pulled out fresh clothes. Shrugging into the t-shirt, he set his gaze on Julian. "Talk."

The other wolf smiled then dropped into a chair opposite the desk, all pretense falling away. "Among the Three Rivers wolves was an Omega. She has joined with Willow Bend."

Not that he cared, but Diesel nodded. "Mason's pack has recovered nicely from Toman's mishandling." He'd never cared for the other Alpha on the two occasions they'd met. The man's dominance had always been a question, but his politics had been solid and predictable. Mason Clayborne had not proven so easy to read, a good thing for most packs. "Why do I care?"

"Because she's Dallas' pup."

The name aroused an old memory in Diesel. Leaving the jeans for later, he walked over to the bar and poured them both a drink. Like him, Julian preferred whiskey, so he didn't bother to ask before he slid a drink across the desk before he took his own seat. "Well, that should make tracking her easier for you."

"She won't roam into Mason's territory." The unspoken accusation lingered between them.

"She was due to give birth, Julian. I wouldn't send out my worst enemy to birth a pup alone." Nor had he informed the Enforcers, which remained point of contention between them.

"You knew I was hunting her."

"Not my problem. If you can't catch her, maybe you shouldn't share your constant failure in that department." It amused him. Dallas was Julian's white whale—he wouldn't stop until he found her. "You didn't come all the way here to talk about old business."

"No, I didn't. I have other news. Your wolf, Colby, passed away overseas several years ago."

"So, you have confirmed his death." Diesel long suspected it. He only sent word to the Enforcers after three years when Dodger—his name amongst the pack—had not returned.

"Yes."

"How?" He knew the wolf passed, had felt the snap of the too-thin tendril of connection. Not knowing where he was or what he'd been doing, Diesel had not acted on the knowledge. It could have simply been time and distance that eroded their connection.

"A fire," Julian said, before taking a long swallow of the whiskey. His expression shadowed. "He saved many lives, according to his daughter."

Daughter. The information jolted Diesel. "His mate?"

"A latent, like their child turned out to be. Both are in Hudson River."

"They have a place here, if they want it." No hesitation slowed his response. Diesel would care for Dodger's mate and their pup, although she had to be a grown woman by now.

"Unnecessary, but you may wish to reach out to Brett. Colby—the daughter, not your wolf—is his mate."

Mated to an Alpha. Dodger would be proud. "Latents don't always do well that high in pack structure."

"She's also a healer… and no longer latent. She's shifted." Julian shrugged. "The rest is their story to tell, so if you want it, reach out to them. The mate has remarried, a human this time, and seems settled. Your wolf saved many lives and is remembered well."

"To Dodger, then." Diesel raised his glass. At the door, Grinder put a fist to his heart and Julian held his glass high as well.

"To Dodger."

They slammed back the whiskey and it was Julian who stood to retrieve the bottle.

"Thank you for bringing the information." It cost him nothing to show gratitude.

"You're welcome." They were silent a long moment as Julian refilled their glasses then resumed his seat and set the bottle on the desk between them.

"How bad was the attack on Cassius' pack?"

"Significant. More than a two hundred wolves dead—many women and children." The information had Grinder growling, but he got himself under control.

Diesel swirled the whiskey in his glass. "What do you know of the Russian wolves involved?"

"Not much." Julian reached into a pocket and pulled out his phone. He pulled up something on the screen then slid it across to him. "This one is nearly identical to the wolf taken in Cassius' territory."

Nearly identical. Diesel studied the image. The man had a Slavic look to him, light hair, dark eyes.

"The next image is of the child they used in the attack on Sutter Butte."

Child? Diesel swiped his thumb across the screen then studied the delicate looking girl with the dead eyes. The lack of any emotion or animation sent a ripple of distaste through him. Only one pack in Russia he knew of used children as infiltrators. "Volchitsa."

"You know them?"

"Not them, specifically." Diesel slid the phone back. "But only one of the Russian packs would use someone so small to do so much damage. They raise them to be infiltrators—usually orphans, with no family group to protect them. They are trained from infancy then sent out to other packs to gather information." *Information. Targets.* The little ones could do so much damage. "Malyutka have no future, no desire, no goal, save for the one they are given. Where is this one now?"

"Serafina Andre has her in Delta Crescent."

"They should kill it." Harsh, and even saying it aloud made him sick.

"She's only a child." Julian took the phone back.

"No, she is Malyutka. If her goal is to create chaos, she will try in Delta Crescent. If it is to kill an Alpha, she will do that as well." His southern brethren would not understand, as with the damn Italian wolf they'd allowed to take up residence with her sixth pack. They would never see the child as a threat.

"It doesn't matter what name you give her." Julian's tone suggested he didn't disagree with the sentiment. "She's a child. They will not kill her. Besides, she's young enough. Perhaps in time..."

After draining his whiskey, Diesel set the glass down on the desk. "The only thing time grants them is it allows child to gather more information and grow. She will only get stronger. More determined."

"Nothing we can do about that." Sober understanding passed between them. Perhaps Julian had not strayed so far from who they'd been as boys. "I will carry your words to them, cousin." The reminder of who they were to each other didn't soften his stance. "They will not follow that advice any more than they followed it about Three Rivers."

So be it. "What of the male?"

"Cassius agreed with your take on that one. My last contact with Brett said he was interrogating the wolf. Afterward, they'll execute him. It may already be done."

Good. Then the threat near the child of his pack had been eliminated.

"He won't take chances with Colby's safety or his pack. Not after what all has happened before." Julian eyed the bottle, so Diesel uncapped it and refilled their glasses.

They saluted then drained them, and Julian refilled them again. The spread of the whiskey in his system heated his blood and chased away the last remnants of the chill. Diesel leaned back in his chair. "They will not come for me, Julian."

"I know." The other wolf shrugged. "Your fellow Alphas don't understand. Most are too young to know the reasons why."

Diesel smiled faintly. "Good. Don't educate them. It was a long time ago." Too long, and too forgotten by time. They needed to leave it there. "How much longer do you plan to stay?"

"I can leave in a day. We have to identify where the wolves are coming in…and deal with Three

Rivers." The admission didn't surprise Diesel.

"So, they have finally come around?"

"To a point," the Chief Enforcer admitted. "If they are being used as a launching point, they have already signed the writs of their destruction." If they weren't, the other Alphas might change their mind.

"I care not for their fate any more now than I did then." Diesel had other things on his mind. Another someone, more specifically. "I will vote to the majority." If it changed the sway of things, then he would let it happen.

"And if they are split?" came the dry response.

"Then kill them so I don't have to have this discussion again."

They locked gazes, and Julian didn't disguise his disapproval. He shook his head and took a long drink. "We shall see what we shall see."

Done with the conversation, Diesel stood. Julian didn't leave his chair. "You will be returning alone."

"That is up to her, isn't it?"

"No, *cousin*. It is not. For now, you may inform Mason she is to be my liaison, so she stays." A bold move, but he wasn't finished. Meeting the Enforcer's stare, he smiled. "If he doesn't go for that, you can tell him she is my hostage—by way of the old laws."

"Do you really want to pick this fight with him over the potential that she is your mate?" *So, Julian knew.*

"If he hadn't wanted it, he would never have sent her. Grinder will be your escort—and he will show you out. Safe travels."

"And good luck to you," Julian said, not turning

when Diesel strode out. "You're going to need it."

Chapter Five

Her escort guided her through a hallway decked out in fresh, green growth. The scents surprised her and—though he set a sedate pace—she almost hated to make him stop. "Is this…mint?" Touching two fingers to the plant, she spared a look at the healer.

"Yes," he said, a smile on his face and in his voice. "We had to get creative down here for the long months. It's taken a few years, but we have a lot of growth these days. This is the herbal route, mostly for teas and tinctures. We also have the vegetable path and the fruit orchard."

"You grow them all underground?" Would the surprises stop coming?

"We have to. Can't grow them above this time of year, and we have rotating lights which provide different radiances of UV as well as sunlight. The plants provide us with nutrition and medicine…"

"…and oxygen." *Holy crap.* She would kill to see the schematics and how they'd handled the construction. Her brothers might be the builders, but she loved designing. Her phone went off, and she jerked in surprise. Did they really get signal this deep? Pulling it out of her pocket, she frowned at the alarm. She'd barely remembered setting it.

"Yes, and oxygen. Our engineers refer to it as a natural carbon dioxide scrubbing system. They remove the excess and produce oxygen for us. We have six areas in the underground compound, though we do plan on future expansion. Each area also acts as fertile ground for the crops and vegetables we need. Meat we can store all year, and do...but fresh fruits and vegetables? Herbs? Growing them gives us the best of both."

Delighted, she tried to identify the other herbs as they resumed their path. "Do you mind if I ask you an awkward question?"

The wolf grinned. "Well, you have to ask it now, because awkward questions are usually dirty or funny or both."

Amused by his very direct and gentle response, she couldn't help her answering grin. "Why are you called Chowder?" What parent did that to their child?

His bark of laughter erased any possible sting. Curling his fingers, he beckoned her to follow him along the path—which turned out to be cobblestones. Frankly if she didn't know she was underground, she'd be tempted to look upward for the sky. Curious, she glanced toward the ceiling and found it to be mostly rock, with the same kind of lights set within them alongside nozzles for what must be water pipes.

Huh. If they run the piping through all of it, they can regulate temperature using running water... They passed another one of the shallow pools with water splashing down over the rocks. Some lichen grew along the sides, a distinct green against the grey stone. The water had to drain below, and across from it were more herbs—and the rich smell of moisture, fresh soil, and growth. It was alive and vivid, better than a greenhouse. Her thermals were too warm for their environment.

"Not all packs live by the old ways, and not all packs live by our ways," Chowder began as they wound through what had to be private chambers, though the hallway widened into circular areas that reminded her of terraced parks then narrowed to walkways between. Everywhere she looked though, plants were in abundance, including flowers which could serve no other purpose than being beautiful. "Consider," he continued. "When we are born, our parents name us. These names are important. They define us as our parents see us and sometimes even possess their hopes and dreams. As we age, we earn nicknames…sometimes even before we have any idea of who we are."

Her eldest brother had been A.J. for as long as she could remember. No one except their mother used his full name. "My brother calls me Squirt sometimes." It was an affectionate name.

Her host gave her a sidelong look. "Because you were smaller than him?"

"Yes."

With a grin, he nodded. "It is much the same here. But, as we grow older, sometimes we change our name to represent who we've become. Perhaps a Sentry will seek a stronger name, something intimidating, while an engineer or a teacher may want to be remembered for their task."

"So, you chose the name Chowder?" It didn't matter that she didn't want to be rude, she couldn't keep the skepticism from her voice.

Another soft laugh rumbled from him as he paused in the last circular area— as far from the center as they could go and no pathways led farther. Unlike the other terraced sections, only a stone pool sat in the center. No plants or greenery decorated the surroundings or invited anyone to stay. Frankly the courtyard was rather boring and spartan. She'd hoped for something more elaborate for Diesel's quarters.

Then again, she shook off the wishful thinking. The man himself didn't seem all that much more decked out either. He was strong, gorgeous, old and tough. What else did he need to be?

"No, I didn't choose the name." He put his hand to a similar security plate to the one she'd seen outside then entered a code. "Go ahead and put your palm on there."

Obeying more out of curiosity than the need to do as she was told, she raised her eyebrows when the plate turned green.

"Now you can unlock the door without an escort." The explanation, so calmly given without an ounce of judgment, worried her more than Diesel telling him to take her to his rooms. How long did they think she was going to be there, that she would earn the right to roam without an escort?

She was a Hunter of Willow Bend, not a Yukon pack member or mate. Scowling at the idea she'd been granted far more access than she desired or deserved, she couldn't help a fresh wave of curiosity when the door panel slid inward smoothly.

Wait... Ranae paused to glance around then back up the tunneled path they followed. Chowder watched her, but if her behavior troubled him he didn't say so.

Listening, she could hear nothing but the water, and even that seemed to fade to the background. Along the path, she'd heard a lot of things—the hum of the water pumps, the buzz of the lights, even the faint voices of other occupants inside their stone dwellings. Why nothing here? Because no one came here? Or maybe no one wanted to be here?

"You were saying about your name," she prodded him, uneasy with all the reasons why this area was so different. At home, Mason's house had very quickly become the center of the pack, much as Toman's great house had been before it. It wasn't uncommon to drop in on the Alpha and his mate— well, not uncommon for most. Ranae didn't think the welcome extended to her as much anymore. She had to earn that right back, and she'd been working hard at it.

"Ah, yes," Chowder said with a nod, as she passed him to step inside. The interior seemed to be made of the same stone, but instead of cobblestone floors, the interior had grass for carpet.

Stunned again, she simply stared at the rich, verdant grass everywhere. There was furniture, too, but it was all spread out. Like a great conversation area set up for a party, but not designed for coziness. Water flowed around the walls, the air was sweet…was that vanilla she could smell? Orchids? Really? Or something else? Her nose seemed to go into overtime trying to sort the various scents. Once more, she felt transported to a whole other world.

"As I said, we choose our names but sometimes, and as is most common in this pack, we earn them, too. I had a particular affinity for clam chowder when I was younger." The explanation tugged her back to the present. Not orchids, but something far more tropical than she expected to find in the Yukon.

"They call you Chowder because you like clam chowder?" *Really?*

"Like is too mild a word," the healer said with a chuckle. "I loved chowder. It was all I ate it for months at a time, breakfast, lunch and dinner."

The explanation made her stomach roll. "Seriously?" She pivoted to face him, aware of the sweat beading her brow. If she'd thought her thermals were too warm for the hallway, they were positively cooking her in the suite.

"I'm afraid so." He wore a rueful smile and spread his hands wide. "What can I say? I really liked it. My brother started calling me Chowder and it stuck."

"What was your name before that?"

"My parents named me Benjamin." He didn't seem to mind discussing himself. "Occasionally, some of my friends still call me Ben, though I think if you were to ask for me that way, most wouldn't know."

"Nice. Your brother is…?" What the hell had Diesel called him? "Grinder?"

"Yes, and if you want to know how he earned his name, you should ask him." He hesitated a moment then raised a single finger. "Don't ask Fluff."

Somehow, she didn't even need to ask him the why on that one. The spikey-haired woman was the least *fluffy* person she had ever met. "I won't, but let me guess…not everyone's nicknames have to do with what they like or what they do?"

"Of course not."

Which meant Diesel was also a nickname. Interesting. What had his name been before? "If I were to ask you about your Alpha?"

"Again, I would advise if you want to know, you should ask him." The man wore an almost beatific smile. "I think he'll tell you."

Not really what she wanted to hear. Eager to change the subject, she glanced around again. "Where should I put my bag?" Hopefully the bedroom looked like a bedroom and not a park.

"You may have your choice of the rooms, I'm sure." Though he kept his tone light, he hadn't ventured very far into the room. Was he worried she'd lunge for the door or something? "Or you can wait until Diesel arrives, and he can show you to his."

The hint of probing question clung to his last sentence. "We're not mates," she announced, though whom she wanted to convince, she wasn't sure. "He just said so to shut me up." It was her story and she was sticking to it. "I'm only here to handle Willow Bend business then I'll be leaving."

"Interesting." Chowder didn't offer her an argument. "The kitchen is to your right. It's not fully stocked, but I'm sure Montana will correct that. In addition to myself, Montana, the cleaning crew are the only other wolves with permission and access to enter this suite besides yourself and Diesel. As you are in residence, the door security will announce our arrival rather than simply admit us. Diesel and I can both override it, should you not answer. No one else."

Her gut churned. Not a cell, but she couldn't bolt the door against her host. *Well, that sucks.* Clearing her throat, she fought a grimace. "I'm going to find a room, and a shower. I assume you have real showers here?" The guesthouse shower had been akin to drilling a hole in the ice and jumping into Lake Michigan in January. She'd done that once on a dare. *Never* again.

Chowder smiled. "Of course. You will find it down the hall near the bedrooms. Give it a moment to warm up. The heated water must travel farther to reach this suite. My suite, by the way, is at the last junction we passed. Most of our phones don't work here, but we do have intercoms." He pointed to the panel by the door. "I'm the first button, Montana is the second." He paused a beat. "I doubt you'll need any of the others, but the red one will connect to the surface cabin, and the green one to the Sentries assigned here."

She nodded. "Thank you."

"I'll let you settle in and bring a tray over until Montana can stock your cupboard. Is there anything you don't like?"

Ranae didn't tell him it wouldn't be necessary. "Chowder," she admitted and he laughed, a rich, redolent masculine sound which invited her to join him. After a beat, she did and shook her head. "Sorry. Not big on most sea foods, but my mother taught me to eat what was in front of me, so whatever doesn't put you too much trouble."

"No worries at all. I think you and I will be good friends, Miss Buckley."

"Oh, please, call me Ranae. If you knew anything about us Buckleys, there are far too many of us to rely on that alone."

"As you wish. Would you prefer coffee or tea?"

Whiskey might be better for her nerves, but the last thing she needed was to get smashed. "Coffee would be fantastic." As he turned to exit, she raised her hand. "Thank you, Chowder."

"It is absolutely my pleasure." He touched a hand to his chest over his heart then turned and left. The door closed behind him with a hushed sound, and she was alone.

Alone in an Alpha's quarters that reminded her of her parents' backyard. "Well, Ranae, we are definitely not in Willow Bend…"

Reminding herself she was a Hunter, trained and capable, she fisted her grip on the bag and padded through the grass towards the stone step path leading down a hall. The first bedroom turned out to be a small, rather spartan room with a single bed. It would more than do. She dropped her bag on the bed, then sat to strip off her boots.

After pulling out some clean clothes, she went in search of the bathroom. Located at the end of the hall, it also adjoined a much larger bedroom. The room was nearly as big as the living room and it boasted a fireplace—enormous, like one in a ski lodge—and an oversized king bed covered in what her nose told her was an actual bearskin blanket.

The dark brown on white reminded her that there were more than grizzlies to be found in Alaska. Curiosity nibbled at her… but she hesitated in the open door. What secrets did Diesel hide in his most private room? She detected only the faintest trace of scent other than the blanket and the snow on fur, but the lack of strength said he didn't use it often.

Shutting the door on temptation, she turned away. The bathroom was spacious, and well-lit, much like the hallway and living room. Closing the second door which led into the bedroom, she turned to inspect the shower.

It was doublewide with two showerheads and a tile floor. The room also boasted a hot tub-sized bathtub which could easily accommodate two...*and all the activities two healthy adults could get up to.* Ranae stilled, then pinched the inside of her elbow hard enough to make tears spark in her eyes.

The last thing she needed to think about was sex with *anyone* while in his suite. Wolves could sort scents out like that in nothing flat. He'd already made one declaration; she didn't want to give him any false impressions.

Continuing her mental chastisement, she stripped out of her clothes. The shower didn't have a door or any curtain, so anyone walking into the bathroom would see her. Annoying, but she was hardly body shy. She could always lock the—she glared at the handles on the doors. No, she couldn't lock them.

Stop it. She told her reflection as she finally freed herself from the thermals. Flushed from the heat, *and only the heat*, she reached in to switch on the water. As Chowder advised, she waited because the first streams were most assuredly cold. When it reached tepid, she stepped under it and let the water cool down her overheated system.

By the time it warmed, she was ready to sigh. Hot water pounded her muscles, and she braced her hands against the wall and turned her face down so it would roll down her arms and back. The water offered her respite and a chance to catch her breath.

She'd learned so much about the Yukon in such

a short time.

Too much. Why show her all of this? Why let her into their secrets? Secrets the other Hunters couldn't possibly have known. No way they would have kept it from her when sending her on the mission. Dylan had even warned her about the icy showers.

Her gut tightened. The only reason to let her see everything had to be Diesel wasn't concerned with her sharing it with her pack. Would he ask her to keep the secret for him? Or would he let her leave at all?

Anger surged beneath the rising tide of fear. Holding her hostage would only piss off her Alpha. As far as she knew—and as far as the histories told—none of the southern packs had ever warred with the Yukon. No, Diesel wouldn't invite an invasion to his inhospitable climes.

Of course, Mason may not go to war for me. Unease coiled at the base of her spine. She'd infuriated her Alpha, and he'd sent her away—banished from the town of Willow Bend for months while she underwent training and what he liked to call attitude adjustment. She'd barely been allowed to return to see her brother off after his mating before she'd been sent out again.

What if Mason had solved his problem totally by sending her to the Yukon? If Diesel decided to keep her, maybe her Alpha wouldn't care.

Hurt exploded in her chest, and she couldn't contain her gasp at the sharpness of it. Had A.J known? Or had Mason simply put her out of reach of everyone and everything?

If she were lost to this pack, would anyone

know?

Anya was still in his outer office devouring cookies, so he swooped her up and cuddled her on the way to return her to her year group. The little girl clapped her hands when he found her year mates running a play obstacle course. The difficulty was low, more to let them burn off energy than to provide a real challenge. As soon as they were in sight of them, she wiggled to be put down. Releasing her, he stood watchful until she skidded to a halt at Bridge.

Even at her young age, she already understood the rule of checking in with those in charge. Ranging alone, even underground, was strictly forbidden until a youngling had graduated—for some that meant sixteen, for others it could mean twenty. The maternals decided who had graduated. Even those with the potential to be Sentries couldn't come to him or his until the maternals approved it.

The system worked. Bridge lifted a hand to wave at him and he gave her a nod before leaving them as quietly as he arrived. Having already disrupted their day once, he didn't want to upset the delicate balance created between maternal and her year group.

His route to his rooms took him through some of the more densely populated areas. A choice, really, though he and his wolf both wished to go check on their mate. Ranae was in good hands with Chowder. The healer was the least threatening of the single males present belowground.

Ranae was Diesel's mate, of that he was certain. *She has the potential, it's in her scent.* So strongly he'd noticed it in Willow Bend. Pausing at a group of chattering seniors, he allowed the elders to include him in their group. Not a single wolf among them was less than a century old, and most were half again plus that. His pack boasted over a dozen in that age range, still more between a hundred and a hundred and fifty.

It would shock some of his brothers down south to realize how few he lost to age and time. *Then again, there are those who should be here.* His first mate, for instance, who'd drifted until she never returned to her human form. A pang ached in his soul as he gripped the hand of the wolf who had given her life. The maternal had never blamed him for her loss, nor had she ever said a negative word.

Deidre, once known as Salt, had taken her birth name in her waning years. In part, she told him to honor her own mother and in part because her own mate had passed. How could she be Salt without her Pepper? It had only been happenstance that put him in range of her when her mate went in his sleep. Diesel had gripped her hand and held her to him. If she had asked to be released, he would have done so. As it was, he could no sooner abandon the mother of his first mate than he could the tiniest of their children.

As they reminisced of a previous winter, Diesel's mind wandered. He'd left the Yukon to attend the conference of Alphas in Willow Bend to test Fluff and Grinder more than to be a part of the Three Rivers council. Somehow, during his visit, he'd caught Ranae's scent and it had woken him, at least partially from the gray shadowing his days.

The fight with Mason and the disappointment

that Serafina wasn't his mate aside, he'd still felt more alive than he had in years.

"All family groups smell alike," Cinder announced, her voice raspy. The announcement drew Diesel's attention back to his Elders.

"Forgive me, matron," he said, zeroing in on her. "What did you say?"

"Family groups, Maxim," she used a name he hadn't gone by in many, many years. It mattered little what he had chosen, and he wouldn't deign to correct her. With age and survival came privilege. "They smell alike. Absinthe said you smelled like Irina, and that boy who came in with you did as well."

Irina. His mother. The boy, Diesel refrained from smiling, had to refer to Julian. His mother had been Irina's sister. Both born to the Yukon pack, Inga chose to wander and found her mate beyond their borders, though she and her get had returned periodically to visit.

"So Julian and I smell alike, do we?" He'd never have pinpointed that. Julian always smelled of the different places he traveled, and as often of fuel and oil as wildness and man. Perhaps a deliberate attempt on his part to mask his smell? Filing that information away, he considered Cinder once more.

"Aye, and it's because you come from the same family group. With Chowder and Grinder it is the same." She waved her hand then leaned into Deidre. "I think our Maxim is getting old—see the funny expression he wears?" Then she laughed, a deep bark of sound that was both faintly mocking and deeply amused. "You are slipping, boyo. We can't usually read you so well."

A lie, but one he allowed. "Forgive me, matron. I am distracted."

"He brought a woman in with him," Deidre said, and her comment sobered him. He would never wish her ill or harm from his actions. "Perhaps he has finally found the one he has searched for all these years."

Meeting her gentle gaze, he released a slow breath. No judgment or question harbored in her eyes. "She is a Hunter from Willow Bend."

"Ah, Chowder said you got into a scuffle there, but he didn't mention it was over a woman." Cinder seemed positively gleeful. "Do tell us, so that we have fresh news before tomorrow's tea with the orchard keepers."

"I could, but that would give you an unfair advantage as I haven't been to the orchards today. Perhaps tomorrow, after I pay them a visit." Diplomacy was not a skill he cared for, but where his seniors were concerned? He thanked his mother for her careful tutelage.

They waved him off with mock sighs, but Deidre touched his arm before he had taken two steps. Understanding her desire, he walked with her toward one of the pools. The running water helped them all in so many ways, from heating to cooling to cleaning and cooking, but also to protect them from too much noise echoing belowground. Even Diesel, with his too-sensitive hearing, could relax near the pools.

"You have a question, matron?" He murmured to Deidre, a woman he had once called mother at her request, though his own had long since passed from the world.

"Only to tell you that I hold no objection to you taking a mate, Diesel." Unlike Cinder, she used the name he'd taken upon his mate's passing. With kindness, she reached up to touch his cheek, and he lowered his head so she did not have to stretch. Delicate of frame, like her daughter, Deidre also possessed a steely will. If only... No, he refused to go there. "If this Hunter you have brought into our sanctuary is the one for you, then chase her and claim her. Do not let what others may say stand in your way. You have stood for us for so long, even when it was difficult for you."

"As have you," he told her, meaning it.

"Pfft," Deidre dismissed his charge. "I lived for you, boyo. You came when Pepper passed. You took my hand and you held to me so tightly, I knew you needed me a bit longer. With them all gone, time will come for me soon enough to pass as well and find them hunting on the other side. Until then, I am with you."

Very little surprised Diesel, yet he found Deidre's declaration a strange sort of shock. "You did not have to live for me..."

She silenced him with a finger against his lips. "I did what she we loved so much could not do. You are as much my son as if I had birthed you, so in this you will obey me."

The demand flowed through her tone. A submissive by nature, Deidre rarely issued such decrees. *That she should do so now...* He bowed his head, then brushed a kiss to her forehead. "Yes, matron."

"Better." She patted his chest. "Tell me, is she

beautiful?"

"I believe so, but she is tall and lanky. Broad shoulders and more like the Amazons you used to read stories of when I was little." As different from his first mate as night was to day.

"What is beauty? It's a moment which stops you in your tracks and steals your breath." Deidre tilted her head. "Does she steal your breath?"

"Yes," he could say so without hesitation.

"Good. Now go find her and win her, then bring her to me so I may welcome her to the Yukon as well." Understanding a dismissal when he heard it, he gave her another kiss and a careful hug, both of which she accepted. He waited until she'd rejoined her friends before striding away.

Perhaps he'd been away from the pack too long—not physically, but emotionally. Chowder had come the closest to suspecting, or so he thought. Yet Deidre's words gave him pause. She'd known. Without a doubt, she'd known he'd been fading.

Resolved to make sure he visited them all before he took Ranae up to show her the wildness of his tundra, he took the longer route through the herb halls. Since he rarely used his rooms, he'd agreed to make sure his space was nearest their healer's. Should he require it, Chowder could retreat into Diesel's space for sanctuary.

He hadn't ever needed to do so, in Diesel's knowledge, but it was there nonetheless. It took him nearly an hour to reach his rooms. Time well spent, but he was eager to see his mate and gauge her reaction to his rooms. Chowder stood in his path though, and the healer wore a tense expression.

Not scowling or growling, Diesel halted and raised his eyebrows. "Trouble?"

"Perhaps," the healer said. "Do you have a minute or are you rushing to make sure she is still there?"

Damn healer saw too much. If he weren't so good at what he did, Diesel might consider thrashing him. "I always have time for you, healer." A gentle reminder of his place and privilege didn't seem amiss.

"We can chat here." He indicated the stone garden. Like Diesel, Chowder preferred his privacy when not tending to his patients. More often than not, he would go to them and no farther than the homestead above when the Sentries were ranged out so far. Otherwise, the circle he'd chosen to live in, with its potted plants and rows of herbs and a water garden, he kept to himself. Quarters across from his were detailed to his brother, but Grinder used his even less than Diesel used his own.

Accepting the choice, Diesel followed his healer to where he'd already set out drinks—tea for himself and a hard iced cider for Diesel. Approving the choice, he tested the scent. "You've been working on your fermentation."

"And my cultivation. Those trees you had brought in? They are bearing near-perfect fruit and, with the winter months here, it's perfect for me to use the vats I stored in Grinder's quarters." Pride filled his eyes as he poured himself a cup of tea. The man rarely drank, not when he might be called on at a moment's notice. Though they had two healers, Chowder was by the far the stronger of the pair. The second tended to act as field medic and currently ran with the pack.

Swirling a mouthful around his tongue, he nodded slowly. It held a crispness, like a freshly chilled apple just at the edge of its ripeness. Sharp. Clean. He took a second, longer drink. Refreshing, with enough heat to warm him—unlike the whiskey, it offered a gentler warmth. "Well done." The cider was truly exceptional. "I think this is your best batch to date."

"I thought so. I'll be bottling this round of vats and keeping it chilled for all of you. I thought we'd save them for the spring festival."

A good thought. It would be a welcome treat to the returning wolves and for those who'd be rejoining the land above, a good way to celebrate.

"Tell Montana I approve and requisition whatever you need."

"I already did." Chowder didn't miss a beat, his grin one of a man who knew he had his Alpha's number. "Your guest hasn't left your quarters."

"I didn't expect her to." Nor did he plan on her leaving anytime soon without him. "But you have more to say on the subject, so spit it out."

"She's the one you scented in Willow Bend." He'd only told Chowder as much when the healer confronted him about the fight with Mason. The call of an Alpha could have a profound effect on the wolves around him, and he'd damn near disrupted the peace in the other wolf's pack.

Even in the midst of their fight, Diesel had held onto his sense…more so when Mason's mate intervened on his behalf. The foolishness of the young, turned wolf aside, he would never harm a mate. It had been his gift to Mason and a peace offering to release her unharmed. "She is." The line of thinking returned him to family groups. "Serafina is mated to one of the Buckley family, isn't she?"

"Yeah, one of the brothers to the second of Willow Bend…it's either Tyler or Lincoln, I didn't spend enough time with either to be sure." Chowder shrugged.

"Lincoln." Diesel nodded slowly. If he and Serafina had already begun their dance…and the man had been there that night, it had been Lincoln he scented. *Interesting.* He took another long drink of the cider. "Do you have any bottled already that I can give to Ranae?"

"You want to use cider as a courting gift?"

"Is it not appropriate?" Treating his future mate to the bounties of his pack seemed a reasonable offer.

"How the hell would I know?" The laugh from the healer carried a hint of self-deprecation. "I know how to bed women, not convince them to mate me."

"You have had many a she-wolf set her gaze upon you." Grinder complained about it often enough.

Chowder shrugged. "I am a healer, Diesel. Most want me to care for them, and even those who feel lust are soon tempered by the need they have to protect me, or worse…annoyed by the demands of the rest of the pack. It is a no win situation until I find the mate that is right for me." He took a sip of his tea, before pushing up his sleeves. "Besides, you courted a mate before. Surely you know how to do it."

"In another time, and with a wolf who grew up among us. The Hunter is different."

"Because she is not submissive."

"No." It wasn't all of it, though. "Because she doesn't believe she belongs here."

"Or maybe that she believes she should belong elsewhere." There was something in the way Chowder offered the suggestion that Diesel took note of it.

"Perhaps."

"I will prepare some bottles for you and chill them, but it may be a day or two. See if you can keep her around that long." Was that an element of challenge in his healer's voice?

"You think I cannot?"

Utterly unrepentant, the younger man spread his hands wide. "I think it's going to be a lot of fun to watch, and we've been sorely lacking in entertainment of late."

Not growling, lest the healer realize he hit his mark, Diesel merely rose and gave him a baleful look. "Don't hurt yourself."

"Oh, I won't." Another unabashed grin that took a second too long to vanish under Diesel's glower. Satisfied that his healer at least understood Diesel didn't care for the teasing, he rose, clapped him on the shoulder once then crossed the stone garden to the final hallway leading to his rooms.

"Alpha," Chowder's voice called after him softly. "Good hunting."

Diesel was still smiling when let himself into his rooms, the glow of the day's lights dimming gradually. Ranae stood in the center of the grass, her legs apart and her arms loose at her sides. Her damp hair teased him—if he'd been faster he might have been able to join her in the shower. As it was, her posture didn't promise him much of a welcome.

Before he could greet her, however, the sunlight warmth of the day lamps switched off, plunging them into darkness. He hadn't reset any of the timers since he was so rarely in residence. Ranae made a low sound, one that might come from a panicked animal, and the sour stench of fear assaulted him.

Reacting to the threat she experienced, he was across the grassy room to pull her into his arms. Her skin was like ice and she was rigid and stiff then she gripped him so hard her claws punctured him through his shirt.

She'd been afraid in the descent hallway, too— he'd thought it was due to the narrowness.

"I have you, Ranae," he told her, as the coppery tang of his blood joined with her scent in the grassy room. "You are safe."

Not waiting for her response, he lifted her and carried her toward the panel. He had to get the lights back on. If she were truly afraid of the dark, the pure midnight velvet of night underground would be horrifying for her.

He barely got the switch turned to bring the lights up slowly when she released another of those low moans. The sound abraded him. No one so strong should be brought to such a state under his watch. The first glimmer of light revealed her pale, taut features to him and her dilated pupils warned him of shock.

Worried beyond measure, he did the only thing he could think of to ground her to the present and to him.

He kissed her.

Snow Wolf

Chapter Six

Stark terror held her hostage. Blackness swamped her. The fear clawed through her and her wolf went rigid. They both wanted out. The animal surged and her skin shivered as the change threatened. One moment alone, the next strong arms closed around her. Some distant part of her mind recognized the crisp scent of snow on fur. Winter—but more than that. The darkness choked her and her claws sliced out. Copper stained the scent of snow.

"I have you Ranae. You are safe." *A promise? A threat?* She couldn't distinguish between the two. She needed to get her feet under her.

The first glimmer of light assaulted her but, drowning, she remained unable to find the lifeline.

The faint illumination highlighted his tense features as he stared at her. *Diesel?* The thought barely registered then his mouth closed on hers. Warm, firm lips branded her, their heat blistering away the cold. She opened on a gasp, then his tongue swept through her defenses.

Digging her claws into his shoulders, she could only hold onto him as connection sizzled through her system. The fire blazed in the darkness, leaving a trail of light to chase away the shadows. He lifted his head, breaking the connection and she panted. His eyes were so close, so deeply blue, they seemed incandescent.

He trailed a hand up her back then closed it over her nape. When he tilted her head, she obeyed the silent demand and then he took her mouth again. Where the first kiss stormed her senses, this one teased her. The sweet, gentle massage of his lips across hers and the taste of him flooded her. His tongue sought entrance and, while one part of her wanted to say no, the rest of her longed to savor the taste of him.

Heat unfurled in her belly, and softness stole through the tension of her muscles. She clung to him as she dared to twine her tongue with his. Everywhere his body touched hers seemed to dial the temperature to scorching. All trace of her chill evaporated under the sensual assault.

God, he tastes so good... The thought found voice as her nipples tightened. *He.*

Diesel.

Unclenching her grip on his shoulders, she flattened her palms then shoved. He didn't move, she'd probably have an easier time shifting a boulder. Dazed, she stared into his eyes as he finally released her mouth. Her pulse raced, and she gasped air noisily as he leaned away. Beneath the copper-tinged snow, she detected a richer, far more masculine scent.

Desire.

Son of a bitch... She wanted to swear aloud, but she needed to get away from him. Her whole system seemed to be in overdrive. Passion thrummed through her. God help her, she could feel her heartbeat in her sex, as though miming the need to have him pounding inside her.

"Bad idea," she finally managed, the words as ragged and thready as the rest of her.

Canting his head to the side, he studied her. Bit

by bit, she became aware of his grip on her nape. He held her still, the contact deeply intimate and leaving her in an intensely vulnerable position. Dropping her gaze from him, she stared at the bloody spots on his shoulders—his bare shoulders. She'd shredded his shirt and left deep marks scoring his flesh.

"Oh shit," she whispered. Had she fucked up so colossally that not only had she attacked the Yukon Alpha once, she'd done it twice? What the hell was wrong with her?

"I'll heal." He dismissed the concern with a gentle shake of his head. The contact of his fingers as he shifted his grip from her nape to her jaw left her aching for more. His skin seemed warmer, an odd thought considering his cold climes. Then again, he was a wolf. "Are you well now?"

Well? Considering she'd betrayed a major weakness then freaked out? She tried to shrug, but the action rubbed her chest against his. Tightening her thighs together, she prayed he couldn't scent the effect he had on her. If wishes were horses, she'd be galloping away, too.

The need to flee pulsed with every beat of her heart. Aggravated by the weakness, she raised her chin and tried to free herself from his grip. "I'm fine."

His eyebrows raised. He didn't say anything nor did he release her jaw as he examined her. Never in her life had she experienced the sensation of being prey. The Alpha holding her could be mistaken for nothing other than a predator. He'd melted her resistance and pulled her out of the hellish panic attack, only to catapult her into a far more confusing state.

"No, not yet, but you're getting there." He stroked his thumb against her cheek. "The lights will be reset so that you may control them manually."

Embarrassed, she lowered her gaze to stare at his mouth. A mistake, because she knew what those sensuous lips felt like against her own. Worse, she knew what he tasted of and the heady combination left her hungry for more. "It's not a big deal." She wanted to dismiss the phobia. How many wolves were truly afraid of the dark? It was absolutely ridiculous. When he still didn't release her, she dragged in another gulp of air. "Let me go." Then, because her voice still quavered in humiliating fashion, she added, "Please."

For some reason, she expected him to fight her about it. He hadn't listened to a damn word so far, but he loosened his grasp and she took advantage to retreat a step. Pride halted her on the second step. Yes, he'd already proven he could affect her, but he'd also held her when she'd freaked out.

"I'm sorry." Apologies did not come easily to her, yet it was the second time in their very brief acquaintance she found herself having to offer him one. "The dark caught me off guard."

"So I gathered." The corner of his mouth curved, highlighting the strength not only in his beautiful lips but also in his firm jaw. She hadn't been wrong earlier—when he smiled, he was damned handsome. Seriously, she needed to stop thinking about his kissability factor. "You're still a little shaky. Would you like a drink?"

"Oh, dear God, yes." The exclamation burst from her, and she laughed, the sound somewhere between rueful and humorous. "Please tell me you have something strong? I didn't feel like snooping through your things to find a bar."

And, truthfully, she hadn't had enough time to win the argument with herself. She'd showered, changed, and settled into the small bedroom she'd claimed for herself. By the time she'd wandered back to his grassy room, she hadn't been certain what they expected of her and the lack of real sunlight at the guest house had left her body clock confused.

At least there, she'd been able to keep the gas lanterns lit and the fire turned up. They had electricity, but she and Julian hadn't wanted to run down the generator if they weren't certain how long they would be there.

"I have plenty for you to choose from." He peeled away the remains of his shirt, then balled it up as he beckoned to her. It left all his glorious skin bare. The marks on his shoulders were deep. The punctures would take a while to heal, and the deep grooves left by her claws remained red and inflamed.

Grimacing, she dug around for another apology. "I am sorry about clawing you. I swear, I normally have much better control." If one were to go by her behavior since she'd arrived, she could see how they would doubt her.

"I told you, I will heal, Dove." He strode across the grass to where one of the long easy chairs rested near what looked like a table comprised of crates.

The nickname stymied her response. When he flipped the top open to reveal a liquor cabinet, the contents distracted her from the trembling still shivering through her. "Is this like some kind of glamping for wolves?"

Diesel peered at her, frown lines deepening between his eyes. "What is glamping?"

"It's where people pay a lot of money to go out into the wild, but they have all the luxuries of home." She gave a wave around the grassy room. The color remained a stunning emerald, and it reminded her of the hills in Ohio in spring. "You've got the perfect grassy backyard—indoors and underground, I might add—and you have a liquor stash inside...what are those? Shipping crates?"

Chuckling, he pulled out a bottle of whiskey and held it up. Relief plumed through her. She and Jack were old friends. "You approve." It wasn't a question.

"I do."

"Good." He closed one side, then opened the other and pulled out two glasses. "Come... Sit with me, and we will drink." He nodded to the pseudo-sofa. It was large, round and almost like a bed, but it had a high back. It would force her to slide on and scoot back in order to sit, or she could just perch on the edge.

He waited, giving her no clues as to what he expected. Exhausted, and more than a little raw, she climbed onto the round sofa then crawled to where she could sit and extend her legs.

What the hell else could she do to make the situation anymore uncomfortable?

Once she was in place, Diesel filled a glass about half-full. He handed it to her before filling his own. It might help her if he put on a shirt. Nakedness and wolves was very normal, so why the hell was she spending so much time ogling him? He moved the crates to sit closer before setting the bottle down and settling onto the oversized sofa chair. Near enough she could feel his heat, but not so close as to bring them into contact again.

The weight of his attention had her turning to meet his gaze. Glass held out, he said, "To getting to know you, Dove."

There was that name again. She clinked her glass to his then tossed the contents back in one swallow rather than saying anything. The heat scalded its way to her belly and settled the jangling of her nerves. Even her wolf seemed to let out a sigh. Before she could ask, he reached for the bottle and refilled her glass.

"Thank you," she said, then moistened her lips. The whiskey was smooth, perfectly aged. She could probably kill the whole bottle herself. She might need to if she couldn't get her traitorous reactions under control.

"My pleasure." He took another sip, not tossing his back as she had hers. She tried to nurse her second, but when he gave her another of those amused grins, she said screw it. Draining the second glass helped the first to sooth her ragged edges. Without comment, he refilled her glass again.

Several long moments passed as she sat in the twilight-lit garden of green. Even the chair—sofa? Whatever the hell the thing was they were sitting on—seemed more suited to the outdoors than in. "You didn't answer my question about the glamping."

"We do not need to *glamp*." He rolled the syllable around as though it were unpleasant. "The room was designed this way because I don't care to be trapped inside, much less underground."

Had he just revealed a vulnerability? "I guess if you have to spend months at a time like this, that makes sense." She'd certainly had her share of cabin fever in the long winter months, even though she was just as likely to go for a run in the snow as any other time.

"I don't spend months at a time down here." He shrugged. "My place is with my pack, roaming the tundra as they roam."

"Don't you have pack here?" She'd met the healer and seen others, or at least the evidence of others.

"Yes, but they are young or infirmed or the aged." Pausing, he left it to hang so long she wondered if he had a problem with all of the above. He drained his glass then refilled it and checked hers. She'd managed to nurse the third so shook her head. After returning the bottle to the crate, he rolled his shoulders. The skin already looked better, the deep score marks less red, but they were still visible. "We built the underground compound for them. They are safe here, and I know they are. They also know how to summon me back if I'm needed."

Realization crested within her. "The real threats are outside the sanctuary of the pack."

"Precisely." Economical with his word choice, he still hadn't broached her freak out or their kiss. It seemed altogether a better idea to continue avoiding those topics.

"What time is it?" She really lost track, and the question burst forth because, while she appreciated the quiet, it seemed to be giving her too much time to think.

"What is time but a way to mark the passage through life with another?"

"Okay, Deepok, that's awesome, but I was trying to figure out if it went dark because it was evening or if there are just a few hours on and a few hours off."

"Dove, it is dark nearly all the time during this season." Though he kept his tone gentle, she could almost hear his unspoken laughter. "The light below is more for the plants and the growing season, so they are well fed and healthy."

"So, if they didn't have to grow things, you'd keep this place pitch dark?" Horror crept through her.

"No, they would need some light. We all need some to allow our night vision to work. But living belowground during the winter months only began a few years ago. First, it was from necessity and, later, it has become how the young survive."

Since he was in a sharing mood, and she really didn't want to keep talking about how dark it *could* be, she latched onto the last kernel of information. "What did they do before you moved them underground for the winter?"

Diesel stretched his legs then crossed one ankle over the other. If she didn't look up, she could almost pretend they were in her parents' backyard—of course, there were no crickets or pesky brothers to annoy them. What was she thinking? Her brothers would never let her spend a moment alone with any single male, much less a foreign Alpha. They'd already lost Linc to one—though, admittedly, she did like Serafina—and Ty seemed to have forged a friendship with another Alpha to the extent that he and Claire had yet to return from Sutter Butte.

"I will answer when your thoughts do not wander so far or trouble you so much." The quiet comment jerked her attention back to him.

"I am paying attention."

"Are you?" Challenge layered through both syllables. "Then what troubled you so much?"

She'd rather step on her own tongue than admit considering her brothers' reactions to him. "I was thinking about home."

"You miss it." Not a question.

"Of course, but I have a job to do, and I'm here to do it."

Diesel took another swallow of his whiskey. That sounded like an enormously good idea, so she did the same. "You came only because of the mission Mason gave you?"

"Of course," she said, proud of that the quiver in her voice had finally gone away. "I am a Hunter of Willow Bend." Well, she'd been a journeyman Hunter, but close enough. "I go where my Alpha sends me."

"And he sent you to me."

Yes, he had. "Not to split hairs, but he sent me to your pack to make sure you were still ruling it, to inform you of the trouble we've had with the Russians, and to encourage you to contact him."

"Well, you have done two of the three."

True. "Which means I can leave soon."

"Not until you are successful with all your tasks." Something had changed in his tone and attitude, but she couldn't quite track it. "Very well, the lights dimmed because we are in the night cycle."

A chime sounded, soft as though a breeze brushed by, and she glanced around.

"That will be our supper." Diesel rose, all gracious host despite the wild element which clung to him. "Stay seated, Dove. I'll fetch it then we can see to answering your other questions."

There it was again, that damn nickname. What other questions had she asked him? Closing her eyes, she listened to the quiet whoosh of the door opening and the faint murmur of his voice thanking another wolf. At least when he wasn't sitting next to her, she could take a deep breath. What was she doing with him?

The cushion dipped, and she opened her eyes to find him watching her. A large tray sat on the foot of their sofa, but she barely spared it a half-glance before his gaze arrested hers once more.

"Will you be my guest for supper, Dove?"

For supper or as his supper? Unfortunately, Ranae didn't know which answer would trouble her more.

The gray-green of her eyes sharpened, and the last of the gold of her wolf vanished once more. The kiss exhilarated him in a way Diesel hadn't been in years. Still, when she'd pulled away, he allowed it. He wanted her to come to him in passion, not terror. The sweet scent of her desire surrounded him. No matter how she struggled to contain her reaction, it was a decadent perfume.

Oddly, knowing he affected her gave him all

the patience in the world. Of course, watching her try to talk about anything else also amused him. Frankly, he enjoyed the sound of her voice. A strange observation for a man who didn't like most sounds anymore; his hearing had grown so sensitive in the last few decades. It was why he hated cell phones and most forms of technology. The constant buzz scraped over his nerves.

Even knowing she had a cell phone in her back pocket didn't disturb him. The faint buzz of it receiving a message scraped over his senses. When she didn't reach for it, he couldn't help smiling. The ache in his cheeks, so unused to the constant need to stretch, appealed to him on another level.

"I will join you," she hedged. "If you call me by my name."

"You don't like Dove?" Reaching for the first plate, he took the pressure off of her. Montana had sent them elk steaks and fresh steamed vegetables along with two loaves of fresh baked bread. If his nose wasn't wrong, there was apple pie in there as well. He had a weakness for the treat, one very few knew about. Of course Montana knew. If he'd ever felt even a spark of interest for her, he'd have pursued his assistant many, many moons before. As it was, she was more a younger sister, though she treated him like she was his elder rather than over fifty years his junior.

Dove pulled her legs into a crisscross as she accepted the plate. He took her glass, so she didn't have to move to set it down, and added it to the tray before he retrieved the cutlery his assistant included inside of linen napkins. It amused him that she'd gone to so much trouble.

Candles also sat on the tray. While he could light them, he had no intention to turn down the lights in the chamber. Not after Dove's very visceral reaction. When she trusted him enough, he would find out why the lack of light frightened her and then kill whatever had given her such terror. No wolf with her strength should ever cower or bay as she had done.

Only after retrieving his own plate did he notice Dove's utter stillness. "What's wrong?"

"You're growling." The observation startled him, yet she was correct.

Silencing the rumble in his chest, he inclined his head. "My apologies, Dove. I was not growling that you don't like the name."

"It's not that I don't like it, but... I have a name. It's Ranae."

"Yes, but to me you are a dove." He set the plate on his lap after mirroring her position. When was the last time he sat down to a dinner with anyone and was more interested in the conversation than the food? Most of the time, he hunted his own meal and ate where none could see him. Others, when necessary, he spent with the people who needed contact with him.

Instead of eating, however, she gaped at him. "I remind you of some delicate fucking bird?"

Laughter replaced the growl in his chest, and he chuckled. "Doves are far from delicate and, while I'm sure they engage in their own antics, I've never thought of them as fucking birds."

Her shock turned to rage. Anger put fire in her eyes, and his wolf stretched. Yes, this they preferred far more to her cringing. His shoulders still carried the sting of her claws, and he'd strut everywhere to show them off until they faded. *Strut?* Fresh amusement rolled through him. When was the last time he strutted anywhere?

The clack of her teeth coming together almost caused him to laugh again, though he suspected she'd stab him with the knife rather than the elk steak. "I'm not a damn bird," she muttered, before stuffing a bite into her mouth.

"Doves are beautiful, graceful birds. Though they seem small and fragile, they fly at incredible speeds. They are monogamous in their pairings, they work together to raise their young and they prefer daylight to the night. They range across many different climates, their migrations taking them thousands of miles." He sliced off a cut of his meat. "They are far from delicate in their strength, their determination, or their beauty." They also relied on the male to make a showy gesture during courtship.

He needed to learn more about his dove before he would know what gesture she would appreciate.

Ranae chewed three more bites slowly and deliberately while she wrestled with her temper. Someone had taught her that anger was a bad thing or at least they'd put a chokehold on it. His dove shouldn't be so afraid to show herself. He debated his next move when she said, "I suppose that's a decent description, I'm just not sure you should be giving me so much insider information about your pack."

"Why?" He knew the answer. It irritated him, but he would hear it from her.

"Because I belong to Willow Bend." Better the pack, than if she'd said… "To Mason. *He* is my Alpha, and I am here on his mission."

Maybe Diesel should have killed Mason when he had the chance. "So you have said." He kept his voice calm. Decades of practice made him an expert at burying his emotions. Ranae was the most unique of prey. "Your family must be exceptionally talented for it to be central to so many alliances."

She speared one of the potato slices on her fork then frowned. "I don't know what you mean."

"Your brother is Mason's second, is he not?" *Yes, little Dove, follow the seeds where I plant them.*

"A.J., yes." Her demeanor softened at the mention of her brother. "He's the oldest of the three brothers."

"Triplets?" It didn't matter what he knew, it mattered only what she shared with him, what vision she gave him into her world.

"Oh yeah, identical and all older than me." She sighed as only a younger sibling could. "They were perfectly impossible most of the time but, even when I want to strangle them, I'd have no others at my back."

Yet. He'd prove to her soon enough that the only wolf she needed to guard her back was him. For now, he continued to spread the seeds toward the destination he wanted her to go. "What makes A.J. more remarkable than the others?"

"How do you know he is?" Sibling scorn mingled with pride in her challenge, but she ate another bite and he passed her one of the decanters of water that came with the meal.

"He, not the other two, is Mason's second, so that means there is more to him than to them." An Alpha chose his second for any number of reasons. Montana sufficed in that position for him because she handled most of the day-to-day management issues he wanted nothing to do with.

"True. Ty doesn't want to lead, not really, and Linc's more of a follower. He likes to make stuff happen and to protect...well, they all like to protect. It's one of those annoying male wolf traits." Had he not been watching for it, he would have missed the side eye she gave him. So, she didn't want to be protected.

Too bad.

Still, it was an insight. She had to be capable of protecting herself or Mason wouldn't have sent her, Julian or no Julian.

"So A.J. is the eldest." It wasn't a doubt. If the triplets measured near equal in dominance, other factors would come into play.

"Yes." A shadow crossed over her face and he frowned at the way the corners of her mouth dipped down. "And it's more than that."

His instinct was to order her to tell him what was wrong, but she didn't respond well to those, and he was intruding on the personal matter of her family. "Will you tell me what more there is to it?"

"It's not like it's a secret." Who did she attempt to convince—him or herself? "A.J. spent several years in prison."

While it might not have been a secret, Diesel hadn't known about it.

"Long story short, all three were off on a

weekend to get away and roam, A.J. and Linc wanted Ty to feel better. He'd been—he'd been in a bad place for a while." Her mouth tightened. "Ty's mate chose to leave Willow Bend, followed another man to Sutter Butte."

Some wounds sting deeper than others, but he said nothing.

"Anyway, Ty had been very depressed and A.J. and Linc wanted to make it better. What's better than a good roam?" The smile she sent him didn't touch her eyes. "While they were out, they came across a woman being assaulted. My brothers would never stand for something like that."

Nor would he, but he merely nodded. No good male would allow a woman or child—or anyone weaker, for that matter—to be hurt in their presence.

"They rescued her, but a human was killed in the process, and the police came upon the scene too swiftly for them to vanish."

Diesel frowned. The southern packs had more local encroachment from the humans than he did, but from time to time his younglings got into trouble.

"Our Alpha at the time, Toman…he ordered A.J. to face the human judgment, and we were not allowed to visit him or see him at all." Sadness echoed in her voice. "It broke my mother's heart, but it was worse for Linc and Ty. They were only ever half themselves. Even their laughter was more hollow and their smiles… They weren't real smiles, does that make sense?"

"Yes." He understood the mourning well. The brothers had faded some without their third…as had the rest of the family. Toman Carlyle should have given up his hold on Willow Bend long before Mason killed him. No Alpha worth his salt would allow his wolves to be so damaged.

"Well, A.J. spent six long years in prison, alone and unable to shift. Then Mason took over the pack and Vivian—the woman they saved—she found evidence that could get A.J.s judgment thrown out. He was able to come home, and he was…lean, and hollowed out, as though he'd been ground to what was just the essence of him."

Ranae finished off the last of her elk steak, but continued to nibble on her vegetables. When she held out her hand, he would pass her the water then take it away when she was done.

"Your family healed when he came home?" He had to know, was that where her fear of the dark came from? The sense of abandonment?

"You could say that. Turned out Vivian was A.J.'s mate…now they are together, and he is Mason's second. They're two wolves determined to make sure no one is left behind. Vivian is pregnant with their first child, too." Simple joy lifted some of her sadness. "Claire came home, and she and Ty worked things out. Then Linc mated Serafina."

"You don't like their mates?"

"No," she said with a quick shake of her head. "It's nothing like that at all. Truly. I think Vivian is amazing. She's smart, level-headed, and a game designer. My brothers think she hung the moon. She makes A.J. deliriously happy. Serafina's cool, strong, and confident."

"But your brother is still far away."

"Yeah." She touched his arm, the first time

she'd actively sought contact with him of her own volition that didn't involve violence. It was a light contact, the gentlest of squeezes. "I am thrilled that he's happy, but I miss him. Now, Ty? He and Claire, his mate, are away too."

"You don't like Claire?" Of the three, she gave less warmth to that name.

"No and yes." She grimaced, squeezed his arm again, then released him. He missed the contact immediately, but she was eating so he left it alone. *For now.* "I hated Claire for a long time, because she really hurt Ty when she left. If you ever met him, of the three, I think Ty is the easiest going and the most gentle. He has a great heart, and he cares with everything that's in him. Claire left him, broke his heart, and went off to live in another pack. I know things weren't perfect there, and I know she came back and they found a way to heal—together. I'm happy for them."

"But…you haven't forgiven her for hurting your family, your brother and, by extension, yourself and your other siblings."

Ranae bit her lip, it was the most innocent and hesitant gesture he'd seen her perform. "That's part of it."

Understanding dawned, and it was his turn to touch her. He placed a hand on her shoulder. "If she hadn't left Ty, your brothers might not have gone on the journey that ended with A.J. in prison."

His little Dove lowered her head and, for a moment, he caught the flash of tears on her eyelashes. Thankfully, they did not fall. If she began to truly cry, it would shatter him, and he'd say to hell with patience and claim her then and there.

"It's stupid," she admitted. "If A.J. hadn't gone, he might never have met Vivian, or worse, what happened to Vivian could have gotten her killed." Her care for the other woman spoke volumes. "But, at the same time…"

"How old were you, Dove?"

Her shoulder stiffened beneath his grasp, but she raised her chin. "Eleven when Claire left, fourteen when A.J. went to prison." Which meant she was close to twenty-three. *A baby*.

Diesel hated himself. *Then again, what is time?* A chance to mature and to grow.

"You were a youth when these events happened," he told her. "It is not unreasonable for you to tie them together. Claire is older. By our standards, those who are older hold the responsibility. While she may have been young herself, actions have consequences and we have to live with them."

The sadness in her expression eased. "I don't want to hate her. I don't even think I'm really angry with her anymore. I did…I did something bad because she came back. I attacked her. All this rage inside of me boiled out, and I tried to make her fight me. She wouldn't. She avoided every blow and moved like the wind." Grudging respect reflected in the words. "Some days, I even like her."

"You haven't forgotten or forgiven." He didn't have to wait for her confirmation. "Dove, your brothers are men. From the sounds of it, men of quality. Are they happy now?"

"Yes." Unqualified and unhesitating.

"Then why aren't you?"

Chapter Seven

The wind chimes saved her from answering the telling question. Diesel rose, set his plate aside, and went to the door. Chowder—would she ever get over calling their healer a name more suited to soup?—stood silhouetted in the open door. Without preamble, he said. "We have trouble."

Shoving her chaotic emotions aside, Ranae put her plate down and slid off the sofa. Chowder shifted his gaze to her briefly then back to his Alpha.

"They called down. Four wounded and coming in." Called down? That meant they'd been hurt above.

Diesel glanced at her. "If you're coming with, grab your coat or shift. It will be too cold for you." Considering he was bare-chested and only wore a pair of sweats, she wondered if he ever felt the cold.

Not experiencing any need to argue, she raised her hand, palm forward. "What would be more useful to you? Four feet or two hands?"

Diesel glanced at Chowder.

"Have you ever worked with a healer?"

"Only in a run and fetch capacity."

Chowder nodded. "That will do. Get your coat."

Pivoting, she ran for her room. It took her less than two minutes to throw on an extra layer of clothes and her heavier boots. Jacket, gloves and cap in hand, she sprinted to them. Diesel's gaze swept over her once then he nodded to the door. She exited ahead of him. Her gut churned at the low light beyond the grassy room.

Fuck. She'd forgotten he said it was the night cycle. The blackness wasn't absolute, however, and overhead there was a hint of twinkling which added to the illumination. "Stars."

"Chowder is getting his gear." Diesel said before he took the lead. There was nowhere else to go but toward the next terraced garden. Chowder carried two heavy bags, and he tossed the first one to Diesel then the second to her. She caught it and slung it over her shoulder. It would take her a minute to pull on her jacket, but she would make it happen on the go. Four Tiki-like torches illuminated the patio garden. The flickering light held the darkness at bay and let her nagging fear be silent.

Diesel raised his eyebrows in silent question. It was the first semi-mention he'd made since her meltdown earlier. "I'm all right," she murmured.

He nodded once. After the healer pulled out one more bag, which he slung across his body, he shut his door and fell in as Diesel led the way. They didn't encounter many wolves until they reached a central exchange she recognized from her first pass earlier. She saw no sign of Julian either. Where was the Chief Enforcer?

Belatedly, it dawned on her that Chowder and Diesel both lived in an area dedicated to the wolves who roamed above. Momentarily fascinated by a dynamic that created a place for wolves that likely never used it, she slowed. When Diesel and Chowder pulled away, she had to hurry to catch up to them. The Alpha shot her another look, a hint of reproach, but he said nothing more.

When they reached the door toward the stairs, her heart started to thump. The door swung out to the antechamber, and she could have wept. It was ablaze with lights. Diesel thrust out his hand for her bag. "Jacket."

Obedience was the better part of valor. They had an emergency, and she was rendering aid. She surrendered the bag and shrugged into her jacket. Chowder and Diesel waited. Neither radiated urgent energy, but she didn't take her time, either. Once the jacket was on, she stuffed her hands into the gloves, then pulled the knit cap over her hair. Fortunately, the wild mass was dry. Too bad she hadn't remembered to bring a ponytail holder.

Giving her a critical once over, Diesel held out both bags. "Can you handle them?" It was a fair question. The one she'd carried was damn heavy. Shouldering the first one, she took the second in her free hand and nodded.

"Got them."

"Good." Before she could slide away, he cupped her face in his hands and closed his mouth over hers. It stunned her senses, all wildness and heat. It stormed through her, demanding she respond, and she drew on his tongue as he delved inside. Her nostrils flaring at the potency of his scent. Her heart hammered against her ribs. As swiftly as he'd grasped her, he let her go. "You wear my scent. My wolves will not touch you."

He turned away before she could sag with her confused relief. Her whole body seemed to be a riot of sensory overload. Chowder grinned at her and, for the first time in her life, she might have blushed. Since Diesel had already begun his ascent, she nodded to the healer to go as well and she brought up the rear. Unsurprisingly, no one else followed them. The door hushed closed and she took the stairs two at a time, measuring her pace against the wolves ahead of her.

At the top, the door opened before she arrived and then they were in the antechamber behind the wall. No sooner did she slide inside than the door below closed and the door to the cabin opened to raucous calls and the sharp, telling scents of blood.

A lot of blood.

All thoughts of lust fled in the face of disaster. Chowder stopped next to a young man who'd all but been disemboweled. The stench of blood mingled with feces, and she wanted to gag but refused the reaction. She was a Hunter. These people needed her.

"Here," Chowder ordered, and she dropped the first bag next to him then second. "Grip here and here." He took her gloved hands and put them in place. She actually found herself holding the wound closed.

Blood soaked her gloves, but she ignored the sensation. The wolf in her grip let out another yowl, and his eyes blazed gold as he spotted her. He lunged upward and she twisted, using her elbow to push his chest down while keeping his innards inside his gut.

The healer moved with economical motions. He opened the first bag and pulled out a syringe then injected the wolf she was keeping in place. The struggle went out of him. Within moments, Chowder had an IV hooked up and he directed another wolf who stood nearby to hold it.

"Now we're going to stuff the wound." Chowder pulled out a series of sponges. "Use one hand to put them in, use the other to control the bleeding. I'll get it stopped." With that, he put his hands on the wolf and his face blanked.

It took them the better part of thirty minutes to stabilize the wolf. He sealed the wound with staples—a sound she hoped she never heard again— then clear tape.

"Let's go," he told her, and then they were up. The next wolf had torn and jagged legs and arms. It looked like something had chewed on him. "Fuck." Chowder swore. "Brace him."

Ranae didn't wait to ask why. She peeled off her blood-soaked gloves and pinned the naked wolf. The man had been unconscious, or so she thought until Chowder wrenched the wolf's leg. The audible snap of bone breaking sent the wolf she held upward and it took all her strength to keep him down. The beast in him snarled at her. She met his gaze and let her wolf glare at him. Between her grip and her wolf, they kept him down when Chowder rebroke the other leg.

Only once he'd finished the gruesome task did he repeat the shot and IV procedure he'd done on the first. "Clean these arms and legs, flush them out with the saline then use betadine."

Grimacing at the very idea of pouring that crap on open wounds, she got to work. Sweat beaded along her brow from the intensity of the work. By the time she got to the wolf's legs, she'd stripped her jacket. Someone took it from her, but she didn't stop her actions. Once she was finished, she glanced around and found Chowder across the room working on another wolf, his face gray and his arms stained red with blood.

She pulled a blanket over the patient she'd worked on, then cleaned up her refuse before hauling the bag over to him.

"Take the next one. He just needs his wounds flushed. Exactly as you did with that one…" His words trailed off as a howl split through the noise. It was long, low and mournful. Another wolf joined the song, then a third and finally all the wolves, even those lying around her in damaged and battered condition joined in.

Tears burned in her eyes. She knew the music. It was the call of death. They'd lost someone. Sniffing once, she rose to go to the last man—no, not a man. He couldn't have been more than a boy, all teenage awkwardness, long limbs, and too-lean body. Even his abdomen seemed hollow and sunken beneath his ribs.

His chest was a mottle of bruises, and one near his side concerned her. With as gentle a touch as she could manage, she brushed her fingers against his side. "I need to roll you over."

The youth shifted, his face a grimace as he rolled onto his left side so she could see his back. Dark blue-black and purple discoloration lined his lower right quadrant.

"Chowder," she said quietly because, unless the healer was in deep trance, he would hear her. "I think he might have lacerated a kidney."

"Tend the rest, I'll be there soon."

"You can lay down again," she told him and the boy sagged to his back once more. He swallowed once, then blinked rapidly. "My name is Ranae," she told him as she began using saline to clean out the deep lacerations along his shoulder. What the hell had mauled him? Because there was no mistaking the tell-tale marks of claws and teeth along his trunk and down his right arm. The wrist had been mangled, tearing away the flesh to reveal damaged muscle and tendon beneath.

"Demon," the child said.

"Demon?" Her eyebrows lifted and she tried to keep her tone light. "Let me guess, your mother gave you that name."

A hint of a smile turned up the corners of his mouth. "Yes. She said I was her little demon and it stuck."

"Well, I think that's what all children are supposed to be to their parents." She grimaced at his sucked in breath when she reached the wrist. The saline had to hurt like a bitch. The betadine wouldn't be much better. They were wolves, they could heal a lot of injuries, but they still had to worry about infections.

Tooth and claw had a way of spreading bacteria deep into the body. "I—was—a special—case." Demon put the words out with harsh gasps in between. She tried to move as fast as she could. The last time she'd had to flush wounds had been the summer before when a Kyle Huston's year group set a series of dangerous traps on one of the obstacle courses and two of the boys pissed off a porcupine. It had been ugly. She and three other Hunters spent hours pulling quills and cleaning wounds because Emma told them they had to learn from their mistakes.

The Willow Bend healer might be a gentle, kind soul, but she also believed stupidity should be its own reward. Demon's damage, however, didn't seem caused by foolhardiness. Or at least she hoped it wasn't, because unless he walked up on a bear and took a piss on it, she couldn't imagine what action could have warranted so much hurt.

Another mournful howl split the night. A new song. A new death. Tears fell from her eyes. These weren't her wolves and not her pack, but it didn't matter. The ache she felt for them seemed to encompass every breath she took. Demon let out a strangled sob. She gripped his uninjured hand and shifted so she could block his head from view.

"It's all right," she murmured, remembering all the times her mother had done the same for her. "You can cry on me. I won't melt."

The kid looked up at her then he turned his face into her hip and let a sob free. The cleaning could wait. She held him while he cried, sparing a brief glance at Chowder as he joined her. He took the saline from her hand and went to work while she stroked the boy's hair.

When the song changed for a third time, she glanced at the healer. Her heart ached for him. With the bruised look around his eyes and his skin gone gray with fatigue, he seemed to age three decades right in front of her. "How many total?" She tried to keep voice down, but what was the point? They were all wolves.

"Too many," Chowder answered. He gave the boy a shot, and bit by bit, his sobs tapered off. By the time he set up an IV, Demon had gone to sleep. Ranae brushed the damp hair away from his forehead.

"He's so young."

"It was his first winter to run with them." Chowder sighed, then he rolled his head in a slow circle as though trying to loosen the tension in his neck. "Give me a little time, and he will run with them again." Then his focus was on the youth, and his eyes closed.

Trusting his confidence and taking her cue from his concentration, she glanced around the cabin's main room. A fire burned, keeping the chill away. The makeshift infirmary only housed four patients. Whatever other wolves had been there seemed to have left during her time spent with Demon.

Glancing at the healer, she gave his shoulder a light squeeze before she stood. Diesel was also gone, likely out into the icy night to deal with the dark song of loss. Whatever had done this—whomever—she wished them a painful and brutal death. It wasn't in her to be forgiving and, while adults might settle their battles in blood and fisticuffs, Demon wasn't there yet. He was still more boy than man.

She made a circuit of Chowder's patients, checking each one. They were all in deep, healing sleeps. Satisfied none of them needed her, she went to Chowder's bags of supplies and rooted around until she found tea. During one of her training sessions, Owen explained to her that healers would burn themselves out. It was up to the Hunters with them to make sure they took care of themselves.

Tea in one hand, she found what looked like trail mix and jerky. Both would give him protein and sustenance. She set them aside then washed her hands before setting a kettle onto the fire to heat. By the time Chowder came to sit next to her, she had tea ready for him and pressed the food into his hands.

With a weary smile, he ate and drank but said nothing.

Outside, the song changed again.

Hours had passed since he'd last set his gaze on Ranae, but the wolves he'd left guarding her and Chowder checked in, their song carrying on the breeze between the calls to mourning. He stood in the snow, bare skinned to the brutal cold, and it could do nothing to ease the fury in his chest. Four wolves gravely injured and another four dead.

A family group and two of his Sentries.

The wolves had done what they dedicated themselves to do—they'd given their lives to save the pack. Without a doubt, if not for their sacrifice, it would be eight bodies he stood over, maybe more.

"One escaped," Fluff said. She stood nude and as oblivious to the icy wind as him. They would both need to shift, but he wouldn't leave the bodies there to be picked over. No matter how rustic a life they lived, the bodies of their dead would be honored. Other wolves had gone to retrieve sleds so they could take them in. Until then, Diesel stood watch over the fallen.

Blood shone in her white, spikey hair and an open scrape leaked on her cheek. "Shift, little sister. Go to Chowder, let him tend you."

"It's barely a flesh wound." She waved off his concern. Rage radiated from her, despite her calm tone. "Grinder is still hunting, the Enforcer is with him."

Julian hasn't left yet. Diesel didn't mind his continued presence. If anything, his cousin was a sharp hunter. If the invaders turned out to be part of the Volchitsa, it might prove useful to their hunt down south. "Where are the bodies of the others?"

Fluff pointed east. "At the first turn, near the riverbed." It was frozen this time of year, but he knew where she indicated. They'd come deep into his territory. "We left them to the scavengers."

"I will deal with them after ours are taken care of." The swift sound of paws racing across snow followed by runners alerted him to his pack's arrival. The wolves had been harnessed into the sleds, so he and Fluff took care to lift the bodies of their fallen one-by-one. Once they were loaded, the wolves left. Three sleds in all, with too many bodies aboard.

"Shift," he ordered Fluff when he saw her try to hide her shaking hands. The cold could be too much, even for them. She obeyed and he stood watch over her until she once again stood on four feet. "Go to the cabin. Watch over Chowder and Dove. See that he tends your wounds. Wait for me there."

Her lip curled away from her teeth. She didn't want to leave him, but she was a good Sentry. She obeyed. Once she set out across the snow, he called his own wolf. The rush of fur over his skin a bliss and an agony. On four feet, he shook once then sent up a call. His wolves answered him, breaking from their mourning song to carry his word.

Ears swiveled, he caught Grinder's call—he'd gone west, toward Amaruq. Had the interlopers struck the base camp first? The growl in his chest thundered free. First, he would inspect the dead, and then he would run for Amaruq. His little Dove had passed through that town only a few days ago. Had she been present or even in their guest house…

Cold rage settled in his bones. He had not found his mate after so long only to lose her to foolish Volchitsa seeking war with him. His pack may have made the move generations earlier, but they were still warriors in their blood. He would hunt them all down and erase them for taking such liberties with his people.

Mind set to the hunt, he raced across the tundra. His people had responded to the threat as they should. The roaming pack had swarmed in to Tikaani. They'd surprised the interlopers. When he found the savaged remains, a fierce pride filled him. They'd taken no prisoners. It was a brutal response to an equally brutal invasion.

Hadn't he just told Julian that the Russians wouldn't dare test his borders? Arrogance and pride were the downfall of all men. Stalking through the bodies, he tested them for scent. They were not a family group. Most were male, though he located two females among the dead. All were full adults—battle hardy, none carried more than a passing scent of the other. So no mated pairs.

One survivor. Running for freedom or to warn of their security?

Diesel shook his head. He trusted Grinder. The man had earned his name for his fierce tenacity. He would not let them escape nor would the Chief Enforcer, if it came to that. Julian hated losing a lead more than being proven wrong. Satisfied they would handle it, he continued his inspection of those who'd come for his pack. Only one body reverted to its human state. The others would, but it could take time and the cold might even interfere.

Crouching, he studied the man's high brow, broad face, and long nose. The faintest tilt to the corners of his eyes—perhaps an Asian parent or grandparent? Nothing about him seemed remarkable. The tattoos he bore, however, told a different story.

His clan name, his position. He was a soldier. Not high in rank, cannon fodder, most likely. Diesel sat back on his haunches. Chances were the others were like this one. They'd been sent to attack, to create chaos—to die. What did the Volchitsa not want him to see?

Aggravation edged his consideration. A second wolf split, cracked, and then began the slow unfolding to its human state. Raising, he watched and kept his observation dispassionate. Like the first one, the man's tattoos marked him as a foot soldier. It took more than an hour for all the bodies to resume their human states and, by then, he had the measure of them.

They were a feint.

Leaving the bodies, he circled back to Tikaani. His wolves were in full force in the town. Their mourning song peaked at his arrival then they called out. He passed by each one, nuzzling, nipping and rubbing against them. With a snap, he summoned two Sentries to follow him as he set out for Amaruq. He left the bulk of his pack there, he wanted a wall of wolves between his vulnerable and another possible feint.

An hour from Tikaani, he slowed his pace and sent up a call. Grinder answered from his north, but it was in a negative. They hadn't caught their escapee.

Letting his rage feed his strength, Diesel ran onward. When the lights of Amaruq came into sight, he scented death on the wind.

His Sentries flanked him as they strode into the village. The Inuit who made the village their home had been loyal to his pack for countless generations. Most who stayed in Amaruq through the long dark kept to the old ways. They would care for a wolf who came to their door; they honored them.

It was how the interlopers gained access. In every home they entered, they found carnage. The strike had been swift and bloody. Neither his ears nor his nose told him of any survivors, yet he checked each building. In the last, he found his wolf, a sweet old man who loved to live with the villagers.

Deidre and Cinder would be devastated at his loss.

Fine. If the Volchitsa wanted him distracted, they'd failed.

Shifting, he knelt by the body and closed his sightless eyes. His two wolves stared at him from the open doorway, even as the wind blew snow into the building. "Join Grinder and find the interloper. Bring him to me, alive if possible. If not? Tear him apart, organ by organ. Box them up and then head inland, so you can send a message for me."

They barked their acknowledgement.

"I will send the details when needed. Now go."

The wolves swiveled and raced into the darkness. The task of dealing with the dead was his. He would honor them as the tribe so honored his wolves.

Then he would avenge them all.

Snow Wolf

Chapter Eight

The lack of natural light left Ranae with only her fatigue to determine the hour. Even if her internal clock was off, it had still been several hours since she followed Diesel and Chowder to the surface. Their patients slept and, in between seeing other wolves, so did Chowder. The healer had eaten everything she cobbled together. When more wolves put in an appearance, she began tearing apart the kitchen.

The food stores were sparse in options, but substantial in quantity. Her mother had fed all the men in the house Ranae grew up in for years. She'd learned to cook more out of self-defense and survival than any real joy in the activity. Thawing meat in a pot of water, she got another large pot heating with vegetables and spices.

Taking frequent breaks to check on her charges, she managed to put rolls together with some flour, yeast, eggs, and milk. The eggs were fresh, but the milk had been powdered. One thing they had in abundance was water.

Chowder appeared in the doorway to the kitchen, his rumpled appearance and tired eyes promising he had slept a little. "What are you making?"

"Not clam chowder, I promise." She rinsed off her hands then checked the meat she had thawing. It looked like chunks of steak—elk, bison or maybe something else. It smelled fine and she could brown it then add it to the soup. Once it was all cooked, she could use some flour to thicken the sauce into gravy.

"Damn, I thought you'd run a few hundred miles south to dig up some clams for me. What kind of care for your healer is this?"

Amused, she pointed to the table. "Sit. I have fresh coffee." She stumbled across the grounds when looking at their vegetable stores. Kept in an airtight container, it had smelled like heaven, so she put a pot on to brew. Once she set a mug in front of him and poured one for herself, she eyed the pot. They'd need another one if any of the wolves outside decided to come in again.

They can make that call for themselves. The meat needed longer, so she left the dough to rise before she split it into rolls then picked up her mug of coffee. The kitchen had finally warmed after she got the oven going. The farther away from the fire she was, the more she wished she had her coat. Unfortunately, she had no idea where it had been placed.

"You don't have to cook for us," Chowder said, cradling his mug. "Montana will send food up soon enough."

"Not really doing it for you." She shrugged, then took another sip of the coffee. It was like manna from heaven. "I need something to do and the patients will be hungry, the other wolves might need a hot meal." Diesel might be hungry when he returned, too.

"It's hard to be the ones who sit and wait." The healer sighed, stretching his long legs out and crossing one ankle over the other.

She shrugged. "I'm used to it." Despite the changes wrought over the last couple of years, she'd spent nearly a decade in sit and wait mode. First, waiting for Ty to recover from Claire leaving. Then waiting for her brothers to recover from the loss of A.J. while also waiting for A.J. to come home.

Waiting was old hat. Annoying, but familiar.

A movement in the other room had Chowder on his feet and checking with Ranae right behind him. The front door hadn't opened, but she could hear the wolves out there, even past the thickness of the walls. There were a lot of them.

Demon moaned again, scratching at the loose bandages they'd applied to his torn wrist. Chowder waved her back to the kitchen. "I'm just going to put him into a deeper sleep."

Not listening to him, she followed and crouched near Demon's head to stroke his hair. The healer gave her a wry look, then placed his fingers to the young man's temples. Demon settled at the first brush of her hand through his thick, dark strands. Though neither said a word, she could almost feel the tension drain out of the youth as energy licked at her senses. Healers might not all be soothing people, but they knew how to soothe.

Half-expecting it, she was ready to catch Chowder when he swayed. Bracing him, she rose and helped him stand. "Now you're going to have something more to eat, and then you're going to sleep."

The healer scowled at her. "You're the guest here."

"Except I'm also in charge of making sure the healer is still standing when this is over." The wolf had to be wearier than he let on, because he let her guide him into the kitchen. Once he was back at the table, she turned away and put together a hot bowl of oatmeal. The stone cut oats had also been in one of cabinets. She'd set it aside with hot water before he'd entered earlier. Setting it on the table in front of him, she added a spoon next to it. "It probably tastes terrible, but eat it all then get some sleep. I can check their bandages, and you'll be right there if they really need you."

"You're mean."

"I can get meaner." She folded her arms. "Now eat."

She'd seen Owen do the same to his mate once. She hadn't understood how he could stand there all fierce and scowling at what had to be one of the nicest people ever. Now, she got it.

Chowder picked up the spoon then made a face. "I hate oatmeal."

"Pretend it's clams."

His grimace spoke volumes. "You're right," he said before he ate a spoonful. "You can be meaner."

Ranae didn't smile, but she liked seeing him eat. After he'd devoured four more bites, she returned to the counter, and her abandoned coffee. The wolf song beyond the walls climbed again and she sighed. The mournful notes pulled at her soul. A part of her longed to shift and join them.

"I'm done." The healer pushed the bowl away then stood. "I'll take your advice and sleep."

Rubbing her lip against the edge of her mug, she kept herself from smiling. "I'll wake you, if you're needed."

"See that you do." He pointed a finger at her. "I

think Pain should be your name."

That wasn't much better than the bird, but she'd take it. "Tell Diesel for me, would you?"

The healer grinned. "You'll do okay with us, Ranae."

"Thank you, Ben. But like I said, I'm only visiting."

"Sure." He waved off her rebuttal and wandered back into the room. She gave him a couple of minutes before checking to see him sprawled on the pallet she'd made him earlier. Once he was asleep, she'd go feed the fire.

Until then, she would pretend to be her mother and cook to fill the empty hours. Better to think about food rather than the kiss they'd shared while she waited for Diesel.

Yes, dammit, I said it. I'm waiting for him.

It took Diesel most of the night to care for the bodies in Amaruq. Once he'd completed the work and cleaned the scenes, he used the radio to call it in to his wolves who worked in the Alaska Bureau of Investigations. Timer and Cork spent time as Sentries when not on their day jobs, but both wolves enjoyed the freedom their service offered while also continuing to protect the pack.

Cork answered his call almost immediately. "Sir." His statement echoed surprise across the crackling line. "What can I do for you?"

"Trouble in Amaruq. Complete the cleanup and I'll send a crew in to hold the base camp until we can make arrangements." He waited patiently for the response, which wasn't immediately forthcoming.

The wolf had to be coping with different facets of shock—his Alpha called him in the middle of winter, and the devastation in Amaruq would be felt for at least a generation. The pack took their relationship with the native people seriously.

"We'll take care of them, sir." Cork finally returned over the line. "Home?"

"Your family is safe." He had not seen any of Cork's immediate family in the dead or the wounded. "Others are injured. Find me once you're here."

He wouldn't share more over the radio line.

"Understood. Cork, out." The man signed off and Diesel shut the radio down. It was an old analog way to connect that few relied on in their digital age. It pleased him that it afforded a level of privacy they might not otherwise have.

He made one last pass through the town in his wolf form before he sent up a call and listened. Grinder answered his howl, and he set off in the direction his wolf indicated. The Sentry sent up a howl periodically as Diesel tracked him, but once he had the feel for where his wolf was, he bayed. The order kept the other wolf quiet. He doubted the Sentry would endanger his hunt, but Diesel didn't need sound to track once he'd detected his wolf.

Every wolf in the Yukon pack was tethered to him, some so deep he knew them as he did his bones and others more fragile, but present. The Sentries were blood oathed to him. Even if Grinder hadn't given him a direction to travel in, he would have known.

A faint light touched the horizon. A hint of the sunrise which peaked and set in the same few minutes. The daylight would soon begin to grow longer, but the night still held sway. The snow crunched beneath his feet, a fresh powder though the skies had already begun to clear. Whatever storm front assaulted them earlier, it had passed.

He ran with a careless ease of a wolf who knew his land, and he knew it well. No matter the season, he could name the landmarks, recognized the scents which belonged and those that didn't. Had he not been preoccupied with his potential mate, he might even have detected the invaders before they spilled his pack's blood.

Dismissing the thought as useless the moment it presented itself, his wolf focused on the task at hand and Diesel agreed. Their mate was of singular importance to them. To ignore one for the other would be a thankless war to wage within. Those who'd harmed his pack would be repaid three times as much in kind.

The last thing the Russian packs wanted was a Petrov returning. He would use the leverage to set the dogs on the Volchitsa where they slept. The reminder of blood repaid in blood had his lips peeling away from his teeth.

His Sentries silenced at his approach. They stood in a loose circle around a downed man. They'd taken him in a stone path along the frozen riverbed. Only Grinder stood in his human form, the other pair maintained their animal shape, their snarls keeping their captive contained. Julian had also shifted, and somewhere he and Grinder had found clothing— likely from one of the caches the pack kept throughout their territory.

Their prisoner had been afforded no such luxury, and his skin showed the bluish tinge from his time bare against the elements. Bruises mottled his chest and blood had frozen to his face.

He was still breathing. That affront would only last as long as he was useful. Diesel shifted, aware that he held all of their attention, save Julian. The Chief Enforcer kept his gaze on the wolf at his feet. So many shifts in such a rapid time had left his skin steaming against the cold, and his body aching. Ignoring all of that, Diesel tipped his head.

"He doesn't seem to speak English," Grinder said, frustration darkening every syllable. "Or he's pretending he doesn't. His screams are pretty clear." He kicked the man in the face, sending blood flying and earning a yelp as though to prove his point.

"He doesn't want to speak," Julian added, his tone flat and unreadable.

Studying the man at their feet, Diesel examined his tattoos, the same markings worn by his dead comrades. "He's a foot soldier. Likely he knows little else than his target. Like a good dog, he went to do his master's bidding."

The Russian spat blood onto the snow, his eyes nearly colorless rather than gold of most wolves or even the blue he and Julian possessed. A rare few amongst the American packs didn't have gold-tinged eyes in their wolf form. More confirmation of the bastard's lineage.

"Kill me and get it over with." The wolf said, raising his chin in defiance. "I do not fear death." His English prove impeccable, despite his heavy accent.

"No, you fear failure." It was an old tale, one

Diesel understood well. "Living would be a worse fate for you, wouldn't it?"

His wolves said nothing. They wouldn't challenge his ruling even if their scent radiated disagreement. Only his earlier orders to keep him alive had prevented his disembowelment.

"I drew Yukon blood," the wolf said with a thump on his chest. "I have no failure."

"I don't know. We caught you…slaughtered the rest of you," Julian mused aloud. "That sounds like a failure to me."

The Russian scowled then lunged at the Enforcer. He didn't make it a full step before he landed on his ass in the snow with the Enforcer's boot at his throat.

"Don't kill him," Diesel said, keeping his tone mild.

"Oh, I won't." Julian smiled, but nothing friendly lived in his expression. For the first time since Diesel arrived, he scented fear on the captive. "He's yours to kill."

Yes, the wolf was. "Tell me your name," Diesel ordered. "The name of your clan."

"I won't." The wolf squeezed out the words. Although he gripped Julian's booted foot, he couldn't dislodge it.

"Answer." Diesel let the order bleed into his words. He was Alpha, and his dominance saw no challenge in the foot soldier beneath him. The man squirmed, and fought to hold his gaze then lowered it repeatedly.

"I cannot…" he wheezed.

"You can."

The wolf struggled for another heartbeat, before the fight went out of him and he sagged. "I am Yury," the man said. "Yury Volkov." The surname meant nothing. Many wolves in Russia adopted the last name. At one time, more than half the Alphas of those packs had the same name.

"Your clan."

"Volchitsa." The admission only confirmed what he'd already learned.

"What was your mission?"

Yury squirmed, and fresh blood appeared on the snow where his frozen flesh tore against the ice. "Please, Alpha…kill me."

"Your mission, and don't make me repeat myself." As if of one will, Julian exerted more pressure on the man's throat and he scrabbled against it. Despite his request to die, his need to survive still lived within him.

"Chaos—to make the Americans bleed…" *Chaos. To what end?* Diesel didn't think the wolf knew, or he'd press him on the answer. Foot soldiers were rarely given the larger picture.

Sutter Butte and Hudson River had been attacked, now him. "What is the next target?"

"I do not know." The stench of a lie choked him.

"Remove his hand."

The wolf blanched, but Julian didn't hesitate, his claws extended and he tore through the wolf's wrist. Yury screamed, the ragged sound grating until he choked off abruptly.

The Chief Enforcer sighed, and Diesel shook his head. "Bind the wound, then secure him." With a glance at the two still in wolf form, he said, "Find me something to drag his sorry ass back on."

"Outpost?" Grinder asked.

Diesel nodded. If the man had anymore information, they needed it. Till then, he focused on Julian. "You need to warn them…there are only two targets left."

"Three." Julian replied. "Of the three, only one is truly vulnerable."

Three Rivers. "You have Enforcers in place."

The other man nodded. "They are on observation only, not intercept."

"Might want to change that order." He rubbed the back of his neck, even as the change of weather began to kiss his senses. "Soon. A storm is coming."

Julian took his foot off the unconscious wolf and studied him dispassionately, before slanting a look at Grinder. The Sentry had said nothing since confirming their destination.

Whatever the Enforcer wanted to say, it would wait. The wolves he'd sent off returned in short order. The cache had to be nearer than Diesel thought or perhaps he was tired. The last thing he wanted to be doing was questioning the invader, he'd much rather be coaxing more information from his Dove. Once the wolf was secure, Diesel sent Grinder to watch over them and then shifted. With a glance at Julian, he set off.

The other wolf didn't change; instead he ran alongside, keeping pace with Diesel. They headed for one of outrider lodgings for wolves who wanted to sleep inside, but didn't want to run all the way back to Tikaani.

Both slowed on approach, testing the air for foreign scents or sounds. Detecting none, Julian opened the door and Diesel entered. A faint mustiness clung to the interior, as though it hadn't been used recently. While Julian secured the door, Diesel shifted and dug out a change of clothes from the box of them.

"Coffee?" The lack of dominance games amused Diesel. Out of sight of the others and alone, they didn't have to be Alpha and Chief Enforcer. Just cousins. If Julian wanted to play it that way, it suited him fine.

"I could drink a gallon," he admitted, scrubbing at his scalp. "Actually, what I want is a shower, a meal, and this to be someone else's problem." Not to mention, he wouldn't mind Ranae being in his bed, though he doubted they were anywhere near that capitulation on her part. An Alpha could plan though.

"Grab one, I'll see what crap your Sentries have stocked here." Julian waved him off.

Fifteen minutes later, Diesel felt a modicum more human and returned to find his cousin frying bacon. "Who the hell stocked bacon this far out?" His stomach rumbled. Except for the meal he'd shared with his Dove, it had been a while since he ate a cooked meal.

"Don't know, don't care. I stole it though." Julian gave him a proprietary grin. "Found it buried beneath all the elk meat."

Which meant someone had been hoarding. *Served them right.* Diesel poured his own coffee then drank most of the cup in two swallows. After he poured a second cup, he went into the side room off the kitchen and flipped on the radio gear. Setting it to the current channel, he retrieved the handset.

"Diesel to base. Check in."

He didn't have to wait long. "Montana, actual."

"Report."

"Survivors are healing and remaining stationary for now." *Good news.* "No other incidents to report."

"My guest?"

"Will not leave Chowder or her charges. She's staying on scene and protecting." Though Montana's voice crackled and popped on the radio, her tone suggested approval.

"Keep them that way, Montana."

"Will do. Are you returning?"

Soon as he could. "Will inform. Diesel, out." He ended the conversation and set the handset back in place. The faint hum of the equipment would be annoying, but he left it on in case they needed him.

In addition to the pile of bacon, Julian had found bread and shredded potatoes. He set a loaded plate on the counter for Diesel before filling his own. "I'm not cleaning."

Diesel snorted, but snagged a piece of bacon and pointed at him. "Fill me in on the rest."

"Not a lot to go on…" Julian said between bites of food. Neither man took their time on devouring the meal. "Whatever Russian pack is doing this, it feels at once organized and not."

"Is it a pack or is it strays looking to make their mark?" The foot soldiers made him think the former more than the latter. Volchitsa were more a roving band of vagabonds. Had they bonded together?

"Why would strays protect each other, even on pain of death?" His cousin shook his head. "No, this is a coordinated effort, I just don't think the pawns know what the player's end game is."

"The others have no ideas?"

"No." Julian shook his head. "Mason is the only one considering the possibility that the threat is to all the packs and, to be fair, only Mason and Serafina are sitting on stable consolidated packs at the moment. Brett's is still recovering, and Sutter Butte may be a mess for some time to come."

"My pack is fine." He reminded his cousin. "We will mourn our dead, heal our living, and continue as we have always done."

"Then crush your enemy as soon as you identify them?"

Diesel merely smiled.

"That is what the Enforcers are for. We can and will track these bastards down. If we go into Russia, it begs no reprisals from their packs."

"You don't even know the lay of the land there, cousin…"

"And you do?" Julian raised his brows.

"I roamed there."

"I fought over there."

"You fought in Europe, and it was a different era altogether. I roamed Siberia, lived in the dark forests, foraged into China and beyond." If they really wanted to have a pissing contest, they could spend their whole day on it. "Your Enforcers are needed here to deal with the upstarts and the Lone Wolves." That was their purpose. "You do not fight our wars for us."

Julian scowled.

But if his cousin wanted to persist… "Besides, I

know of only one other wolf that knows Russia better than me." Biting into his last piece of bacon, Diesel waited for him to latch onto the bait.

"Who?"

"Your Dallas." A dark look crossed the other wolf's face and Diesel didn't smile despite his amusement. "Perhaps, if you find her, you'll discover more answers."

"Sometimes, you're a bastard." Julian growled.

"Most of the time," Diesel agreed then shrugged. "You asked. I know she spent time there, on and off, over the years. She may know nothing, but a wolf on the run usually knows all the major players, because they have to know how to avoid them."

Scowl easing, Julian finished the last of his food then drained his coffee. "One disaster at a time. I'm going to see if I can contact Mason and Serafina. Do you want to be present, or would you prefer to continue your pretense of disliking technology?"

"It's not a pretense. I don't like it. It's annoying, but it has its place. Call them."

Julian pulled a larger phone from inside his coat. No wonder he hadn't shifted. "It's a satellite phone," he said by way of explanation.

"I don't care," Diesel assured him, before refilling his coffee with the last in the pot. Julian gave him a dark look because Diesel didn't make more.

The phone rang twice before Mason answered. "Not sure whether to be impressed or worried because you're checking in so soon, Julian."

"Probably both," Julian answered without quibbling as he put the phone on speaker and set it between them. The hum of the electronics raked across Diesel's nerves, but the soft, childish laughter drifting from somewhere near Mason offered a balm.

"Go find Mommy," Mason ordered gently. "Daddy will hunt with you in a little while." Another soft laugh, then the sound of a little girl calling for Mommy as she raced away. "You have my attention," he said once the baby sounds vanished.

"A play was made for the Yukon," Julian began.

"A feint," Diesel corrected. "All foot soldiers, none very dominant. More brute force than anything else. We have one prisoner, who won't live for long."

"Any losses?" Trust an Alpha to go to the heart of the matter.

"Four dead, four wounded."

"And my Hunter?"

Diesel didn't bare his teeth, but that was another matter they needed to settle before the call ended.

"Ranae is fine," Julian answered. "She wasn't involved in the fight."

"Where is she now?" A silken threat flowed through the words.

"Looking after my healer while Chowder tends the injured—behind a wall of two hundred solid fighters." Diesel wouldn't pretend she didn't matter. "We need to discuss this further after we deal with the problem at hand."

"So, it's like that, is it?" Amusement softened the question.

"Yes." He didn't quibble. "I plan to keep her."

Julian sighed, while giving him a bland look.

"How does she feel about that?" Instead of sounding offended, a hint of intrigue touched Mason's tone.

"She doesn't understand yet." Diesel kept it honest. "But we've only just met. Give me a few weeks."

"Few weeks?" Doubt edged his voice now. "Diesel, she is my wolf. Mine to protect, and if she doesn't want to stay there a few weeks, I will not order her to do so."

Fine, if he wants to throw down a gauntlet... "Then I will hold her hostage. The other packs have your wolves, cementing your ties to them. Consider her a promise to good relations between ours."

"Those are archaic laws, not to mention ridiculous. If you try to hold her hostage, she would be within her rights to fight her way out."

"I have no problems with that." The only wolf she would ever fight would be him and he would never harm her—or let her go. *Problem solved.*

"Table it for now," Julian interrupted. "We have enough issues to deal with and, for the moment, Ranae is safe and occupied."

"Fine, I gave her two weeks. By my count, she has nine days left. We will revisit the issue then...but, Diesel, allow me to be clear. If she wants to leave and you make me come up there, you won't like the result."

Nor would Mason, but Julian simply shook his head—a request, not an order in his eyes. Diesel shrugged then waved a hand. "Continue."

"We've questioned the foot soldier," Julian inserted, apparently quite content to avoid further discussion of Diesel's mate. "He claims they were here to sow chaos."

"Arguably, it's what they did in Sutter Butte as well." Mason didn't sound certain. "Though at a significantly bloody cost."

"The challenge Brett faced was only that of an Alpha, they didn't touch his pack." Julian tapped two fingers to the counter. "Not chaos engendering…not really."

"You're missing the point." Diesel eyed his cousin. "You've spent too many years outside of a pack—and, while you rule Willow Bend now, Mason, you too spent too many years alone."

"So, what is it we're not seeing?" The mildness in his question belied any real offense on Mason's part.

"They are targeting their attacks to each specific pack. Cassius' attack was exceptionally bloody and violent, but that is Sutter Butte. Brett seemed the weakest of the Alphas, as he'd already taken damage from the mad wolf, so eliminating him would be the most expedient way to take over." Diesel drained his coffee. "If I were interested in their territories, it's what I would have done."

Silence hung between them for a long moment, then Mason asked. "And if you wanted mine?"

"I'd kill your mate."

Chapter Nine

Nearly a full day after she'd shared a dinner with Diesel in his grassy room, she returned to it—alone. Nothing inside had changed, the remnants of their meal still sat on the end of the oversized sofa, their glasses remained perched on the crate table. Once the door secured behind her, she walked over to pick up her glass and drained the remnants.

Chowder determined the injured could be moved to the sanctuary below finally. Ranae's eyes were gritty from lack of sleep, and the fatigue in her muscles left her sore. Despite the long passage of hours, she'd made do with only snatches of rest. It seemed no sooner did she allow her eyes to close than the healer sat up and went to one of his patients.

He cared for them, she kept an eye on him. As they recovered enough to eat, she provided the stew—stew Chowder even declared passable, despite lacking clams. It had provided a much needed moment of levity when Demon experienced night terrors. They only got him quieted when Ranae sat with him, stroking his hair. He'd curled onto his uninjured side and settled his cheek to her thigh.

Cramps ripped through her for holding position for so long, but she didn't move until he rolled of his own accord. At first she couldn't figure out why they hadn't moved the injured immediately, but once they made the descent—well-lit this time, thankfully—she realized most of the pack was asleep and they could move the injured in without scaring the young.

A female wolf named Montana introduced herself, and advised Ranae she would show her back to her rooms. Ranae declined until she'd seen Chowder to his. The healer had protested, but Montana joined her in telling him to go to bed. The injured needed sleep and safety now more than a healer on hand. Between them, they'd gotten the healer moving.

Setting her glass down, she picked up Diesel's and drained it as well. Despite having showered earlier, she needed another one, but what she really wanted was eight hours of uninterrupted horizontal time. *The big bed is probably more comfortable than the one in the room I picked.*

She considered it—it would serve him right. "And send totally the wrong message." No matter how tired she was, it would be a bitch thing to toy with a wolf's affections, whether she believed him or not. She cleaned up the tray of food then carried it to the door. There she used the intercom and chose the number for Montana. When she received a message, she left one and said she'd put the tray outside. She would happily return it, but she didn't know where it went.

Once she'd taken care of that, she poured herself another drink and carried the whiskey with her to the bathroom. She tossed it back after turning on the water. Stripping off her bloodied clothes and reminding herself she still didn't know where her jacket had gone, she climbed in the shower and rinsed away the last day's worth of sweat and pain.

Leaning on the tiled wall, she pressed her cheek to the coolness. She could go to sleep right there, but what a waste of water. Maybe she should have filled the tub. Ten minutes later, she made herself shut the water off and toweled herself dry. Unwilling to put the bloodied clothes back on, she set them to the side. Her mother would growl and snarl if she didn't soak them.

"Good thing Mom isn't here, then." With only the towel wrapped around her, she left the bathroom and walked to her room. Whatever Diesel had done to the lights kept them on at that dim, but visible setting. She liked it. In her room, she exchanged her towel for an oversized t-shirt and a pair of panties, then fell onto the bed.

Her eyes had barely closed when she heard buzzing.

Peeling an eyelid up, she studied the room. The buzz repeated.

When it came a third time, she groaned and pushed herself up, retraced her steps and stared at her dirtied cloths in the bathroom. Fishing her phone out of her back pocket, she stared at it. A series of messages appeared on the screen.

The sanctuary must have Internet. It didn't even occur to her to check and her phone had connected automatically.

Three notes from A.J. all in response to her she'd arrived message from three days before. Had it really been three days? It felt like a month. The messages were all typical brother stuff—including the last one to remind Diesel she'd had her shots, but she did still bite.

Shaking her head, she fell back onto her guest bed. It was like falling on a cushion of stone, but she really didn't care. She had messages from her parents, Ty, and Linc—both wanted her to let them know when she left the Yukon, and both chided her for not telling them she had landed safely.

"Ugh, you have mates. Go mother them." She skipped answering them for the moment.

The last message had her sitting up again. It was from Mason.

Contact me immediately.

"Really, Diesel? The one time I wished you lived in the backwater wasteland I thought this would be." She wanted to growl, but no way she could disobey her Alpha, especially since he was reaching out to her.

I'm here, she sent back.

Can you call?

She checked her cell reception and grimaced. *No bars.*

Then how are you texting me?

Guilt swamped her. *Internet connection.*

Huh. Crafty bastard never told me he had that.

She kept her opinions to herself about the crafty bastard.

Julian and Diesel contacted me about an attack. Are you safe?

Warmth flooded her, and she blinked back tears. Her Alpha did care. *Yes, sir. I wasn't in any of the fighting, helped the healer while he tended the injured.*

Good job. That's not easy, to stay out of the action.

I made myself useful.

Mason didn't respond immediately. A yawn

cracked her jaw and she took advantage of the delay to drag back the heavy wool blanket and crawl beneath it. The area wasn't cold, but she liked to be warm when she slept.

Thank you, Ranae. I am here if you need me.

Surprise gripped her. Hopefully she wouldn't need him. *Thank you, Mason. Forgive me for asking, but is there anything else? I need sleep. Been up for thirty-six hours.*

Not exactly diplomatic, but... *Sleep. Check in later.*

A good response, but a moment later, he added. *And contact your mother after you've rested.*

Ranae chuckled. *Will do.*

The phone went quiet, and she set it on the blanket next to her as she collapsed once more. A yawn stretched her mouth wide, and her eyes closed. She descended rapidly, her whole body going liquid when she heard the door in the outer room open.

A groan tried to work free, but she clamped it down. She needed to sleep. The barest hush of footsteps, then nothing. Satisfied Diesel had gone to his own room, she curled onto her side and began to sink once more.

The bed jolted and she opened her eyes to see a huge white wolf easing onto the bed. Ranae rolled onto her back and pushed up on her elbows. "What the hell are you doing?"

Blue eyes met hers as the wolf simply stared at her.

"There is not enough room in this bed..."

He tipped his head to the side, his ears flicking toward her.

She groaned and tipped her head back. "I just want to go to sleep. Do you have any idea how tired I am?"

Why wasn't he more tired? Hadn't he gone off to deal with the problem? Diesel didn't leap down but worked his way into stretching out alongside her and then he set his head against her hip.

It was way too personal. She gave him a light push and rolled to her side. It gave him more room and jammed her up against the wall. The wolf seemed to unfold, stretching out into the available space and then tucked his head against her shoulder.

She was too tired for his crap. "I hate you."

He huffed and when he began to breathe long, slow and deep she sighed and closed her eyes.

The dim lighting gave him a perfect view of her face when he finally roused from some of the best sleep he'd had in a while. Initially, he'd planned to let her have the room to herself. No need to force his attentions, and it would be better in the long run if she came to him. He'd made it as far as his own room before the realization that he'd never sleep if he were not close enough to protect her.

Mate.

The knowledge carried a special kind of hell with it. Though he minimized the threat to his pack, he now faced a very similar weakness to Mason. If anyone laid a finger on her, they'd lose the arm if not their life. Walking into her room in wolf form meant he could protect, and she didn't have to feel pressured by a man trying to sleep in her bed.

It was a minor difference, and she would be

well within her rights to slap him down for it. He didn't mind. He'd take the hit. Deserving her chastisement was worth the exchange for ensuring her safety. Though in truth, he'd been after peace of mind.

One did not recover from the loss of a mate so easily and he hadn't—not for years. The chance to move on, the opportunity for hope? His Dove represented all that and more. Montana told him of all she'd done and, when he'd checked on the injured, they'd all mentioned her—especially young Demon. The pup was half-in-love with the she-wolf who'd looked after him.

She slept on her side, one hand tucked beneath her cheek, the other arm extended so that her free hand rested in his ruff. That light contact kept him absolutely still when he woke. Soon enough she would wake and want him away, but he would enjoy the moment's intimacy for however long it lasted.

A hundred questions formed in his mind. What did she like? How long had she trained? Her discipline had been profound. She'd gone right to work when they made it to the top of the stairs. She hadn't slowed and, even though he'd made sure the lights were on, she hadn't even hesitated to follow them into the stairwell.

Courage or brashness? Did it really matter?

She tried to roll over and released a little moan when she couldn't shift his weight. Curious, he didn't move and waited, anticipating the moment she opened her eyes. The dark lashes swept up to reveal the gray-green he'd begun to adore. The shade reminded of the sea when a storm churned the water.

For split second, her drowsy expression held sway until it resolved to annoyance with a frown tightening her brow. If he were a man, he would've grinned. As it was, he let his mouth open so his tongue could loll out and savor every nuance of her scent.

It coated him, having slept so close to her, and his would be on her. More than safety demanded he keep his scent on her clothes, her bed—because until he could embed it in her skin, he wanted it clear he pursued her, and he wouldn't brook any competition. The thought jolted through him…what if his competition was not in the Yukon but in Willow Bend?

His jaws snapped shut and she rubbed at her eyes at the click of his teeth coming together. "Considering you weigh a ton and have all the room, what are you being pissy about?" In the first hours of waking, her voice held a particularly husky quality.

He nuzzled her cheek rather than answering, and she allowed him one small swipe of his tongue before she shoved muzzle away.

"Ugh, morning breath."

He huffed, then sniffed her with deliberate indelicateness and huffed again.

"Not me, smart ass. You." She pointed to the floor. "Get off."

While he definitely enjoyed the challenge she offered, it would suit her well to remember who the Alpha was. She gave him another shove, this time bracing herself on the wall and using her legs. It actually rocked his balance and he shot to his feet.

"Thank you," she said, springing up and off the

bed before he could react. "I have to pee." With that, she sauntered away, leaving him with a beautiful view of her long golden legs and the pale cream panties she wore, since her t-shirt hadn't fallen all the way down.

When his tongue lolled out this time, it wasn't just to savor her scent. He waited until the bathroom door closed before he leapt down and padded into his bedroom. Only there did he shift and bring himself to his full height. Stretching his arms over his head, he listened to each of the vertebrae as they cracked and popped. The release of tension reminded him of how long he'd stayed still.

No one had disturbed them. A good sign. He'd left Grinder and the others to dispose of Yury once they finished questioning him. Afterward, Diesel had then seen Julian to his vehicle to make sure he headed back toward Prudhoe Bay.

Scratching his chest, he considered whether to dress then shower or to simply take his shower then dress. The idea he even considered clothes was in deference to Dove. Most wolves were not body shy. Then again, most wolves wouldn't out right reject a mate claim, either. In the end, it didn't matter what most wolves would or would not do—it only mattered what Dove preferred.

Still debating the matter when she exited the bathroom, he waited for her to notice him through the open door so he could gauge her reaction. Her gaze immediately collided with his, dropped to his body then stared a heartbeat longer than necessary. His cock thrummed to life under her attention. Grinning slowly, he paced forward and gave her time to recover.

Coughing once, she glanced down the hall. "I'll figure out coffee…" Then she all but fled.

Pleased beyond all measure, he sauntered into the bathroom for his shower. She'd noticed. More, she'd liked what she'd seen. Riding the high of being ten feet tall, he took his time with the shower.

The scent of coffee greeted him while he toweled off. Satisfied by her response to his body, he selected lightweight jeans and a simple t-shirt. She wasn't in the arbor.

Dampness met his bare feet with every step. The misters had kicked in to water the lawn and the overheads had brightened for a sunlight effect. Dove stood in the stone garden, with its appliances built into the rock walls. Someday, he would really need to compliment Montana on her efforts to create the perfect parts of their environment in his rooms.

Sadly, Ranae had dressed as well, though her feet were bare. The long, dark pants she wore were a soft cotton and her t-shirt white enough he could make out the line of the bra she'd also donned. Cradling a cup of coffee, she stared at the ceiling.

Pausing behind her, he canted his head to try and see what she saw. The rocks stretched up the walls, then the ceiling widened out. The UV lamps along the day lamps created a brightness which left him squinting.

"A lot of thought went into this construction," was all she said, before pointing at the counter. "Coffee is made."

"Thank you." Giving into the temptation, he rested his hands lightly on her shoulders and brushed a kiss to her cheek. She went absolutely still under the contact, her muscles stiff. Not insulted, he kept the contact brief before releasing her and continuing to the pot for his coffee.

"Do you have to keep doing that?" The quiet question radiated with suppressed anger and more than a hint of anxiety.

"No," he admitted, keeping his back to her. "I don't *have* to keep doing it, but I like touching you."

"So I've seen."

He couldn't help but feel she edited herself. Not a reaction he wanted her to have. "Dove, feel free to speak your mind."

"I would, except you're the Alpha and I'm your guest. I have Willow Bend to think of." A politic answer.

And damned if it didn't aggravate the hell out of him. Containing the reaction, he took his time to fill his cup before he turned to look at her. "Dove." Command filled the syllable, and her gaze jerked to his. "If you obey no other order I give, I want you to obey this one." He held her gaze, letting his power suffuse every word. He was Alpha, but he was also a man. "Always speak your mind to me. Never feel the need to curb your words or dilute the sentiment out of fear that I will react badly. You may say anything to me."

The moment hollowed, even time seemed to slow as her pupils dilated then contracted. Her lips compressed into a thin line, and her scent took on a distinct sharp edge. Anger. A beautiful hot house fragrance, like roses.

"Really?" Skepticism lived within her snarl.

"Yes, really." Keeping his distance, he leaned against the counter. "I want to know you."

"And if I don't want to know you?"

Well, he had told her to speak her mind. "Then it is up to me to convince you I'm worth knowing. I thought we'd gotten off to a good start during our dinner."

"You mean after my meltdown and the kiss where you seemed to take control of my soul?" Flushing, she glanced at her coffee. Her soul, eh? He'd take it.

"Yes. I liked kissing you—I didn't like that you were afraid and hurting. The kiss was not meant to imprint, but to help you find your way back to yourself." For him as well, but that had been the lesser concern at the time.

"Then the second kiss at the stairwell?"

"You needed to wear my scent around the wolves. The attack left everyone on edge, and you were a stranger to them." He wouldn't apologize for wanting her safe.

"Last night when you climbed into my bed to sleep? Who were you protecting then?"

"Me." He took a sip of his coffee as she digested his answer. Shock rippled through her expression.

"You?"

"I'd been away from you for nearly twenty-four hours. Members of my pack died, others are injured. I wanted—no, I needed—the peace of mind that came from knowing you were all right. Since you insisted on sleeping in that room, I wanted to be there, too."

Her mouth opened then closed again twice

before she too took a drink of her coffee. "Alphas rarely admit a weakness."

"Most wolves won't admit to one unless they trust someone."

"How the hell can you trust me that much?" Was it really such a mystery to her?

"Because you are my mate." He loved the way it sounded.

Dove scowled and shook her head. "You don't know that—you can't. You also can't just decide something. Mating takes two people, and I don't know you."

Well, they had come a long way since that first night. Warmth unfurled within him and his wolf stretched. "Then get to know me. For you, I'll be an open book."

"That's a lot of confidence when I'm loyal to Willow Bend."

"Loyalty should be treasured in all its forms. You are a good Hunter or Mason would not have sent you on this mission." As annoying as Dylan had been on his various visits, he'd also proven to be very capable. His choice of an Omega as a mate demonstrated more about the wolf than he might realize.

"I wouldn't assume that. I'm half-convinced Mason sent me here to get rid of me."

No, she didn't believe that…she feared it. "Will you tell me why you think that?"

She sighed then drained her coffee. Even from across the room, he could hear the gurgle of her stomach.

"Perhaps over food? Or would you rather go

hunting first?" The offer was made before he fully considered it, but his wolf wanted to see hers. Wanted to run with her.

"Hunting? You're planning to let me leave your…what do you call this place?"

"Our sanctuary and, of course. You're not a prisoner, Dove."

She made a face.

"This surprises you?" He finished his coffee. "Would you like another cup or to get out of here?"

"Yes and yes—to another cup and to getting out of here." Extending the hand with the mug, she crossed the room. "I'm not human on only one cup."

"You're never going to be human on two. You're a wolf," he said, refilling the mug.

The corners of her mouth curved and the frown abandoned her expression as she chuckled. "Okay, that was funny."

"Thank you." After he filled hers, he filled his own. "Why does it surprise you?"

"Cause the pack was attacked, your people were hurt and you think I'm your mate…but you're just going to let me go running with you without fear of something happening?"

He returned the pot to its stand before he answered. "The sanctuary is meant for our vulnerable and for any wolf who doesn't wish to travel to the cities or roam with the pack during the long winter."

"Exactly my point."

Oh, he understood her point. "Do you see yourself as vulnerable? In need of my protection and shelter?" She had his protection, whether she needed it or not.

"No."

"Nor do I." He let those words sink in a moment. "You are a Hunter, you are trained, yes? You understand combat? The need to stick together on a hunt? To work with the other wolf?"

"Yes. I used to tag along with my brothers when I was younger. They never let me do anything, but I watched them. I learned. I've done requisite apprentice training and, for the last year or so, I've been working as a journeyman assigned to different circuits with the other Hunters."

"Then you're more than capable of joining me on a hunt."

"You're not what I expected," she said, then leaned against the counter near him. Close, but not touching.

"What did you expect?"

"At the risk of being insulting," she said, staring at her coffee cup. "An old wolf, set in his ways, who wouldn't bother to shift or have more than a shack and a pot to piss in."

He laughed. "We have some who live like that, Dove. In the summer months, I have a cabin not far from here, deeper into the woodlands. It has no electricity, no… modern conveniences. It has all that my grandfather had when he first built it. It's peaceful. The game is plentiful and the river is well-stocked with fish. But I am one man, and I have an entire pack to protect."

"You make that sound natural, yet you do everything to make sure no one outside knows about it. But you let Julian come here."

"Yes, Julian has been here before. He's my

cousin. His mother, my aunt, could return to our pack whenever she desired."

Dove stared at him. "I didn't know anyone would willingly claim to be related to Julian."

"He's not so bad. Old, set in his ways—and I am fairly certain he also has more than a shack and a pot to piss in despite never letting anyone see it."

She bit her lip then, one-by-one, giggles escaped.

He held up two fingers and a question danced amidst the laughter in her eyes.

"That's twice I've made you laugh. If I can do so a third time, will you give me a prize?"

"Maybe." It came out almost coy. "Depends on what you want."

"To see your wolf."

She grinned. "Very well, if you can make me laugh a third time, I'll go hunting with you and you can see my wolf."

"Excellent." *Small victories.* "Breakfast?"

"Do you have anything in here?"

"Possibly." He pursed his lips and turned to study the counters. Montana likely had the cabinets stocked as soon as he told her where Ranae would be staying. He'd rather take her out for fresh meat, but he set the coffee cup aside and began to inventory the cabinets.

"Don't you know where you keep things?"

"Not particularly. I don't stay below often. I prefer the freedom to roam." He found the cold storage stocked with different cuts of meat including… "Bacon." He held it up like a triumph and eyed Dove. She burst out laughing.

Well that proved easier than he'd expected, but her enjoyment pleased him.

"You approve, yes?"

"Oh, I like bacon fine, but you look like a little boy who just discovered the cake hidden in the fridge."

"Why would anyone hide cake in the fridge?" He set the bacon the counter. He could fry up all of it, but likely they should add something else to it.

"It's just a saying…" She waved off the comment. "If you have any mix or flour, I could make pancakes, maybe."

"You would cook for me?" It humbled him.

"Aren't you going to cook for me?" She pointed at the bacon.

"Fair point. We'll cook together."

"In that case…" She returned to the coffee maker. "I'll get another pot started, and you can explain Diesel to me."

"Me?"

"No. Well, yes, eventually I guess, but I meant the name. Chowder told me how he got his, but please don't tell me you liked to eat gas and that's why you have the name." The mock horror in her tone elicited a laugh, from him this time.

"Perhaps you'll have to earn that answer."

"That sounds like a challenge." Despite her earlier reservations, she didn't seem to mind. The coffee started, so she began rummaging through the cabinets and he joined her. They needed pans, and at least one plate—maybe two.

"I like challenging you," he said, not minding when she squeezed around him and her fingers brushed his back.

"Not sure whether to be worried or excited by the prospect."

"Be excited." He advised. "It's more fun."

Her grin lit up the room and Diesel and his wolf both wanted to sigh. It had been a long time since he enjoyed something so mundane as cooking or searching for cooking utensils.

"Do you mind if I ask you about what happened last night?"

A darker cloud than he cared to cast, but he'd told her to speak her mind. "Not at all. What do you want to know?"

"Everything?"

He nodded as she set a bowl on the counter and began to mix ingredients together to create a batter. "Better we discuss this before we eat."

Setting the pan on the stove, he turned on the heat and began laying strips of bacon along it. Once it began to sizzle, he told her of the attack, the hunt, Amaruq and his plan for Yury.

Definitely not a conversation for a meal.

Chapter Ten

Not only did Diesel answer her question about the attack, but he gave her intimate details of the deaths in Amaruq, his suspicions about the Russian pack behind them, and his plans for the wolf they'd captured. Settled on the sofa once more with their pancakes and bacon, she listened in quiet awe as he laid it all out for her.

When he finished, she said, "So that's it? You're going to send each of his organs to one of the packs in Russia, along with a personal note?" She wasn't sure whether to be horrified or impressed.

"It's a kind of blunt honesty they will appreciate. Dipping into the North American packs might seem a sport to some of their young, but older wolves understand that if we do the same to them— we would be wise to wipe them out." Diesel shrugged. "My ancestors were Russian. I know how they think."

At this point, she should be used to the shocks but they kept coming. "The Yukon pack is Russian?"

"Some, not all." He tipped his head. "Is that a problem for you?"

Opening her mouth, she started to say 'no' then paused. As direct as he'd been with her, he deserved honesty. "I don't know. I've heard a lot of horror stories about Russian packs."

"The brutality? The way they take over another pack through assassination of the males and the conquest of the females?" Maybe he was too direct.

"Yes." The dark terrified her, and the Russians reminded her of the dark. A boogeyman waiting to ambush them when they least expected it. "We don't really know much about them other than avoid them at all costs…a few of Willow Bend's wolves have gone overseas and staying away from them is on the top of the list."

"It's a wise piece of advice. They don't like outsiders and tend to kill first and ask questions never." The ease he had with the danger soothed her in a way it shouldn't. "It comes from having limited resources and very difficult winters. Survival depends on access to resources, and outsiders can chip away at those resources."

"You don't have that problem here?" Winters at home could be hard, but she couldn't imagine the long hours of night they endured in the deepest part of winter, not to mention the brutal cold.

"We don't have much competition here." Though he'd finished his meal, he sat with her as she nibbled her way through the bacon.

"Was there competition here when your people migrated?" Sober thought. "And…didn't the other packs have an issue with Russians moving in to this area?"

"First, no wolf pack was displaced when my people migrated. One of the reasons this region was chosen was for the lack of all but maybe a small handful of lone wolves. Most of those moved on of their own volition."

"Or at least that's what you were told." Over the years, she'd heard her share of tall tales. Toman had told her family it was better for A.J. to do the penance asserted by human law for his killing of a human rather than bring him home where he would face certain execution.

"I will grant you, it is what I was told. The migration happened in the early part of the 19th century, the other North American packs weren't here. It wasn't considered a very hospitable region then."

That earned him another laugh and she pointed her bacon at him. "I have news for you, it's not considered much of a hospitable region now."

Leaning forward, he snagged the bacon with his teeth and she tugged. He won more than half of the crispy slice. The way he chewed it sent a frisson of awareness through her, but she ate the rest of her piece herself then shook her head.

"Perhaps it's not, but we like our isolation. Even with the changes wrought by technology and many of the younger members of the tribes moving on, we still have the many."

Rubbing her jaw, she held out her plate with a few slices of bacon left. "I'm full if you're still hungry."

"I'm hungry for a great many things, but I will settle for bacon." The playfulness wasn't her imagination. He caught her wrist before she could withdraw it, then fed himself from her hand.

He nibbled all the way down the slice. Though loose, the warmth of his grip on her wrist kept her still. She could pull away, but he'd been so giving and open—she didn't want to. His eyes were so vivid blue, and even though she was aware of his breath and nearness, the lap of his tongue against her fingertips made her shiver.

"Delicious," he sighed with satisfaction, stroking his thumb over her pulse point before he released her.

Her face warmed and she wanted to growl, but the laughter in his gorgeous eyes silenced the rejection. "I hate that I'm blushing."

"I don't." He stood then, setting the plate down and extending his hand to her. "Come…let's go run, I've won the right to see your wolf, and I would show you my territory."

Accepting his hand, she let him pull her to her feet. "I don't know where my jacket went."

"You won't need it." He padded on bare feet to the door.

"Or my shoes."

He chuckled. "You won't need those either."

At the door, she tugged once and he halted. When he turned and faced her, she studied his expression. "Are you for real?"

"Define for real." If not for the earnest way he studied her and the careful way he cradled her hand in his she might have thought he was joking.

"Most of the males I know…they can't help themselves. They have to protect me from everything, even myself. Are you for real about going out there? To run on the tundra? Even with the danger?"

"If you mean do I trust you to be capable, yes. If you mean do I trust myself to watch your back, then also yes."

Her heart sank. Watch her back? Of course, he was just like…

"Dove," Diesel said, closing the distance

between them and cupping her face. He urged her gaze upward, and stared at her with that same earnestness. "I trust you to watch my back as well."

Surprise buoyed her above the disappointment. "You don't know me." All the wolves in her life who did, yet this one stranger, *he* believed in her.

"When you've lived as long as me, you become a good judge of character." With a squeeze of her hand, he guided her through the underground compound passing groups of chattering children and more.

They waved to Diesel, called out greetings, but none intercepted them. His pack seemed confident and calm. Even with all the people calling out greetings and the peace in their scents, something still struck her as odd. Keeping her questions to herself, she padded barefoot along the stone and grass pathways winding through the sanctuary.

At the door to the stairs, she braced herself. She needn't have worried though, because the lights were on. "You're going to run the bill up at this rate." It wasn't exactly a thank you, but he grinned at her nonetheless.

"So much doubt," he said. "You are going to really put me through the ringer to prove my worth, aren't you?"

Her face warmed once more, but she couldn't help the soft laugh that escaped as they took the stairs at speed. He matched strides with her so they stayed side by side. At the top of the stairs he released her to open the door for her. No one remained within the cabin, and all the signs of their patients had been cleaned away. She couldn't even smell the blood.

"Damn," she murmured. "Your cleaning fairies are way impressive."

Diesel snorted and gave her a light nudge. "Shift for me in here, where it's warm."

It wasn't exactly hot in the room; a low banked fire gave the room a warm glow and a couple of oil lanterns added to the illumination. "I see, you brought me to a freezing room to get me naked."

Folding his arms, the Alpha leaned against the wall nearest the outer door. "Delay all you like, I will wait."

Pivoting, she faced him and pursed her lips. "I'm not shy."

"I never said you were."

Gripping her shirt, she tugged it off over her head, then freed the bra before she stripped out of her yoga pants and panties. Nude, she eyed him and raised her chin. One thing having three brothers taught her—*don't back down from a challenge.*

Ever.

For several long heartbeats, Diesel kept his gaze zeroed in on her face. While she'd never been an exhibitionist, she expected a little more notice than he gave her. Hands on her hips, she tapped one foot and waited.

"Problem, Dove?" The faintest curve to his lips betrayed his entertainment at her predicament.

Dodging the bait, she reached for her wolf and the rush spilled over her. Faster than nearly anyone in her pack, save perhaps her Alpha, though she'd never compared it, she went from two feet to four in a twist of blissful agony. Her bones didn't crack and snap like others; she'd always been far more fluid.

"Oh, Dove, you are a beauty." He'd abandoned his post at the wall and approached her. The praise had her lifting her head and testing his scent. He crouched before her and brought his head level with hers. His wolf was huge, hers was far more average. One exchange of being so swift to shift was she didn't quite have the bulk of her brothers.

She might be smaller, but she had strength and speed. With his hands on her head, he canted his to study her and she took advantage of his distraction to slurp his face. Dancing away, she bounded around the room then skidded to a halt at the door.

The freedom of being in her wolf form offered a wild pleasure. It had been far too many days since she'd had the opportunity.

"As my lady wishes." Diesel stripped out of his clothes and she didn't pretend to look away. The wolf assessed the male as only a wolf could. He was tall, broad shouldered, and densely muscled. She expected more scars, but the flex of his thighs distracted her.

His change was a revelation. Deep breaths carried the rich, masculine scent of snow on fur. When he completed his transition, he stalked forward and she flicked her ears toward him. He butted his head to hers, then rubbed all along her side. If his nose went anywhere near her…he nipped her hip and she whirled and snapped at him.

Undeterred he pounced her and they tumbled. She slid free, and rolled over to land on her feet. Twice more they faced off, pouncing and breaking apart. He was more than a third again larger than her, but not once did she feel the threat of his age or his dominance. It was downright liberating.

More than ready to abandon the cabin, she raced over to the door then back at him. With a bark, he ordered her to follow and she fell away from the door to let him open their exit. He hit a pad with his paws, then they were inside the mudroom antechamber and the heat shut off and the red lights began to tick down.

Antsy, she danced back and forth. Diesel flicked one ear to her then the door. At the hiss announcing the door release, she focused and readied to face whatever challenges awaited them. Diesel strode through the open door first and she gave him a beat then followed on his heels.

They emerged into the darkness of the day, and Diesel halted three steps from the door to let her eyes acclimate. She made a fierce, compact and definitely beautiful wolf. Her pelt had hints of gold and brown mingled with white and grey. The mottling affect reminded him of the hint of freckles he'd spied along her torso and arms. A sprinkle of them decorated her nose, but her soft golden skin tone rendered them nearly invisible.

He'd spent a lot of time studying her face earlier and counted each one. Dove paused then turned in a slow circle, her nose rising to test the breeze. The bulk of his pack still roamed near Tikaani with a select few having encouraged their younger members to return to the sanctuary. The rest? They would do as they'd always done, but they kept their numbers up to avoid ambush and his Sentries stretched themselves out to keep the pack protected.

Dove slowed her circle then paced to his side

and bumped him. When he nipped at her muzzle, she rewarded him with a show of teeth. Yes, she proved a delight. Her simple joy at not being closeted away firmed another opinion within him, one he'd understood all of his life. To be a mate to an Alpha was not the same as choosing him as her Alpha. He could be her mate or he could be her Alpha—he far preferred the former to the latter.

Together, they set off across the empty village. The storm he'd scented the day before must have blown through while they slept. Fresh powder puffed beneath his feet and only the faintest of breezes stirred his coat. It was a perfect day, one he intended to spend exploring. The sun rested on the horizon, a sliver of light to illuminate the day. It would dip again soon, but he kept watch over his companion.

If the shadows bothered her, she didn't let on. For now, he would keep watch and, if necessary, angle their path toward Tikaani again. Though he didn't doubt her strength or her skill, he didn't believe her ready to roam for days on end.

His wolf snapped at his wandering thoughts and Diesel halted. The breeze carried no scents he didn't recognize. Flicking his ears, he listened. Some change alerted his senses, and he refused to allow surprise to cut into their day. Dove stilled next to him, her position moving to cover his flank. Her side brushed his, and it was so natural, bliss filled him.

Too long he'd run alone, with an emptiness in his soul that not even the care of his pack could fill. The same void pressed him to walk closer and closer to the fade—an urge he no longer experienced. Dove filled the vacancy within him and it overflowed the brim.

When he claimed her...

Movement sharpened his focus, and he swung his head that direction. Something roamed the woods he'd been leading her toward. His woods. His territory to roam.

Slapping her with his tail, he glanced back to catch Dove's golden gaze. The weight of her regard struck him with a potent force. He flicked his ears toward the woods then her before he flattened them and peeled his lips from his teeth. He expected her to understand the body language.

She'd cocked her head at his initial request then gave him a single nod.

Ferocious delight fisted in his chest. No argument, no stubborn refusal, merely acceptance. Certain she understood, he set off on a diagonal trajectory into the woods. Dove followed behind him, her path settling directly into his footsteps in the snow. Clever girl. If someone detected his path, they'd only see one wolf.

If he'd been human, he might have paused to kiss her for the intelligence in her action. His wolf ignored the side of him turning into a blithering idiot, his ears focused on where he'd heard the movement.

A whisper of snow, followed by stillness too unnatural to be an accident. Whatever waited for them was downwind, which meant either it heard them or scented him. Increasing his speed, he shifted his angle sharply and Dove stayed with him. They flew through the woods, curving so close to the trees, he left strands of his fur behind. The deliberateness would spread his scent in wider distribution.

These were his woods. He'd marked them many times. During the roaming months, his pack rarely troubled him when he vanished into the woods or along his part of the tundra. He went there for solitude, and now he intended to share it with Dove. Whatever interloper thought to make itself at home would be sorely disabused of the notion.

A change in the wind brought him the scent of wolf. Not one of his. Flashes from Amaruq and of his fallen pack members in Tikaani raced through his mind kindling rage. The wolf didn't belong in the Yukon. His anger fueled him, adrenaline flooding his body and he ramped his pace, the sharp turns and winding path he ran through the woods leaving the trees almost a blur.

His target heard them, his own paws scrabbling as the bastard raced away. Diesel filled his lungs with the scent of the intruder. Dove stayed with him, her compact body moving with a grace as she came alongside him, though she never went for the lead. No sense in hiding their numbers. Three miles vanished beneath their feet as they pursued, and he cut in front of Dove when he spotted their prey waiting for them in the deepest shadows of a grove of tightly woven trees.

The wolf leapt forward and Diesel crashed into him at speed. They went down in a tangle of raking claws and snapping jaws. Dove jumped over him, landing on the bastard's back and her teeth sank into the thicker muscle at the back of the wolf's neck.

Nearly a match for him in size, the invader was a dark gray, nearly invisible against the dark. Locked in combat, he dug his back feet into his opponent's belly, spilling blood.

The gray reared back and Dove jumped free, neatly avoiding the tree the male had tried to slam her into. Diesel bared his teeth as he closed on the other. Dove angled across him, her head beneath his at his throat and she echoed his snarl.

Outnumbered, the gray eyed them then lunged for Dove. If the gray counted on using his larger size and considerable jaw strength to harm the smaller female, he was gravely mistaken. Dove went low and Diesel leapt, going over her to slam into the gray and he closed his jaws over the bastard's nape.

With one vicious shake, he slammed the other into a tree, then a second one before flinging him away. The wolf rolled, halting to shake his head dazed, but Diesel gave him no quarter. The invader initiated the call for death when he ventured into his lands and signed his death warrant by trying to take out Dove.

His mate-to-be didn't slow. She raked her claws over the downed wolf's face, splitting it open and spilling more blood. When the beast lumbered up, Diesel struck and tore out his throat.

The wolf gurgled, then toppled onto his side. Dead.

Throwing his head back, Diesel howled in triumph.

Riding the high of victory, he swung around to check his mate. She didn't stare at him, but instead faced the darkness, her nose lifted and her ears flicking back and forth.

Guarding him.

Pride swelled within him and he checked his kill once, verifying the death before he went to her. She withstood his inspection well then lapped at his muzzle, the rasp of her tongue against his fur grounding him. He rubbed against her then she repeated the move, circling him once and rubbing along each of his sides then his flank.

Belatedly, he realized she inspected him for injury. She found one, one his hip and nuzzled at it. He wanted to snap at her that he was fine, but when was the last time someone took such care in checking him over? She had not a scratch on her, and more than proved her skill in fighting alongside him. When she reached his neck, he lowered his head a fraction so she could sniff him.

Taking advantage of the position, he filled his lungs with her sweet scent. The roses he'd tasted in the cabin were still present, as was snow and wood—and him. Beneath it all was a layer of concern and undiluted joy.

She cared. The confirmation acted like a panacea to his soul, quieting the rage the invader's presence had provoked. His Sentries called to him as they raced through the woods, tracking them. Answering their call, he flicked his ears to listen for any other sounds which didn't belong.

A split second before Grinder arrived, Diesel swung to face his Sentries. Dove took her cue from him and as she had when they fought the invader. She settled in at his side, her head below his throat. He'd never cared to have any wolf there, not even Amara. Though she'd never tried—in similar circumstances, she'd stayed utterly out of the battle.

She hadn't even liked hunting.

Dismissing thoughts of her from his mind, he focused on his wolves. The same two he'd sent to deal with Yury accompanied Grinder. They must have completed their tasks and returned to Tikaani.

With a toss of his head, he ordered them to the body. A part of him wanted to steal away with Dove, celebrate their victory together with a hunt or better…in his bed. Those needs would have to wait. Verification of the assailant was paramount. If any more of those fuckers roamed his territory, he would call open season on them and send the pack on a real hunt.

Grinder snapped an order at the other two and the three worked in concert to lift the fallen wolf. Dove started forward as though to help, but in this, Diesel blocked her. The three were used to working together, and she didn't know them well enough yet.

He also didn't want any of the unmated males that close to her. Possessiveness swarmed through him, a primitive desire so fierce he didn't even try to explain it away or make an excuse. Though she didn't press the issue, she did snarl at him. The baring of teeth reminded him of his earlier promise.

Nuzzling muzzle, he licked the sharp canines she displayed even as he curved around her. Having his Sentries at his back didn't bother him in the slightest. After a moment, his Dove relented with her snarl and nipped his jaw.

Amused at how quickly she forgave his demand, he checked on his wolves. They worked together to carry the oversized beast on a more direct trajectory for Tikaani. Dove settled in at his side, neither trailing nor moving ahead, although he caught her checking their flank nearly as often as he did.

His Sentries gained speed as they matched pace, the perfection in their steps another source of pride for him. Grinder led the Sentries, and he'd done a damn fine job with their training. If Dove wanted to continue on her Hunter path, he would discuss Grinder taking her on as his direct apprentice. Fluff, though nearly as skilled as Grinder, was nowhere near as good of a teacher.

Filing the idea away, he listened to his wolves sound off as another Sentry sent up a call. His howl would have warned them of potential threats and drawn outliers closer to Tikaani once more. The Sentries would have divided and went off in quadrant searches.

They knew their job. He checked the internal compass alerting him to his pack. The first week of any winter roam involved a lot of time spent among his people, renewing bonds and reconnecting. No one else had fallen to the intruder, so either he'd been skirting the Sentries or he'd deliberately lain in wait for Diesel.

Foolish maneuver, whatever his goal.

At the edge of Tikaani, Grinder changed direction for the riverbed rather than the town. Dove danced along the edges as Diesel showed her a better spot to descend to the frozen landscape below. A hint of her blood touched the air and he swung around to study her, halting his progress entirely. She bumped into him then stopped.

Droplets on the snow had him ducking his head to her paws. She lifted one after the other for him when he released a sub vocal sound. Her right rear paw bled sluggishly.

Too long on the brutal cold, and his gut instinct was to send her inside. He fought the more primal urge and raised his head to meet her gaze, ears forward he whuffed.

She twisted and lifted her paw to inspect. Smart wolf, she didn't lick at it. The moisture on the open wound might do more harm than good at their temperatures. Lowering her leg, she took a step, then another. Rather than give him an outright refusal or turn away to head to Tikaani, she tested her balance and her paw against the icier snow.

No pain discolored her scent, but she lifted her paw nearly as soon as she put it down. Another step and she raised it again. A low growl hummed in the back of his throat, but she brushed her nose against his muzzle. A request. Slanting a look to where his Sentries waited with the body, he judged the time since the beast's death and the length of their travel.

If the man didn't transform within the next fifteen minutes, he would take Dove back to the sanctuary. He could always return or have Grinder photograph the body. Bumping his head to her side, he granted her the privilege she requested. With careful steps, she finished her descent, careful to keep her right rear paw elevated.

Some wolves looked ungainly when they navigated on three legs, not Dove. No, she made it seem like a graceful series of leaps and bounds. She paused a couple of feet from the body, and Diesel settled in to sit next to her. When she leaned into him, he soaked in the contact but didn't relax his vigilance.

The Sentries took up cardinal positions opposite his stance at Dove's side. The wolves correctly assumed he could guardian her flank, so they handled the other possible approaches.

One minute before he prepared to herd Dove inside, the corpse began to relax into his human form. She seemed to anticipate his need and rose to hold her own weight so he could stand. Instead of approaching with him, she waited as he studied the body. The tattoos told him the wolf came from the same clan as Yury, but this was no foot soldier. He had the markings of a lieutenant.

It was this wolf Yury had sought to protect with his refusal to answer, and evasiveness. The lieutenant also confirmed that it wasn't only strays wandering into his territory, but a coordinated strike.

If there was one, there could be a second.

Straightening, he snapped a look toward Grinder then began his own shift. The Sentry hit his feet a few scant seconds after Diesel. Their skin steamed in the cold, but the banked fuel of his rage kept Diesel from even feeling it.

"Be ready to double security, reach out to our Sentries throughout Alaska and those down in Vancouver." He had wolves everywhere. His Dove limped over to him, and Diesel sank his hand into the fur at her nape. Then he released the call—it would summon his wolves.

An Alpha's call was a provocative talent, limited to those who were bound to him by blood, birth, and choice. His Sentries went to their bellies even as Grinder knelt. At his side, Dove leaned into his thigh and he kept her on her feet as he sent the pulse along the connections tying him to his wolves. He wanted them all in. Tikaani's sanctuary would soon be filled to the brim and family reunions not expected for another few weeks would populate it with joy.

Then they would steel themselves for war.

Chapter Eleven

Prior to the conflict in the woods, Ranae would never have considered herself an adrenaline junkie. Still, the battle with the Russian wolf left her feeling more buzzed than afraid. Diesel's acceptance of her decision to remain despite the slice to her paw elevated the sense of exhilaration cascading through her. So much so that when he gripped her scruff and issued the Alpha call, she wanted to throw her head back and howl in answer.

Together, they loped back to Tikaani as his Sentries diverted to rounding up the pack or deal with the body. Once back inside the cabin, she continued to vibrate like a tuning fork to an internal hum only she could hear.

It took her longer than him to shift once they were inside the warming antechamber. The wolf was truly incredible. His shifts seemed as natural and easy as hers and he'd shifted twice as much as her in a relatively short amount of time. As soon as she hit her feet, she turned and threw her arms around him.

He accepted the embrace, the contact of her naked breasts to his chest electrifying her senses. Beyond the initial lust lay something much deeper. She pressed her face to his throat, drawing in his scent. He hit the wall behind her, and then he dug his fingers into her hips, keeping her fast to him. The heavy weight of his engorged cock pressed against her belly. Shuddering, she drew in a ragged breath even as he fisted her hair and eased her head back so he could meet her gaze.

Submission to the desire blazing in his brilliant blue eyes lay on the tip of her tongue, but he closed his mouth over hers. The savage hunger in his kiss fed both her need for contact even as it stoked a hotter fire within her.

Scraping her teeth over his lower lip, she pulled back from the exchange and stared at him. The same incandescent fire she'd glimpsed in his eyes from the battle burned in them as he locked gazes with her. "I want you," she admitted, unabashed at the very real passion leaving her pussy damp and her internal muscles clenching. She wanted to climb him until his cock rimmed her entrance and she could slide down on him.

As though reading her mind, he lifted her hips and pressed her against the wall, his hungry mouth descending to take hers again. She fisted his hair, straining for contact as she wrapped her legs around his hips. He nibbled a path down her jaw, even as his hands massaged her ass.

The room flooded with the scent of male desire and aggression, the provocative nature clogging her lungs. She wanted to drown in it. He slid a hand along her side then cupped her breast. Arching at the contact, she gasped as he pinched the peaked nipple with deliberate force. Pain accented her pleasure and she almost forgot to breathe when the stiff, erect length of his cock rubbed along her slick labia. The bare brush of force against her clit sent a riot of sensation to pulse along her nerve system.

He lifted her higher and she wanted to whimper as the friction stroked her up his length to the tip. She wrapped her legs around his sides. Liquid warmth escaped her and she squeezed as he rubbed the ridges of his abdomen against her—the contact a tease, amping her excitement while not delivering the pleasure she craved.

His tongue traced over the rapid beat of her pulse at her throat. The precarious nature of her position struck her even as he sucked lightly on the skin. All he had to do was sink his teeth in, lower her to his cock, and she would explode.

Instead of feeding her the carnal fantasy, he licked and sucked a path down to her breasts. She wanted to protest, but his mouth locked over one pebbled nipple and her mind blanked. The hard suction seemed to connect with her clit, and she throbbed with renewed need. He teased her with vicious accuracy, then switched his attention to her neglected breast.

His hands seemed to be everywhere, massaging her breast, stroking her side, gripping her ass and the sensory overload pummeled her.

"Diesel," she managed to squeeze out past the hisses and gasps as he seemed to devour her.

"I want to play with you," he growled. The dark declaration damn near proved to be her undoing.

"I need you." The admission burst from her on a cry as he lowered her a fraction. She felt the head of his cock press against her entrance. She wanted to play with him too—to touch and stroke the engorged member with its thick ropey vein running along the underside.

She wanted to lick him, taste his essence, and sip at the combination of salty and sweet. The first press of his head stretching her had her scratching at his shoulders as she opened her mouth to cry out. He swooped in, capturing her with another fierce kiss.

His tongue thrust in to tangle with hers as he slammed home. She locked her thighs, trying desperately to pull him deeper. The sensation was so fucking incredible, she stopped thinking and let him drive the rhythm, even as she moaned into his mouth.

When he braced her back on the wall and sucked her lower lip out in a mind-bending scrape of teeth and tongue, she trembled on the verge of orgasm.

He held her there, teetering, then whispered. "Open your eyes, Dove."

Desperate for him, she obeyed without question. He drew out of her, then thrust home again and she cried out.

"Eyes open," he snapped, and she forced herself to meet his gaze. Wolf and man stared at her, their passion a wildfire in her veins. "Tell me what you want, Dove."

"You," she admitted. "I need you."

"You have me," he said through clenched teeth. His hips began a slow, grinding piston that drove him in and out of her at an agonizingly delicious rate. She wanted to weep. She tried to drag him in faster, but he was stronger and held her to the pace he'd set. "I am going to bite you."

Her inner walls spasmed as he dragged his cock out.

"I want you to bite me."

Her mind seemed to blank for a moment, and she dug her nails into his shoulders, uncertain of whether she wanted to pull him closer or push him away. He was driving her absolutely mad.

"You're not ready for me to claim you," he said, his breath a whisper against her lips as he nudged her nose with his. "Trust me?"

He could—she knew it and so did he. He could press the issue while the raw sensuality between them overwhelmed her. Even as her body demanded she give into him, fulfill the intensely sexual craving, her mind resisted. She was a Hunter of Willow Bend, but it wasn't her pack she thought of or anyone else. The mingled scent of their lust in her nostrils, her body and arms full of Diesel—all she wanted was him.

"Yes," she confessed. "I trust you."

"Then hold onto me, Dove, and we'll answer this need." It was the last words he spoke, his mouth claiming hers once more as his body began to pound into her. The rugged thrust of his cock against her sensitive flesh consumed her. The sound of their bodies slapping together, the feel of his chest against her breasts, the taste of him on her lips and she lost all reason.

The fast, furious nature of their coupling left her damn near mindless. When his teeth sank into her shoulder, she pitched over the edge and sank her teeth into him, desperate to hold onto him. Her orgasm seemed to stretch out as pure heat ballooned inside of her and then she shattered.

His raw snarl as he shouted his own release was the last thing she heard.

The strength of his orgasm left Diesel shaking with pleasure. Dove clung to him, almost boneless.

The rapid race of her heart and the ragged nature of her breathing filled him with another primitive kind of pride. From her kiss-swollen lips, to her disheveled hair, to the ruddy red flush on her skin—he'd done that to her.

Her internal muscles flexed and closed on him, spasms which seemed to jerk through his over-sensitized cock, but he didn't pull out. No, he needed the overload, the contact—the intimate connection. Taking her for the run, he hadn't anticipated a battle or the violent need for coupling they'd both experience afterward. Thank all that was holy, he'd secured the doors when she'd embraced him.

Not claiming her had been the most difficult moment he'd ever experienced. The bites brought them close, but without the mutual decision—it wouldn't take. Patience, he reminded himself. Glancing down at her still closed eyes, he had to smile. Bliss radiated from her, as aftershocks ricocheted through his system. Still, he'd marked her and pounded his scent into her. She'd left fresh scratches on his back and a deep bite on his shoulder. The pain had edged his pleasure to perfection.

The thought had his cock stirring with the very real need to play with her. Rolling his hips, he ground himself very firmly against her clit. Her gray-green eyes opened, gold bleeding into them as her wolf stared at him—as drunk on him as he was on her.

"You will sleep in my bed tonight." He gave voice to the demand of his wolf.

She merely smiled then slowly raised her hand to rest against his throat. Though her grip was gentle, she pressed her fingers to a point of vulnerability.

"Who gets to be the wolf?"

A chuckle rippled through him and he kissed her again, putting his hand to her throat and mirroring the gesture. Trust. He'd asked if she trusted him and she'd given it to him. He would nurture the precious gift for what it was. The lazy stroke of her tongue along his teased him, and it was with reluctance that he broke the kiss. The perfume of their lust filled the antechamber. All the wolves he'd summoned home would pass through there and every single one would know she belonged with him.

It was utter self-indulgence to thrill at the thought, but who cared? It could only be better if she'd welcomed his claim and he'd asserted himself as her mate. Still, it had been a spare amount of days, and she'd already accepted him into her body. They would dance. They would play.

She could run.

He would most assuredly chase.

After one, long slow kiss he made himself ease from her body. They both hissed at the loss of contact then her gaze collided with his, a smile on her lips and in her eyes. "Thank you."

"Oh, you're more than welcome, Dove." He pressed a kiss to the wound on her shoulder then lapped at it to ease the sting. The sharp slice of his teeth had imprinted the mark deep. She would wear it for days.

It wasn't a mating mark, but it settled his wolf in profound ways.

"Thank you," he said against her skin, another kiss to the unmarked skin of her left shoulder. When he took her again, he would bite her there. So many sweet places he could graze with his teeth.

He would find them all.

Only when she was steady on her feet, did he release her. She had the look of a woman thoroughly used and loved. It suited her wildness to perfection. Catching her fingers in his, he raised her hand to his mouth. Awareness of their mingling fluid trickling along her leg sent another possessive wave through him.

"You were exquisite out there today," he said before pressing a kiss to her knuckles. "Perfection on the hunt."

"You were pretty badass yourself." The ease with which she delivered the compliment did wonders for his ego. "Thank you for trusting me."

"How could I not?" He had no words to express the depth of his admiration for her. Though young and untried, she possessed a rare gift. She complemented him in so many ways. Wolves he'd known for years could not fight alongside him with such effortless ease.

"We have to walk now, don't we?" she said by way of reply.

"I will carry you, if you like." He couldn't help it, he still held her hand and threaded their fingers together. Though slenderer than his blunter, squared digits, she possessed real strength.

Her form showed pure athleticism, yet another testament to her strength and training. She carried nothing spare and, while her curves were soft, they only enhanced her femininity.

"I can walk." Her free hand closed over his gradually thickening length. The heat sent electricity scorching along his nerves. The tender squeeze she gave him had him closing a hand on her breast. "I just wanted to feel you," she told him. "In my hand…maybe later, in my mouth."

The admission sent his blood flow south, and he grew steadily more erect against the slow cupping stroke of her hand on him. "You can have me wherever you want me, Dove." Since two could play at that game, he circled her pebbling nipple with his thumb. "I want you on your knees before me, my mouth buried against your cunt as you come so I can taste you. The I want to slide into you as you orgasm, and fuck you all over again."

Her pupils dilated. "This is a dangerous game."

"But very fun." He nipped her lower lip. "I promise."

"Do we have to go in right away?" She glanced down at his cock in her hand and she licked her lips.

"No," he whispered. The pack needed time and, even if they didn't, they would wait for him. Hunger flared through him anew, but when she tried to drop down to her knees, he caught her. "This time, Dove, we do it the way I want." He spun her and put her hands on the wall. Bracing her there, he nuzzled the shell of her ear. "I will touch, and play. You will grip the wall."

She shuddered, and he scented the freshness of her arousal. His cock seemed to pulse in time with his heartbeat. Despite his declaration of play. He simply wanted to slam home inside of her and take her until she couldn't forget him.

Ever.

Closing his mouth over the mark he'd already

made on her shoulder, he fisted his cock. After nudging her thighs apart, he began to torment them both by running his cock against her nether lips. Every push and pull was pure, sensual torture.

Palms flat on the wall, Dove arched her head and the action bared her throat. He played with her breasts, teasing, tweaking her nipples, caressing them even as he continued to mime pushing into her. When she locked her thighs together, trapping his cock against her in a fierce grip, he growled.

This time he nipped her throat, then moved his mouth to her wound-free shoulder. "Bad wolf."

Not remotely cowed, she laughed and thrust her ass against him. The action elongated her body and gave him the perfect view of her pert nipples and enveloped his cock the promise of her heat. "Will you punish me?"

"I should…" But who was he kidding? They were both so hungry for each other. He could virtually taste her need, and his rose within him, a wild beast desperate for satisfaction. "I will—later." He pressed her thighs apart, strength on strength, then settled his cock at her entrance before he thrust home without further preamble.

They found their rhythm by the second stroke, two wild beings straining to join together. He wrapped one hand around her breast, then dipped his free hand do her pussy. With two fingers, he began to stroke her clit and she came apart beautifully in his arms.

Once.

Twice.

And as a third set of tremors shook her, his

world narrowed to a single focus as everything boiled down to the way his cock drilled into her. He bit her a second time and she came, the hot sweet nectar of her orgasm filling the room with its perfume as he followed her over the edge. His spine went white-hot as he melted from the inside out.

He barely caught her as she collapsed, and he went to his knees, still deep within her as his own orgasm continued to wrench free.

His wolf wanted her, demanded they take her. Their will, their dominance could overwhelm her. They could subsume her pack bond, stealing her once and for all to be at his side forever. Yet the man resisted his more bestial side.

No had been a complete sentence. It needed no explanation or justification. She'd taken him as a lover. They would dance.

The chase was already on.

Snow Wolf

Chapter Twelve

It took a full hour before they let go of each other long enough to step into the cabin. Diesel wore a smirk, and she couldn't really fault him for it. She'd never orgasmed so much or so forcefully. While she could blame her limp on the small remnant of her ice cut foot, she didn't bother. The sensual soreness left her wanting to strut. Still, she dragged on her abandoned clothes—which the cleaning fairies had folded neatly for her in their absence—and turned to watch Diesel, only to find him eyeing her with same kind of hunger.

"Oh no," she wagged a finger at him. "We have to go back to work now."

"The pack is safe." An easy declaration, since he'd summoned them all. But as much as she wouldn't mind dragging him onto a bed to play, she didn't think she was capable.

"I need a time out." She smoothed her shirt down. "Need to let my muscles recover long enough to go for round four."

"Five," he corrected with a smug smile.

Delighted, she burst out laughing. "Five. Until then, you wanted to see to your pack and I'm rather hoping you'll explain what you saw on the body."

His proprietary grin faded a notch. "The tattoos he wore are similar to the other wolves who attacked. They tell me what clan in Russia he hails from and more…they told me his rank."

Using her fingers to comb through her hair, she

padded closer to him. "Significant?"

"Enough." He touched a finger to her cheek, a simple yet terribly intimate gesture. The door to the antechamber opened to admit seven wolves, a family group from the look of them. She glanced at the new arrivals, and they gave her a smile in passing, each reaching out to touch Diesel lightly as they split around him like a stream flowing around a rock.

Diesel nodded in acknowledgement, but he didn't remove his touch from her cheek nor did he look away. When the grouping disappeared down the access stairs to the sanctuary, he said, "The wolf was a lieutenant. The foot soldiers would likely have taken their directions from him." Another group passed through and, like the first, they gave her wide, friendly grins. The tension around their eyes eased as they each touched Diesel on their way through.

When that lot were on their way downstairs, she studied her partner curiously. "Do they all touch you each time they see you?" Wolves were tactile creatures. They needed the regular contact for comfort and bonding.

"They are unsettled," he told her, though she understood that. "It is rare that we abandon our wolf form this early in the year."

Fresh curiosity spearheaded through her, more questions she wanted to ask. They would wait for a quieter time. "You know, you have this reputation at home—the back woods Alpha, primitive, aloof…but you're not like that at all."

His eyebrows rose a fraction in response. "No?"

"No," she grinned, dropping to sub vocal as the hatch began to swing inward again. "You're an

Alaskan teddy bear."

He didn't respond verbally, but he didn't have to. His eyes held the promise of retaliation later. Once that lot went through, she added. "I think I shall call you Bear."

This time, he did laugh then bent his head and kissed her. He held captive with just the sweet taste of his lips on hers when the next wolves streamed past them and while she wasn't sure whether they smiled or not, she didn't mind.

For two hours, they stood there, not saying much as his pack trickled in—some groups large, other groups small. Only when the numbers trickled down to one or two, did he nod toward the door. "Time to descend."

Before he even opened the door, he caught her hand in his. "The additional population will strain resources and energy, so the hallway…" *Was dark.* She glanced down the long stairs, the light from the antechamber not truly penetrating all the shadows below.

"Fun." The tension knotting her gut tightened, but Diesel squeezed her hand.

"I am with you," he promised. "We'll descend together."

Trusting him on his word, she held fast to his grip as they took the steps. A distant part of her mind counted the number. It might help if she ever had to take these steps in the dark without him. Her gut clenched at the very idea, but she didn't stop counting or walking down.

By the time they reached the door to the underground village, sweat left her skin damp. The cool air on the other side offered a welcome relief, along with the lights.

Pausing, he turned to take her other hand in his and faced her. "I have to meet with Montana and the Sentries."

Understandable. "I can find my way back to the rooms or somewhere else, if you think I would be more useful…"

He considered her a long moment. "You are welcome to join me at the meeting."

The invitation carried too much inherent promise on her part. "Thank you," she said, finding she meant it. "I think it's too soon for that."

"As you wish." He lifted their joined hands then kissed her knuckles. "I'm sorry I didn't get to show you much of my land yet. I'll take you out again, as soon as we're able."

"I'd like that…and, Diesel?" She squeezed his hands, trying not to make too much of how her voice cracked slightly. "I mean it. If I can be of use, put me to work."

"I will. For now, stop and see Chowder on your way to our rooms. I'll send food to you—"

"I can manage with what you have in stock," she interrupted, returning the affectionate kiss to his knuckles. "You're bringing in a lot of mouths to feed, let them all settle."

"Very well. See Chowder about your foot."

"It's not that—you know, he's on the way." At the stubborn set of his jaw, she simply amended her protest. It wasn't a lot to ask. "I've got one more question." It was one she almost didn't want to ask.

"Speak," he kept his tone even, but a hint of

impatience crested beneath the word. To be fair, he'd told her to always speak her mind.

"I need to check in with Mason." She showed him equal respect and kept her tone calm and even. "Is there anything you don't want me to share?" It was utterly disloyal to ask the question, and she grimaced. Yet—she'd been privy to the inner workings of his pack, to the resources they had. The conflict between what she'd learned and who she told—she didn't want to betray him. A wolf couldn't be loyal to two Alphas.

"I trust you." The absolute sincerity in his simple pledge left her blinking back tears. He touched a finger to her lips. "I'll see you soon." Then he was gone.

Awareness of his absence swept through her. Fast on its heels was the acknowledgement that not only had he *said* he trusted her, he'd shown it. No escort waited to follow her back to their rooms. The only order he'd given was that she stop and see Chowder. Flexing her right foot, she felt a twinge. It stung a little, but it didn't hurt.

Of course, he'd drowned her in pleasure so maybe she could have amputated her foot and it would barely have hurt. She was still grinning at the idea when she reached Chowder's quarters. She paused and considered the panel to find a button that would alert him she was outside.

After depressing it once, she glanced around the courtyard. It really was rather lovely. If she didn't look up and see the enclosed ceiling, the combination of plant life, trickling water and natural light had her half-convinced she was outside.

Even the vague emotional discomfort she associated with traveling through dark places like the steps had passed. The door opened behind her, and the healer's chamomile and mint scents tickled her nose.

"You're one more courtyard over," he said with a grin as she faced him. Then he paused, and his smile grew even wider. "Hot damn. Go, Diesel."

If the absolute joy hadn't shown in his smile, she might have blushed. As it was, she grinned. "You know I could absolutely have been the one to jump his bones."

Folding his arms, the healer leaned against his open doorway. Still smiling, he said, "Well, then hot damn. Go, Ranae."

Another laugh burst from her, and she shook her head. "You're a terrible man."

"Oh, I have my charms. What can I do for you?" Even as he asked the question, he glanced at her bare feet. "Why do I smell blood?"

"I think I broke it open on the walk here," was all she managed before he tugged her inside and urged her to sit. In short order, he'd poured them both cups of coffee before he sat in the chair opposite her and pulled her foot into his lap. Next came the cleaning with saline then betadine. She managed to endure it without hissing. "Hmm, it's not deep and your shift seems to have helped, but you did reopen it. I'm going to give you a bit of a boost on the healing and put a light bandage on it."

"I think that's a lot of fuss for a cut." Still, she didn't pull her foot away and let him patch her up.

"We're allowed to fuss." Chowder gave her

foot a gentle squeeze. "I'm just going to grab you some clean socks for now."

"Like you said, I'm one hall down…"

The healer pointed at her. "Stay. I'll only be a minute."

Ranae scowled after him. "Sit, Ubu, sit. Good dog."

"I heard that," he called back. "Just remember who was barking the orders night before last."

"Touché." Despite her grumbling, she couldn't help but grin. Yes, they had fought a Russian wolf. Yes, it had interrupted her exploring. But they'd won the fight, she'd had amazing sex, and Diesel offered her his trust and given her freedom to be herself.

All things told, it had been a pretty damn awesome day.

Diesel's office was full. In addition to ten senior Sentries, Fluff, Grinder, and Montana were also present along. That left over a dozen still on patrol outside sanctuary.

The conversation in the room halted at his arrival. Montana stood from her perch on the corner of his desk and eyed him as he strode in to face them. Most had passed him on the way inside and had already given him shit-eating grins. Dove's scent clung to him, and it settled his beast even though she had declined his invitation to attend at his side.

Eyeing his wolves, he had to admit she was probably right to decline. He could await Dove's decision with patience. His agitated wolves, however, needed action.

"We have a problem." He got right to it. "All

the evidence suggest the attack was a preemptory strike. We have issued one response." He spared a glance at Grinder for his permission.

"Bobbin and Tock are en route with the coolers. We found a great way of getting them over there using organ donation." He bared his teeth as though mimicking a grin. "What do you want to do with our most recent catch?"

Preoccupied with Dove, he hadn't fully decided what course he would take with the lieutenant. "Remove the tattooed fingers and carve away the tattoo on his right pectoral muscle. Box them up for transport." He would send them to the Moscow pack with a bottle of whiskey, and a promise. The last he'd heard, Alexandrovich still ruled Moscow. He would not enjoy the gift.

"I'll take care of it," Fluff offered.

Grinder gave her a long look, a wordless tension hanging in the air between his Sentries. Diesel left them to sort it out. If it proved problematic, he'd involve himself. Grinder nodded then jerked his thumb toward the door. "Go now. If the temperatures drop much more; you'll need an ice pick. Boone, back her."

Fluff scowled at the offer of a backup, but Grinder didn't relent.

"From this point forward, all Sentries move in units of two or more. I prefer three, but we'll work with what we have." Even as he made the statement, Grinder shot him a quick look. As security measures went, it had a sound foundation.

Diesel nodded his approval. "For a time, we will all experience a certain level of discomfort as we break with our normal patterns. It is for the good of the pack, and it is a sacrifice we can all make."

His wolves didn't disappoint him. A resolute Fluff touched a fist to her heart before she left with Boone to deal with the issue of the lieutenant.

"Head count?"

Montana rested her fingertips on the edge of his desk. "Nearly everyone has checked in. We have some family groups who migrated deeper into Canada. We've left messages for them at their way stations. Do you prefer to call them home or let them continue to roam?"

The distance provided a double-edged sword. They were not in the immediate vicinity the Volchitsa seemed to be targeting, but they were also beyond direct assistance.

"If they're close to Willow Bend territory, send them in that direction. I'll handle those arrangements. For those in the more remote regions, give them a choice and explain the situation."

His second made a note. "We'll also have issues with supply and energy if you keep the bulk of the pack within sanctuary for longer than a week."

Zipper raised a hand. The youngest of his senior Sentries, he'd only been promoted to his current position the year before.

"We don't raise our hands, dumbass," one of the wolves behind him hissed, and Zipper shrugged. Not much got under the wolf's skin.

"We made some arrangements for laying in extra stores for Amaruq if the winter proved problematic." The wolf continued. "It's mostly dried goods and freeze-dried emergency supplies."

Montana drummed her nails. "That'll do, in a pinch."

"I don't expect us to require them," Diesel assured them. "For now, I want to be certain our young don't have a bloody winter to remember." Quiet finality echoed in the room. "Patrols will continue. Grinder will assign you to quadrants. I want to be certain we have no more surprises waiting out there for those who prefer to return to their roam."

"Forgive me, Diesel." Montana shifted her attention to him. "Does that mean you won't be returning to *your* roam?"

Silence rippled across the room, and the weight of his Sentries' regard came to focus on him. "Not immediately," he said. "I have other concerns I need to address."

"Is she your mate, then?" Zipper's enthusiasm flooded the question. Blade, the wolf nearest the young Sentry, slammed an elbow into his side.

Diesel slowly began to smile. His cheeks ached from the possessive grin he wore then he laughed. The shock on his wolves' faces told him exactly how long it'd been since he showed such humor. "She is mine. That's all I have to say on the matter." Once Dove accepted his pledge, he would declare it before the whole pack.

"Then she is ours to protect," Grinder said, rising. The Sentries in the room followed suit, every single wolf fisting a hand above their hearts.

"She is also not to be coddled," Diesel stated, command in every word. "She's a capable fighter in her own right and a Hunter of Willow Bend. We will respect her strengths, support them, and if she is willing, she may very well need to apprentice to the Sentries." The last, he said directly to Grinder.

"It would be my privilege to train her." His wolf didn't disappoint, though a hint of mischief rested in his expression. "To be clear, if we're battle training, how many hits do I have before you rip my head off?"

More amused than concerned, Diesel spread his hands wide. "Why don't I surprise you?"

Laughter adjourned the meeting and the Sentries filed out, each pausing only long enough to clap him on the shoulder or shake his hand. Their easy acceptance spoke volumes for the respect Dove earned during her time looking after Chowder and the injured. Once the last stepped out, Montana dropped into the chair opposite his desk, and he leaned against the wood.

The smile faded from her expression, and she studied him.

"Spit it out," he told his second. What made the she-wolf so incredibly good at her position was the way she looked at the angles, more domestic than martial, but also with an awareness of all the wolves in play.

"What will you do if she doesn't accept you as her mate?"

Diesel scrubbed a hand over his face, then shook his head. Montana never pulled a punch, attacking her points with surgical precision. "Whether it takes one day, one month or one year...she will."

"Your confidence has never been an issue," Montana began, raising her hand in a request for him to allow her to finish the thought. "But, prior to your journey to Willow Bend, you'd begun the fade."

So, Chowder wasn't the only wolf who'd noticed.

"If she declines, rejects your proposition, will you once again begin the journey away from us?" No condemnation reflected in the straightforward question, but her scent altered, subtly detailing her worries. *Fear.* Montana was one of the most capable wolves in his service. If she was afraid, he needed to fix it.

"No," Diesel reached for her hand, then tugged her from the chair. Pulling her into his arms, he hugged her. Though stiff at first, a hint of embarrassment discoloring the worry and fear underscoring her scent, she gripped him tight in return. "I am a patient man, Montana. No may mean no, and I will accept Dove's repudiation should it come, but no doesn't mean always and forever. I waited decades for this opportunity, what are a few years more?"

She squeezed him her relief palpable, then sighed. "I will keep you both in my thoughts that she does not reject you." With a sniff, she pulled away and eyed him. "Though from the smell of you, you've already made some headway."

Another grin stretched his cheeks. "She's a good woman, but like most of us, very set and determined. It's a privilege to chase her."

"Poor thing," Montana said, shaking her head as she withdrew and collected herself. "She won't know what hit her."

"That's the idea." He winked, and his assistant's shock added another layer of enjoyment for him. "Life goes on. But, tell me, what arrangements have you made for our fallen?"

She poured herself a mug of hot cocoa from the sideboard. Most of the Sentries had cleared whatever food had been waiting, though he scented coffee in another of the urns. "Normally we would wait till spring, so we could honor all who left us during the long dark."

The Yukon pack held two great gatherings each year. One at the start of the long dark, when they came together and celebrated their summer, shared news, and oftentimes celebrated any matings or births which occurred during the year. The second came after they returned from their roam, a reaffirmation of life and a time to remember those who had moved on—whether from life or the pack.

"These deaths are a cost to us, and they should see our efforts to prevent further disaster as well as celebrate the lives we lost." Montana cradled her mug in her hands. "To that end, there will be a gathering in the circle tonight, nothing formal—but we will have music, food, and a place for memories to be shared."

"A good plan," he approved, then helped himself to a mug of coffee. "What else has transpired that I need to know of?"

Montana settled into a chair as he circled the desk to take his own. It took the better part of an hour, but she gave him a solid sketch of life in sanctuary, of the mate potential discovered by two of the youths and the guidance the matrons had taken to let the two explore. It was good to know his wolves still lived and loved, found joy in the simpler things.

When the conversation turned to Amaruq, the

well of sadness in her voice didn't surprise him. Montana had been fond of the tribe members who called the base camp their home.

"One small ounce of good fortune for the whole mess—Ambrose reached out." The head of one of their most loyal Intuit tribes lived more often Ketchikan. He and his family had many deep ties to the Yukon pack, including mating into their bloodline. "Demon is his cousin twice removed. Since Demon's parents were among the lost...Ambrose is sending his son and several other members who want to stretch their wings to take over Amaruq."

Good news, indeed. Ambrose was a good man. "His son—Jasper?"

"Yes, the second son. The oldest is still away living in Chicago and practicing law." The oldest had been one of their communication points via Willow Bend's attorney when necessary, though Diesel rarely called on the younger man to do the task. "Jasper's been working as a bush pilot, ferrying tourists around. He's actually a good selection for the post. He's old enough to be experienced, young enough to be adventurous, and he has a crush on Fluff."

The last was a surprise, which made Diesel laugh. "Fluff? Has he met her?" The tough as nails Sentry didn't take crap from anyone, and acted so contrary to her nickname, it had burrowed in and she couldn't shake it no matter how she acted.

"Several times," Montana's amusement grew. "According to Ambrose, Jasper volunteered as soon as they received the gruesome news. He also asked me to keep an eye on him, since he believes his son is desperate for heartbreak."

"If he pursues Fluff, he'll need more than us watching out for him." The boy would need balls that clanked. Leaning back in his chair, he toyed with the idea even as his thoughts drifted to Dove. Hopefully she was resting. He didn't plan on much sleep for them that night. Sleeping next to her while in his wolf form had settled him, easing the fist of loneliness and despair which had been his constant companions for too long to count. Tasting her, however, had only left him hungry for more. "When they arrive, send Fluff to protect the base camp. I'll want her to winter quarter there for the time being."

"So your idea of looking after the boy is to put him in the wolf's sights?"

Diesel shrugged. "If they are meant for each other, it won't hurt to give them a nudge."

"And if they aren't?"

"Then better to wash the potential wound clean before it gets infected." If Fluff wanted nothing to do with Jasper, better he find out early on. "Then, if it is the boy's only reason for coming, we can make different arrangements."

"Very well." Montana didn't approve, but she also didn't argue. Sometimes his second possessed too soft a heart, then again, he hadn't had one for so long he'd not really noticed. "Do you want to go over the financial projections?"

"Not really," he said with a grimace. "But it needs to be done."

The next two hours dragged on as Montana went over all the information she'd maintained from their financial reports to their stores as well as any issues with discipline—only one case. All told, the pack remained in solid shape.

When she finished, he waved her out, then settled in to consider his next move. The packages to the various packs were on their way. The organs would be delivered, in all likelihood, Alexandrovich would deal with the problem for him.

Yet he didn't dare leave anything to chance. What he needed was information.

Alphas didn't travel from their packs, that was the accepted rule. They had representatives they sent out to handle interpack relations. The council they'd convened in Willow Bend had been an exception. Packs needed the comfort of having their Alpha close by, they had to know the Alpha secured them and that they could secure their Alpha.

The problem was whether the incursions were being directed by a pack or acts of desperation on the part of displaced wolves. Rising, he left his office and began to roam the sanctuary. His wolves needed to see him. All he really wanted to do was see his Dove, but like those who followed him, he needed the chance to reaffirm their connection.

Death was a normal part of life, but that was cold comfort for the affected—for those who'd lost a friend, a mate, a child or a lover. Diesel knew his pack understood why connections were important. More, he knew they would come together to care for each other.

It didn't surprise him to find Deidre with the family of one of his fallen Sentries nor to see Grinder with another. Diesel took his time with each family, listening more than speaking. They wanted to tell their tales, and he absorbed them. Knowing his wolves meant Diesel had an awareness of them all, but hearing the personal stories? It detailed for him what they had lost.

So he made his circuit, passing through each area and sitting for a time with any who needed him. The echo of surprise in their responses proved Montana's concerns. Drifting through life with only the most tenuous of connections had created a vulnerability in his wolves. One they likely hadn't been able to name, as he couldn't. Seeing him, talking to him, and even simply having him pause to shake a hand or give a hug—it reminded them he was still there.

For Diesel, it reaffirmed his own commitment to the pack. The drive to return to his Dove followed him, but even his wolf understood the need so they took their time. When he reached the section leading to his rooms, he checked on the injured and stilled as he caught his mate's scent as he paused to study the room. Most of the injuries had been grave or Chowder wouldn't have kept them close at hand.

The healer sat with one of the gored wolves, his attention and focus on addressing the last of the man's injuries. Chowder's resources had been stretched thin and he'd not leaned on Diesel while he'd been hunting their enemies. Taking a moment, he put a hand on the healer's shoulder in an offer of support. He let his strength flow into the healer's body.

"She's with Demon," his healer said in lieu of a thank you. "The youth has taken quite a shine to your mate, and he's grieving."

Of course the boy was. Barely old enough to join them on the roam, it had been his first winter dark to spend with the pack, and he'd lost both of his parents. Diesel spotted her sitting on the edge of Demon's bed. The young wolf leaned against the pillows, his pallor and stricken expression a testament to his sadness.

"How is his arm?" Bandages stretched from the boy's biceps to his wrist.

"It will take time. They damn near severed his wrist and ruptured a kidney." Chowder placed two fingers on the wolf he tended's forehead. "Most have an infection. Wherever those bastards came from, they were sick."

Diesel frowned, swinging his attention to the healer. "How sick?"

"I've got the fevers under control, but it's taking me time to leech the illness from their blood."

"Contagious?" His mate sat with one of the affected. Her compassion and strength being a balm to the boy aside, they couldn't afford an illness to invade the pack.

"I don't believe so." Chowder's answer didn't improve his mood. The healer didn't hedge his bets or play with cagey answers. Rising, he faced his Alpha. "In most cases, the injuries would have been made better when they shifted. Even grave ones repair with regular shifts."

"And these aren't?" They kept their voices low, near sub-vocal. When Chowder moved away from his patient, Diesel followed.

"Not entirely, no. The natural healing has been slowed, almost to human levels." Which didn't bode well. "I've got the fevers controlled, and I'm purging them, but for now…isolation is best."

Then why was Dove there? He didn't have to verbalize the question.

"Demon doesn't sleep well. He's been plagued by nightmares and the fever seems to affect him more than the others."

"His age." Not a question.

"Probably, but the night they were brought in, your Dove kept him settled. She could chase away his bad dreams and he likes her—enough so that I think he's imprinting."

Given the loss he'd sustained; Demon would have reached out to someone stronger to give him strength. Ranae Buckley possessed those attributes in spades. Her dominance wasn't a question, nor was her compassion. "You haven't told Montana yet." If he had, his second would have alerted him.

"Nothing to tell yet," Chowder rubbed the back of his neck. "When I have more, you'll know it."

"Make sure you rest," he said, eyeing his healer. "You're exhausted. Lean on me if you need to."

"I will." Chowder grinned. "Course, you sound like Dove." Somehow, Diesel suspected Demon wasn't the only one taking to his Dove. "She was all over me to rest, and she kept making me food to eat."

"Well, maybe you'll listen to her if not to me."

Chuckling, Chowder shook his head. "Doubtful. But go see them. It might do Demon some good, and she's checked where you were twenty times since you walked in."

Pleased, Diesel pivoted to go see his mate and

her charge. If Demon had imprinted, he would be *their* wolf and not just his. Despite the sad circumstances, it boded well for the future.

Dove glanced over and their gazes collided. His wolf surged within him, and her smile welcomed them.

Yes, the chase continued, but in that moment, the gap between them narrowed.

Chapter Thirteen

"Diesel is coming," Demon warned her in a whisper so quiet she barely heard him. The youth had been tense, drawn and angry when she'd first come to see him. During her visit with Chowder, the healer mentioned going to visit the patients and she'd played tag-along. After getting a good look at Demon, she was deeply grateful she had. The boy had dark circles beneath his eyes and his skin felt hot to the touch.

Chowder mixed him a tea and given him some healing, but the boy hadn't really risen to either. For her, though, he'd at least made an effort, and she'd almost gotten a laugh from him before Diesel entered. She was aware of him. It was as though every hair on her body stood up when he came into the room. If she closed her eyes, she could still find him. That thought gave her a jolt. Demon's total awareness of his Alpha was natural.

The animosity, however, had no place. Covering his uninjured hand, she gave him a squeeze. "Good, he wants to check on your well-being."

The youth shrugged, and closed his eyes. Curiosity sharpened within her, but she glanced at Diesel as he bumped her with his hip ever so lightly. His hand brushed her cheek and she smiled. Strength rolled off the man, it was as though he changed the temperature of every room he entered. Tempers cooled, comfort warmed. His eyes held a much brighter smile than the gentle one he wore.

Ranae moistened her lips, waiting patiently

until he swooped a little lower and brushed her lips with a light kiss. Excitement flowered in her chest, and she cradled the sensation close. For the first time in her life, she might understand the need to fan girl someone. Not that she intended to tell him.

At least not now.

"Hi," she murmured.

"Hi." He hooked a chair from near the wall and pulled it over. Sitting, his thigh rested against hers and the contact left her wanting to sigh.

One good, hard tumble and she'd turned into a sighing moron. Shaking off the reaction, she bumped his leg and nodded to Demon. "He's having a difficult morning."

Diesel covered her hand on Demon's, his expression sober. "I know. I am very sorry for the loss of your parents." Though he directed the words at Demon, Ranae's heart fisted and grief flirted through her.

Why hadn't Demon told her?

"It's done," Demon said, not opening his eyes. Defiance, though, not sadness marked the gesture.

"It is, and they will be honored." Diesel agreed.

Scowling, Ranae glared at him and the Alpha raised his eyebrows in question. Focusing on Demon, she said, "I am sorry as well, I should have realized you would have been with them." They weren't among the injured and she hadn't seen them. *I guess a part of me hoped they were Sentries and working somewhere else.* Her parents had always been there for her, even when they didn't always understand her or drove her crazy. The knife to the gut it would be to lose them even to natural causes at her age couldn't compare to the violence ripping them away from someone as young as Demon.

"You didn't know them," Demon said, only he opened his eyes to look at her.

"That doesn't matter. I know you." The reminder earned a reluctant smile from him. To be so young and so full of anger. "It's okay to be mad," she told him. "It's also okay to be sad and to want to cry."

"Warriors don't cry." Blind, youthful faith in his sentiment aside, his voice cracked.

"Bullshit," Ranae replied. Diesel echoed the statement in the same breath. Demon's eyes widened, and he jerked a look at his Alpha before returning his attention to Ranae.

"They don't…real men don't."

"If that's true, none of my brothers are real men." She smirked, filing that little jab away for later. Her brothers were wonderful, vibrant, overbearing Alpha males and occasionally needed to have the wind knocked out of them. As their younger and only sister, that duty fell to her.

"You know what I mean," Demon protested.

"Yes, she does," Diesel thrust himself back into the conversation. "She's also wise."

The challenge from his Alpha arrested his attention and Demon finally looked at him, though he couldn't bring his gaze higher than Diesel's chin. "She's not a man."

"Thank all that's holy for that." Leaning forward, Diesel pressed his leg into hers and she remained silent. "She is wise, however, and she has experience. Do you truly believe I have never cried?"

"Um…" Demon grimaced. "That's a trick

question."

"No, it's a direct one. Do you think I've never cried?" Patient, Diesel studied him. Though confusion rippled through the aggression roiling in Demon's scent, Diesel's remained calm, cool and rich. She really could drown in the scent of him. Like her, he hadn't showered, so she scented herself on him and butterflies batted around her belly.

A strange sense of possessiveness invaded her, and she had to wrench her mind back to the present. Demon needed her attention, not her lustful meanderings toward Diesel.

"I can't really see you crying, sir." Demon sounded almost apologetic.

"Fair enough, and I don't do it often, but our tears are not a sign of weakness. They show we cared. They admit we are honoring those who lost, not because they are gone so much as because we will never see them again." The quiet solemnity in his words struck Ranae, and she blinked hard to keep her own tears in check. "Sometimes we mourn when a wolf moves to another pack. Parents will cry when their pup grows and is successful. They are not saddened by the child's success, but by the transformation of child to adult. Their child will never need them again, not as they once did. When our parents leave this world, we miss them."

Demon sniffed hard, his voice thick. "I do miss them…and I feel like I failed them. I'm young and I'm strong, but they tore into my mom and I couldn't get them off her."

"You did your best and those that took her from us have been executed," Diesel said. "I cannot give your parents back to you, nor can I give you direct revenge on the ones who did you injury. I can promise you though—*everyone* involved in their loss will pay that loss in blood." Pure steel infused every syllable.

Sitting up, the boy reached for Diesel and the Alpha gripped him close. When Demon began to cry, Ranae had to wipe the tears from her eyes. Demon stretched out a hand blindly, and she caught it. At the requesting tug, she closed against his back to hug him, and her arm brushed Diesel's.

Wolves needed contact. They needed connection. They needed to know they weren't alone. Demon needed love, understanding, and comfort. Ranae could give him all three, and so could his Alpha. Demon cried himself out, the sobs becoming low and punctuated by hiccups. Only when they ceased altogether did Diesel loosen his hold.

Ranae followed his lead, leaning away as Diesel studied the red, blotchy-faced kid. "Better?"

"A little," Demon admitted, though some embarrassment crept into his scent. "I'm guessing I shouldn't have made your shirt so wet."

His Alpha chuckled then gave the boy a light chuck under his chin. "Shirts dry. Eventually, so do tears. If you ever need to cry, you can find me. I have no problem with being there for you."

"Thank you." Demon sighed, then looked at her. "Can you come back to see me? Chowder won't let me leave the infirmary until my arm finishes closing."

"Every chance I get. Maybe I can tell you stories about what I got up to when I was your age, and you can tell me about the best pranks you've ever pulled." It was an easy answer, but she meant it. The kid had gotten under her skin. If she'd had a younger brother, he'd probably be a lot like Demon. Then again, he'd also have the triplets for siblings too, so he'd turn into a pain in her ass.

"We don't pull a lot of pranks. The matrons don't approve." Demon rubbed at his face with his good hand.

"Pfft," Ranae waved off the concern. "That's half the fun."

"Hmm," Diesel said with a hint of a smile. "Maybe I shouldn't let you encourage bad behavior."

"No letting about it." She grinned. "I always encourage bad behavior, but…" She returned her attention to Demon. "*You* need to eat your food now, and get some rest or I'll get in trouble with Chowder for inciting a riot." Because Diesel was right there and it was fun to tweak him, she leaned in closer to the youth and said *sotto voce*, "I'd be more afraid of the healer than your Alpha, if I were you."

Across the room, Chowder snorted loud enough for the sound to carry, and one of the adults on the other bed actually chuckled. Soon, broken laughter echoed from around the room and Ranae straightened. Accomplishment filled her and she let Diesel grasp her hand as they walked through the ward. He paused at the different beds, checking on his wolves.

In that, he was like Mason. She'd seen how concerned Mason was with all of his wolves. Even Felicia, the mate of their former Alpha—he'd worked hard to keep Felicia Carlyle with them. The disparity between his rule and Toman's had an effect on the pack.

Outside the infirmary, Diesel slanted a look at her. "Did Chowder tell you about the infection?"

"He did," she admitted, and though he'd expressed mild concern, she hadn't let it deter her from visiting. "If there was a danger, I've already been exposed. I'm sorry I exposed you, though."

"I'm not." They followed the winding path through the stone gardens, the trickling water accompanying them as they headed toward his rooms. "Even if I'd known, I wouldn't have tried to stop what happened between us."

Her toes curled, and he glanced at her feet. "Chowder's?"

They were powder blue with acid green touches to them. Obnoxious and over bright, but they made her smile. "What was your first clue?"

Diesel chuckled, and pressed his hand to the panel. The scanner released the locks on the door and it swung inward. "I don't smell blood, so I am assuming you did as I asked and had him look at it?"

"I did," she admitted. "He cleaned it, treated it and put a Band-Aid on it. I think if I'd let him, he'd have kissed it, too."

Inside the grass-carpeted room, he scooped her up into his arms and she gave him a baleful look. "I can walk."

"I know." He carried her across the grass and toward the hall. "I can carry you, too."

Looping an arm around his shoulders, she canted her head. "So now that we've both proven ourselves capable, do I get to ask where we're going?"

"The shower," he told her as he carried her into the bathroom. "Then to bed."

When he set her down, she pressed her hands to his chest. Diesel playful was fun. "I still need to check in with Mason."

"He can wait." Diesel opened the shower door and turned on the water.

"And he has been." She wasn't looking for a fight, but this was important. "I spent the last few hours with Chowder and the patients."

A rumble expanded in his chest as he stripped off his shirt. Her bite on his right shoulder stared at her like an accusation. That fluttery feeling of possession ramped through her again.

"Of course, I suppose another hour or two won't matter." She tried to do the time change in her head, but she had no idea what time it was.

"Not at all." Diesel said, desire thickening his voice. He'd already stripped off his pants, and her gaze dipped to the length of his cock jutting upward toward his belly. "In fact, he can wait until tomorrow and the news will be the same."

A flash of guilt stabbed her as Diesel spread his fingers beneath the hem of her shirt. The light touch against her skin sent an entirely different kind of flutter through her system. "Well, we did already take care of the problem."

"Yes," he said, urging her shirt up and gliding his hands along her sides. She raised her arms so he could peel the fabric off her.

"And I cut my foot on the ice, not in combat." So, it wasn't really something she needed to report.

"Absolutely," he dipped his head and nuzzled a

kiss to her the corner of her mouth before working his way toward her throat. She rose on her tiptoes as he unclipped her bra. "And if it was truly serious, you would have already told me."

Her nipples beaded as he sucked on the skin just above her pulse point. The slow, lazy heat inside of her began to roar to great flames. "It's probably too late there…"

"Agreed," Diesel said, nudging her yoga pants down as he dropped to one knee and kissed the tip of one beaded nipple. Thoughts scattered as he laved his tongue over it.

"Okay," she shuddered when he added a scrape of his teeth to the lazy strokes of his tongue. "I'll call Mason tomorrow."

Her panties vanished, then Diesel held her hips as he kissed a path down her belly. Anticipation swept through her when he eased her thighs apart. "Then we are done discussing him?"

"Yes," she exhaled the word. He closed his mouth on her clit, and she had to grip his shoulders to keep from falling.

All done.

By the time they made it to his bed, Diesel had to carry his mate again. He didn't mind the slightest. Boneless and spent, Dove let him towel her hair and curled right up to him when he sprawled next to her. She fit him perfectly, the weight of her against him glorious.

One arm behind his head, he studied the ceiling. The loving had relaxed his body and for a time, his mind, but the problem with the Russians began a slow replay as he lay there. Dove curled her fingers against his pec, then traced the bite she'd left there.

"Shh," he told her, stroking her shoulder. "You can sleep."

"I'm not really that tired," she admitted, her voice low and husky. The sound caressed his senses. "And something is bothering you."

Tangled with her was not a place he wanted to bring a discussion of bloodshed and pain. Yet, he had already done it by letting it take over his thoughts. "I am considering my options."

"About the Russians?" Smart and aware, she zeroed in on his issue.

"Yes," he said, giving her a light squeeze before resuming the petting of her arm. Just having her pressed to him gave him a much-needed clarity, but it also sharpened the blade, which could now be held to his throat.

After several long moments of silence, she rose flattened her hand to his abs. "You can talk to me about it if you want, and as long as it doesn't directly affect my pack, I'll give you my word that whatever is said in this bed is not free for discussion with my Alpha."

The offer flattered him. Her loyalty belonged to Mason, and if he didn't think about it too hard it didn't bother him. The desire to keep his secrets warmed him, but it could tear her apart. "I will not hold you to that conflict of loyalties," he told her and pressed a kiss to the top of her head. The offer alone a far more valuable gift than he could measure.

"You can, though." She lifted her head and looked at him. Her swollen lips still as beautiful to him as when she'd wrapped them around his cock. The depth of passion she possessed could take him years to explore. "I want to do that for you."

Her damp hair fell over her shoulder, brushing his fingers and he savored the touch of it. The admission she would be willing to compromise herself a sweet, if dangerous offer. It told him she was nowhere near as unaffected by the desire to mate as she'd expressed. Mates owed loyalty to each other above all. "You wanting to is enough, Dove."

"Like I said earlier, the potential of getting in trouble is half the fun." Though she kept her tone light, it didn't neuter the devotion she'd shown him. Loving her was so easy. "That said, you don't have to tell me."

"I don't have to do a lot of things, Dove." The name truly did suit her, whether she believed him or not. "I'm debating the most efficient way to get my message across to them."

"Huh…not sure what flower says *fuck off and die*." The deadpan delivery jerked him from the dark twist in his thoughts and he laughed. Yes, so easy to love. Grinning, she settled her head against his shoulder and continued to pet his abs.

"I hadn't considered flowers." Still chuckling, he stretched until her leg slipped onto his thigh and he could slide his leg between hers. *Mine*. The possessiveness belonged to him as much as she did. "The problem is not what to send, the problem is finding the correct one and making sure I never have to respond again."

"Would you do to them what they have done to you?" No judgment echoed in her query, but he paused regardless.

"Kill the innocent?" Attacking a pack's children, its vulnerable, always put them on the defensive. Assassinating the strong, and most often all the males, allowed another pack to claim the territory and the women left behind. Still, eradicating them all meant no one grew up to become an enemy. It was an ancient fact of war. No matter its place in history, however, it did not make it any less ugly. "I would like to believe I wouldn't."

"So you haven't discounted it as a method you might use?" She wiggled, then rolled onto her belly and crawled over until she could lay across him. Her chin rested on folded hands over his breastbone. The position put her on top, and vulnerable, should anyone burst in the room. Quelling the instinctive need to roll her onto her back so he could take any potential hits, he studied the genuine curiosity in her eyes.

"War is rarely pretty. I would like to think I'm not a wolf who could shed the blood of those who are caught in a conflict, but the reality is—they would be caught in the middle whether I put them there or not." Catching a lock of her damp hair, he twined the sandy blonde around his finger. "Why do you think the packs created the Enforcers to begin with?"

"To police the Lone Wolves? To give the more dominant among them something to do because they weren't constrained by a pack?"

"Yes and no." Still mulling the rest, he watched her eyes. As guarded as she was, she never hid her feelings from her eyes. He had to wonder if she was aware of how much she gave away? "Lone Wolves have existed since the first pack was formed. Not everyone is suited to a pack lifestyle or to following an Alpha." If he had not won his right to lead the Yukon, he didn't know if he'd willingly follow another. "In the old days…"

"…when you were a boy?" The tart response had his lips twitching, but he ran a hand down to her sumptuous ass and delivered a light swat. Her impudent grin grew and her eyes softened in the same instance.

"*Before* I was born, Dove. *Before*." His protest only served to deepen her humor, apparently, because she laughed. The musical sound was worth any poke at his ego. Tempted to play with her ass some more, he curved his palm over the part he'd slapped—in part to cool the heat and in part simply to touch the softness of her skin. "War between packs hasn't been fought in your lifetime and only touched upon once in mine. But, in previous centuries, disagreements over territory, over mates—over anything, really—could erupt, and the innocent were always caught in the crossfire. While getting two Alphas to agree on anything is a challenge, it is the rare Alpha who will not want to see the vulnerable protected. Even the vulnerable of an opposing pack."

"But it still happens."

He nodded. "Yes, it still happens as it happens in any war fought, be it with wolves or humans. There are those not suited to war, those who wouldn't wage it even if they were capable, and those who cannot fight. The charge of the Enforcers is first and foremost the defense of the packs. They act as custodians for the Lone Wolves as part of the defense of the packs."

"I get that. It's part of why Julian came. The issue with the Russians is an Enforcer problem, too."

"Yes," Diesel traced the curve over her buttock. Her muscles remained loose, though another smile flirted about her lips. "In particular because they are threat to the packs. Pay attention to the wording, however. They are charged with the defense of the packs..."

"...but not the Alphas."

"Precisely." It was a very fine distinction. "It is why an Alpha challenge demands no outside interference and the rules of that combat are well-established."

"Yes, if someone enters our territory and declares Alpha challenge we escort them to the Alpha."

"Escort, but not confront."

"I know." She made a face. "It's punishable by death to interfere or at best expulsion. But if a challenger is attacking our people..."

"Then you act accordingly. It is entirely possible the lieutenant came here to challenge me." Possible, not probable.

Dove made a face. "I interfered."

"Pfft," he dismissed the concern immediately. "He didn't declare shit, sweetheart. All he did was lunge out of the shadows to attack. You had every right to assist me in the combat—not to mention, you were magnificent."

A blush pinkened her cheeks and she glanced down, an air of shyness to her. "Thank you. You really didn't need me, but I couldn't let him just attack you without helping."

Tracing a finger along her cheek, he marveled at the way she took the compliment. Had he not told her how well she'd handled herself? "Never denigrate what you have to offer. In every combat, there is an element of chance. A lucky strike, a miscalculated dodge…it only takes one claw or tooth in the wrong artery to end a battle. You fought not only with grace, but with intelligence. You didn't intervene or get in my path, yet you harassed him and kept him off balance. It was a thing of beauty to see."

"Well, I don't have poetry to describe you, so I'll stick with my earlier assessment." She pushed higher against him then kissed him soundly. "You're a badass."

Perhaps. He hadn't ever considered himself such. For her? To keep her? To protect her? To see that gorgeous smile and hold her in his arms? He'd burn down the world. "We shall have to work on you accepting compliments."

"I can take a compliment." Her blush removed the conviction from her protest.

"Not really, no. However, for someone so skilled and valuable, I shall endeavor to compliment you daily until you learn to accept them for what they are."

"Besides a way to change the subject, what are they?"

Definitely intelligent and savvy, though he meant every word. "They are the truth, Dove. And, my apologies, I had not intended to change the subject. I have no answers for what troubles me."

"You can't just let the Enforcers handle it?"

No, he couldn't. "If they were handling it, three packs wouldn't have faced attacks." Pressing a finger to her lips, he quieted whatever response she had been about to make. "If they *could* handle it, I trust Julian would have already done so. He is not a man to waste time or effort. In truth, no one knows precisely where the attacks are coming from. That means they have to deal with the information after the fact. The wolves who came here are dead. We have only a small amount of information. Does that mean more are coming? I can't ignore that threat, nor can I overlook the potential that they may go after Mason's pack or Serafina's. I cannot worry for that, because I'm not there to defend them and they're quite capable of handling it themselves."

"But you just said accidents can happen and the element of chance…"

"Precisely. It is always in play. A lucky strike, a mistake—the death of a mate is a very big distraction, and one that could serve the invisible enemy well."

Dove paled, and her eyes grew huge. Diesel wanted to kick himself.

"I do not believe they will target your brother," he assured her, even as he wrapped his arms around her. This time, he did tumble her onto her back. Covering her with his body, he wanted to show her she was safe. "I know he is mated to Serafina…"

"They're all in the firing line, though," she admitted quietly. "Linc, because he's the mate to an Alpha, A.J., because he is Mason's second and if there is a fight, he'll be right there. And Ty? Ty's off with Claire in Sutter Butte. She's damn capable in a fight, and I don't doubt for an instant that Ty wouldn't be right there at her side."

She swallowed, the convulsing of her throat pulling at every protective instinct he possessed. Though she had not included herself on that list, Diesel knew his need for her made her a target. If— no, when—he claimed her publically, their enemies would understand harming her could remove him from the equation. Cradling her face in his hands, he nuzzled her with a kiss. "I will do everything in my power to prevent that being an issue." No sooner had he uttered the declaration than he recognized the absolute truth in it. That truth decided him.

"I adore that you are promising me that, but you can't…you're here. And they are in other packs…"

Did his mate not understand the lengths he would go to for her?

"I can if I go to Russia and take the bastards out at the source."

Snow Wolf

Chapter Fourteen

"You can't go to Russia," Ranae repeated the same sentiment she'd been arguing since Diesel brought up the idea in bed. She followed him from the bedroom as he stalked down the hall toward the kitchen.

"It is a solution that offers us the maximum advantage." The calmness with which he stated the idea baffled her.

"It's insane. You'd be heading into enemy territory without any idea of your actual target."

Opening the cupboard, he pulled out a couple of glasses then reached for the whiskey. "I will not take your lack of faith in my abilities to heart or as an insult."

"Oh, please. I'm not insulting you." Her heart raced too damn fast, and she put her hands on her hips. One of the lessons Collin and Zane drilled into her Hunter training included getting her temper under control. Deep breaths brought her rebellious heart to heel.

Diesel filled the glasses then held one out to her. "Don't rein yourself in, Dove."

Lover or not, she was the also the representative of Willow Bend. *Discipline. Focus. Calm.* She needed all of those elements to handle the situation at hand. *When in doubt, reason it out.* Her mother's words echoed in her mind. *Worst case scenario, punch them in the face.* Linc's advice sounded better, considering the situation, but far less likely to earn her the desired result.

Flicking a look at him, she accepted the glass. "As I said, I'm not insulting you. The choice to go to Russia seems imprudent as it would leave your pack vulnerable and may earn future reprisals from packs we're not already dealing with."

"Few if any would dare come here…"

Raising her hand, she stopped him. "It's not *just* your pack facing these wolves. Fine, you had a skirmish. You want to end the likelihood of future attacks before they can happen. You go to Russia, you kick over the anthills, maybe you break open a few heads. Fantastic. Word spreads—don't mess with Diesel of the Yukon. Let's say you even make it home alive—that's the *best* case scenario. They leave you alone, but they don't leave the other packs be." Despite the steady thrum of her own heart hammering in her ears, she clung to rational thinking.

"You think that's the only best case?" No anger reflected in his eyes. If anything, they'd grown chillier as his manner stiffened. Even his scent vanished, leaving only a nip of frost to touch her nose.

"I think you're a powerful Alpha determined to do everything you can for your pack, but if you go over there—you will be seen. Word may also get around that there is a foreign wolf on their soil…fair game to anyone. Do I think you're capable of taking on a dozen wolves no problem? Sure. What about a hundred? What about an entire pack?" She drained the whiskey. "You said it yourself, luck plays as much a part in battle as skill and strength. If the wolf that kills you there comes here to claim this territory?

Who will defend the Yukon? Do you have anyone here who can hold your pack if you fall?"

"My mate can."

Her stomach plummeted at the soft declaration. "Don't put this on me. We are so not there yet. We're lovers and, while I—I am enjoying what we're doing here…" Her wolf whined within her, struggling with the dissonance between her growing affection for Diesel and her devotion to the pack which birthed her. "My loyalty has to be Willow Bend."

"Understandable." An unreadable mask settled over his expression. If she'd thought it chilly before, the cold left goosebumps all over her skin. He refilled his glass and padded into the grassy room. Even though he seemed intent on freezing her out, she couldn't help but admire the taut pull of muscle as he moved. Neither of them had dressed, but instead of feeling exposed or vulnerable, she felt like she belonged.

The realization sent another tremor through her. She couldn't be loyal to two packs—nor two Alphas. The temptation to throw her glass across the room and hear it shatter waged war with the need to keep her calm. "You know it's not fair, right?"

"What isn't?" He didn't look at her.

Setting the glass down, lest she give into the urge, she followed him onto the grass. It was soft beneath her feet, almost warm and yet cool. It reminded her of the first soft blades in spring. "You want me to hold nothing back, to not rein myself, but the moment I don't agree with you—you're freezing me out?"

Tilting his head a fraction, he glanced over his

shoulder at her. "I've held nothing back. I told you my bloodline migrated from Russia. I have connections there, and I understand the customs."

"Well, your words say one thing, your tone says another." It wasn't hostile. Hell, it wasn't even moody. It simply rang false, and set off every alarm in her system.

"I am Alpha, Dove. The needs of my people come before all." Except his mate. He didn't say the words aloud, and he didn't have to. They echoed loudly through the room.

She'd told him they weren't there yet.

Frustration twisted her gut into knots. "How soon are you planning on leaving?"

"Who's asking?" He faced her. "My lover or Willow Bend's Hunter?"

Hurt lashed strips off her soul, and she raised her chin and met his cold gaze. Fire burned in her, fire to his ice. "Does it matter?"

"I believe I have already shown you that *you* matter. The rest is for you to decide."

Between the hurt and frustration welled fresh anger. Pivoting once, she stalked down the hall to her room and clothes. Dragging on a clean set of panties, then jeans, she elected to skip a bra then pulled on her t-shirt. Dressed, she checked the charge on her phone and barely made a mental note of the number of messages before she shoved it into her pocket.

Her right foot ached, but she stuffed her feet into boots she'd brought before leaving the room and striding across the grass to the main door. Diesel stood exactly where she'd left him.

He didn't ask where she was going and she

didn't tell him. Outside the room, she concentrated on gulping deep breaths of air and putting one foot in front of the other. The desire to run off her anger vied with the need to not show weakness to the pack around her. From the moment Diesel walked into the cabin, he'd dominated her thoughts and her time.

He also made me feel welcome... Despite the fact he held nothing back and showered her with attention, she was not his pack.

Nor his mate.

At the exchange between the herb hall and the trees, she cut to the right across a common area. Few wolves seemed to be about and what ones she did see, she didn't recognize. Choosing a stone path at random, she walked along it.

There's no such thing as a fated mate. Of course they all loved the fairy tale of love at first sight. Or she had, right up until Claire sundered Tyler's heart into a thousand brittle pieces, walking away from him and not glancing back. Tyler had declared Claire his before Ranae had been born. Her whole life, she'd seen the devotion Ty had for his mate only to see the ugly remains when Claire left.

Yes, she came back. Yes, they were happy *now*. But it hadn't been love at first sight for Claire. She hadn't agreed to mate Ty. It didn't matter his sincerity, and Diesel could mean every word he said...*But I'm not ready.*

Whether it meant she wasn't ready to be his mate or to leave her pack or both—she didn't know. Barely a week in the Yukon, and the man seemed to have changed the course of her life.

"You're her." A woman's voice jerked her out

of the internal conflict that had her chasing her mental tail. Halting, she found an older woman staring at her. Based on the silver in her hair and the deep grooves wrinkling the corners of her eyes, she was old.

Older than Diesel by more than a little.

"Forgive me, Elder." She inclined her head a fraction to show the deference and respect all elders were due. "I was not watching where I was going."

"Hmm," the woman said, holding a large basket of laundry under one arm easily. She studied her. "You've quarreled with him. Good. Disagreement leads to clarity."

Uncertain of what to say precisely, Ranae gave her a small smile and spread her hands. "I'm just out for a walk…" Not entirely the truth, but also not a lie.

The older woman laughed. "Then come walk with me, child. I'm Deidre."

"Ranae." She fell into step with her, manners long ingrained by her mother made it hard to refuse the request. Elders earned their place through long life and service, it didn't matter that she was of the Yukon, she deserved whatever deference Ranae could offer her. "Would you like me to carry that?"

"No, dear. It's good for me to stay independent." She turned down a tree-lined path. They really did have fruit trees growing in their underground paradise. Never could she have imagined this. "What did you quarrel about?"

Not entirely comfortable discussing the subject of the woman's Alpha with her, she slipped her thumbs into the belt loops of her jeans. "As I said, I was just out for a walk."

As the woman diverted into a doorway, Ranae

paused. Deidre leaned out to stare at her. "Come on in, I can't possibly talk to you in private if we're yelling to be heard."

Biting back a smile, Ranae trailed her inside slowly. The interior of her rooms was as different from Diesel's as night was from day. It looked like a cabin, all hardwood interiors, right down to the logs tucked to each other to frame the walls. Even the ceiling hung lower without the affectation of natural light though a faux window on the back wall offered the illusion matched by the real one which gazed onto the stone path they'd just walked.

"Have a seat, child. I'll make us some tea and you can tell me what he's done that's upset you so much."

"Deidre, ma'am…" She tried to keep her voice even. "I appreciate the concern, but I really have nothing to say." As pissed as she was at the cavalier attitude Diesel seemed to have adopted toward his own safety, she didn't have any intention to share the information with a woman she'd just met. Hell, she didn't even know how or what she would report to Mason.

Setting her hands on the back of a chair, Deidre smiled at her. The woman truly had a kindly appearance, a grandmother. She also carried about her an air of timeless wisdom. The stories she could probably tell… "You do not want to betray confidences. I respect that. Let me confide in you so you may understand why I wanted to talk to you."

The urge to pace rippled through Ranae, but she wrestled it away to show courtesy. "If you want."

Deidre gestured to the empty chair across from

the one she held and Ranae had no choice but to sit, even if sitting still was the last thing she wanted to do. Deidre didn't join her immediately; instead, she retreated into a cozy little kitchenette. Scenting no other wolves in the house and putting that together with the tiny appearance of a one-bedroom cabin, Ranae guessed the older woman lived alone.

Perhaps all she wanted was some company. The idea settled some of the unease in her gut. The elder wolf returned with two icy bottles and set them down on the table. "Hard cider. Chowder makes it, and he sent me a fresh batch yesterday."

The sharpness of the apples touched her nose the moment she opened the bottles. It was like summertime fermented and captured in the container. Testing a sip, the coolness of it soothed her parched nerves and the tart taste left her thirsty for more. "It's good, thank you."

"You're very welcome. He never shares his recipe with any of us, but he's grown quite talented at the process." Deidre took a seat. "Thank you for joining me."

"You're welcome," Ranae managed with a straight face. In some ways, Deidre reminded Ranae of her own mother—without the friendly yelling and affection head slaps. "Thank you for allowing me into your home."

"Probably strikes you as strange, but then you don't know me. Amara was my daughter."

The statement didn't mean anything. "Forgive me, ma'am. Amara?"

"Oh." Deidre's expression sobered, and she set her bottle aside and folded one hand over the other.

"Forgive me, Ranae, I thought you knew. Well, that will make this far more awkward."

And uncomfortable, but Ranae refused to complain, at least aloud. "It's quite all right, ma'am. To be honest, I haven't met very many of the pack— at least not on a name introduction basis." No she'd been too busy following Diesel around like a poodle, coming to heel under the weight of his tender attention.

"I understand. As I said, this might make things awkward and, if you will forgive an old woman her directness, I'm not going to drag this out for either of us."

Thank God.

"My daughter Amara was Diesel's first mate."

The world bottomed out on her. Although she tried to school her features, Ranae couldn't disguise the surge of jealousy scoring her insides. Taking a drink of the hard cider, she concentrated on the cool taste. In the back of her mind, she'd known Diesel had been mated before…that he'd outlived his mate. But this was her mother?

"Please forgive me if the bluntness hurt you."

"I'm fine, and it did not." No the hurt came from wanting a certainty and being angry at her own divided loyalties. "I'm sorry for the loss of your child, though."

"Thank you. Every parents' worst fear is to outlive their young. In many ways, Amara was a special girl. Diesel adored her," Deidre continued, then raised a hand as though asking for time. "Again I am not saying this to cause you discomfort or sadness, but because I think it is important for you to understand."

Accepting the explanation, Ranae nodded once and took a drink of her cider. The alcohol might help her digest the tale.

"My Amara was a gentle soul, far too gentle for a wolf who was not submissive. Her only ambition from the moment she set her gaze on Diesel was to be his mate and stay forever and always at his side. Even when he encouraged her to go away to school, to broaden her horizons and to see the world, she declined. Nearly every wolf goes on a roam at some point their young adulthood...as I'm sure you have, yes?"

"Yes." Ranae could answer that easily enough. "I went to college, and I did my share of partying and exploring." Though truth be told, she'd always put herself in controlled situations. She'd lost A.J. to his roam with their brothers. Three had gone and only two returned. She didn't dare risk anything to chance.

"Amara never wished to go, she saw no purpose in it when she knew that Diesel would need her. He held off claiming her until she was almost twenty, then...well, mates want what they want. He was a good mate to her, always considerate and always strong." The picture she painted left a lump forming in Ranae's throat. "But I fear my daughter was not always a good mate to him."

"I don't understand." She hadn't meant to ask. She *shouldn't* ask. Taking what the woman wanted to share was certainly enough.

Deidre leaned back in the chair and shook her head. "Diesel is a strong, determined man as you have noticed. Even then, he was a fierce protector and one of the strongest Sentries our pack had seen in a generation. Our Alpha at the time knew Diesel would be the one to take his place. There was no question of challenge. Instead he groomed him, taught him and, over time, began to transfer authority to him. The night Jorgen passed, the pack mourned, but not a moment of discomfort did we experience as the leadership settled expertly atop Diesel's shoulders. The Sentries swore to him, and so did the pack. We'd all known, you see, so there was no need to settle it through combat or challenge."

A shockingly clean and easy transition of power—and one she'd rarely heard of before. Even the most tacit of challenges could be offered when no combat was required. "It sounds like he was born to be Alpha."

"Yes, and Amara threw herself into being the perfect mate. Yet there is no such thing…" Deidre caught a hint of condensation along the side of the bottle and traced it up the glass. "You see, mates should always challenge each other, provide a sounding board, and support—and be capable of telling someone when they are being too stubborn or are wrong. Arguments are healthy, debate is healthy…Amara did none of these things."

"Ma'am, I don't think you should have to tell me this…" It was too personal. Too intimate. Diesel hadn't shared the information with her, and she had no right to intrude.

"Of course I don't have to, but you've quarreled with him and now you're tying yourself into knots. I'm telling you this because you should know—to be the mate to an Alpha means you have to stand up to them, especially when you don't agree with their course of action. To be mate to an Alpha is to make them clarify their stance. No one else is in a position to challenge their authority without challenging their position. A mate, though? A mate is uniquely suited to the task."

"I'm not…"

"It matters not that he hasn't claimed you or you haven't accepted. He has declared himself. His heart knows you, child. If your heart needs longer to decide, let it have the time."

Chastised, she nodded.

"My Amara was many things, but challenging others simply wasn't in her nature. Even if something terrified her or made her ill, she wouldn't dream of expressing any wish contrary to that of her mate's."

A coldness gripped her spine, a sense of apprehension.

"You understand the pack transforms to run wild as our wolf halfs every winter during the long dark?"

"Yes." She couldn't imagine it, but she did understand the idea.

"Our young don't begin to join us until they are sixteen, sometimes seventeen. In my youth, we did not have this sanctuary. Those of us who did not turn with the pack stayed with our tribal neighbors. The Inuit have ever been kind to us and always protected us. The majority of the pack would roam, and we would winter elsewhere. When the spring comes and the light returns, we made our way to Tikaani. Amara's first full winter didn't happen until she was nineteen."

Caught up in the tale, Ranae frowned. "Why so late?"

"As I said, it was determined individually for each wolf. Neither my mate nor I felt Amara was ready, but shortly before her twentieth birthday, she mated Diesel."

"And she went because he did."

Deidre inclined her head, a soft sigh escaping her. "Sometimes I think I failed her because I didn't teach her to speak her mind. That first winter was truly difficult for her, yet she insisted nothing was wrong when I asked. To Diesel, she hid her upset and discomfort. The next winter, it was worse. By the third…the third she did not return from."

"Something happened to her?" No way Amara roamed alone. She had to have traveled with Diesel. He would never let anything attack her.

"She faded. In three short winters, the time spent as her wolf consumed her and there was not enough of her to return. When we all came together, Amara disappeared into the Tundra. Diesel spent nearly two years tracking every pack…but she was gone. Neither he, nor I, nor any of the Sentries, could find her."

"But he's Alpha and she's his mate…how could he not sense where she…oh." *Oh God.* The grief when the tether between Alpha and pack had to have broken—which meant his mating connection ended too. There were tales told in Willow Bend of the occasional wolf who faded, went wolf and never came back. Sometimes surviving mates did that, sometimes it seemed to be related to a disturbed personality or the mentally unstable. Other times it was purely depression. No one true cause.

"Exactly," Deidre said with a sad smile. "He is a good Alpha, he lost his mate and he did not leave us, though over the last few years…I think he had begun to fade himself. There was no joy in him, no happiness, merely the work and obligations. Even his contact with the outside world became a thing of intricacy and demand he simply didn't want to deal with…and in the few short days since you arrived, he's come back to us. All of us."

The burden threatened to crush her. "Thank you for telling me the story of your daughter and I'm sorry for her loss."

"Darling child, I told you this because you quarreling with him is good. He has carried the weight of this pack alone for far too long. He needs to be shaken and good. So revel in the fact that you can stand up to him, and don't give an inch unless it is what you desire." For the first time since she'd run into Deidre, Ranae had the most unreasonable urge to hug her.

"I'm really good at arguing," she admitted. She wasn't always so good at doing what she was told, yet Diesel hadn't given her orders. He'd left the decision in her hands.

Her hands.

The thought crystalized. He refused to order her. At every step, he'd wanted it to be her decision.

"Deidre, would you excuse me, please? There is something I need to take care of."

The older wolf smiled. "Of course. Please…come see me again when you have time."

"I'd like that." When they both rose, Ranae

gave into the desire and gave her a quick, if fierce hug. "I would really like that."

After leaving her, Ranae retraced her steps to the public areas and pulled her phone out of her pocket. Diesel wanted her to make her own decisions. Fine. She'd made one.

If he wanted to go to Russia, no way in hell was he going alone.

Checking her signal strength, she fired off a text to Mason.

Sir, we have a problem...

Disliking the distance he'd forced between them, Diesel remained in their rooms long after she'd walked out. She hadn't taken her things, but she'd left all the same. Drinking and brooding were two things he tried never to do at the same time. Pushing his Dove had been a calculated risk. The same calculated risk he planned to explore in Russia.

None of his Sentries possessed his knowledge of the landscape, either political or social, not to mention cultural. Few wolves knew he'd been to Russia. Even less knew he'd been there several times in his long life. He hadn't told Dove the whole of it, but her immediate concern for his safety and the security of his pack both pleased and annoyed him in equal measure.

If he had to leave his pack to anyone, she'd proven to him she had the measure if not the awareness or knowledge as yet. When Jorgen took him under his wing, he'd told him that he'd always know his successor when he met them or at least the wolf most capable of becoming his successor.

Mates didn't typically rise to fulfill the duties of their fallen lovers, but he and Dove weren't fully mated. She could survive his loss far more easily if they weren't. So, he poked at her like he would a bear, incited her temper and sent her storming off.

It had worked as he'd expected, so why did he find himself sick with the idea it might have worked too well? She had no way to flee across the tundra or to return to Prudhoe Bay. Julian's vehicle had returned with him, per Grinder.

He drained the last dregs of the whiskey then stood. Wolves didn't need vehicles to travel overland. They didn't need anything more than their own four legs. The worry pricking at him, feeding his agitation was his own wolf's awareness of the stubborn nature of their mate. If she were well and truly pissed at him as had been his intention, she might have taken that course of action.

The moment the thought took root, he snagged a pair of pants and strode out the door. He'd lost one mate to the snow, to her inability to tell him what she needed. Challenging Dove then not accepting her declaration for what it was because he wanted her to say the exact words to him rather than the sentiment alone was simply pride.

Furious, he strode along the pathway toward the central gathering point and the ascension stairs. Three steps from the door, her scent arrested him. Pivoting, he searched the area until his gaze found her sitting on one of the benches near a splashing fountain.

She typed swiftly on her phone. Relief curbed the worry curdling in his soul. Angry with her for being safe seemed an absurdity, yet there he stood experiencing the idiotic. The wolf clawed at him, eagerness to see their mate overriding his irritation. The man...Diesel drifted back a step until he could lean against the wall, tucked into the shadows.

Watching over her would simply piss her off further. He wanted her to fight him, fight for him—fight to be with him. Overhead, the light began to dim and his anger evaporated. He'd fixed the settings in their rooms, but the sanctuary would go into the night cycle on schedule.

The glow of her phone illuminated her face as the low wattage street lamps turned on one by one. Pushing away from the wall, he was already walking toward her when she lowered the phone and glanced at the fall of night. Anger, he wanted. A desire to fight and claim, he needed. Her fear? No, that he forbade.

"It's all right," he told her. Strain showed in her expression and her knuckles went white on the phone. "The lamps are coming on, see?"

Dove blew out a breath as she followed his direction. Her scent tickled his nostrils, sweetness, strength, and apples—apples?

"You had cider." Irked, he didn't bother to disguise his disappointment that someone else had introduced her to the joy of Chowder's product.

Surprise marked by a hint of guilt widened her eyes. "Is that against some rule?"

"Of course not." He slung himself down on the bench next to her. She turned off her phone and slid it back into her pocket.

"Then why so miffed?" She folded her arms then leaned back against the bench and the arm he'd slung behind her. The sensation of her resting against him settled his agitation.

"I'm not miffed."

"Pfft." The snort mocked him, but he spied the hint of a smile. "You sound miffed."

"Chowder's cider is a bit of a delicacy around here. A sweet treat with a bit of a bite and a—" He paused when she leaned into him, her nostrils flaring.

"Did you take a bath in a bottle of whiskey?"

"No. That would be a waste of good whiskey."

Her laughter tugged a reluctant grin from him "Good. As for the cider, I blame Deidre. She saw me storming around and insisted I sit and talk to her."

It was his turn to jerk with a hint of surprise. Amara's mother? "What did she say?"

"Can't tell you. Girl code."

Girl code? "What?"

"Girl code. It's invoked whenever two women discuss private subjects. Particularly if it involves those of the opposite gender." Sass decorated her tone. Sass and amusement rather than her earlier anger.

"You do know she would tell me if I asked." He infused far more confidence in that statement than he felt. Deidre would do as Deidre damn well pleased, and he would no sooner order her to betray a confidence than he would force Dove to mate him.

"Then go ask her." Was that an invitation to play?

Suspicious, he eyed her. "Why are you in a better mood?"

"Am I?" Leaning against his arm, she canted her head so that she could look up at him. The act also gave the impression of baring her throat to him. Impression, not act. It was an invitation to play.

"Yes," he said, dipping his head down to nuzzle the sweet invitation of her lips. "You are."

"Maybe I had time to think the whole thing out."

"Go on," he beckoned, nibbling a path along her jaw.

"You wouldn't go into enemy territory if you didn't have a plan." She released a little sigh when he tugged on her earlobe.

"Clever wolf," he whispered, then traced the shell of her ear with his tongue.

"You would never abandon your mate—even if she hasn't reached the same conclusion as you." Beautiful words from a beautiful woman.

"Yet," he added for her as he nipped her throat just above the pulse point.

"Yet," she conceded and his wolf wanted to burst free and howl. It wasn't an outright declaration, but close enough to satisfy his absolute need for her.

"Thank you, Dove," he whispered, raising his face so he could gaze into her eyes.

"Don't thank me yet." She nipped his lower lip, then laved the injury. "I said I understood you have a plan and that you have every intention of returning to me. But I think you need to know I have a plan, and I know exactly how you're coming home…"

Intrigued, he raised his eyebrows. "How is that?"

"Because, I'm going with you."

Not a chance in hell.

Snow Wolf

Chapter Fifteen

If she'd thought Diesel's cold rejection difficult, his very real fury at her involving the other packs in his plans proved to be red-hot. Though they still shared a bed, he'd barely spoken a word to her since she'd informed him they would be meeting a flight in Prudhoe Bay, from there they would follow his lead—but no, he wasn't going alone.

At first, she worried he would leave her behind, but he hadn't. On the other hand, three days with his barely saying a word even as he made arrangements to leave, then as they journeyed to meet Julian in Prudhoe Bay. She climbed back into that tin can and sat in the back while Diesel rode up front with Julian.

The flight sucked even more going back to Seattle than it had on the way up. They landed to find Etienne Andre of Delta Crescent, brother and second to Serafina, Trask, a huge, brutal looking wolf from Sutter Butte, and Luc Danes, second to Brett Dalton of Hudson River waiting for them at the private airstrip.

Diesel's grim reaction had set her teeth on edge, but she sucked it up. Informing Mason had been the right choice. Her Alpha shocked her when he not only agreed with her assessment of the situation but also Diesel's. The fact he made arrangements with the other packs to get representatives onboard, all ordered to let Diesel take the lead seemed a thing of miracles. Of course, she represented Willow Bend, but even if she hadn't…she planned on going.

"We'll be landing in China within the hour," Etienne said as he rejoined them in the cabin of Delta Crescent's private plane. The males had all taken residence in various sections of the cabin, all seated in chairs facing each other. She sat near Diesel, but he still didn't say anything to her.

I am with him, and I will stay with him. The need to protect him, protect her family, protect their packs overrode all else.

"Once we land, we proceed under Diesel's command," Julian actually managed to say the words with a straight face.

"If we're going to use the buddy system, I've got the lovely Ranae's back." Luc winked at her. Though he definitely fell in the good-looking category, she wasn't interested and she simply ignored the comment to glance at Diesel.

"A party this large will stand out." Diesel said, he wasn't looking at her but at Julian. "So I've made arrangements with a friend." The low gravelly hum of his voice was a balm to her senses. She thought she could hold a grudge, but Diesel could teach a master class in it.

"How are we planning to cross the border?" Etienne's deep brown skin reminded her of polished ebony. "And if little sister needs a partner," he glanced at Luc. "You won't be it."

Save her from dominant males.

Diesel tapped his finger once. "We have permission from a small enclave of Chinese wolves who keep a landing strip in Northern China. They have an arrangement with the government, they keep guard on the border and the army leaves them alone.

We'll cross there."

"Does the plane stay or go?" Etienne made no assumptions. He was all business, understated, but clever. At least that was how Linc described him. *At times he seems more like an accountant or a manager than a second to an Alpha. Then someone does something stupid...* It wasn't the words so much as how her brother described it which made her laugh.

At first, Diesel waited so long to answer, she thought he might ignore the question. He'd ignored several since they'd met with the other wolves saying only the absolute minimum needed. "Stay, have the Hounds remain on board. The wolves will provide a refueling truck, but they should stay with the plane."

"Done." Etienne leaned back into his seat.

"So what is the plan?" Luc asked. "Not that hanging out with all of you in a foreign country doesn't sound like loads of fun... but it really doesn't."

"You follow me and you do as your told." Diesel pinned him with a look. "Or you can stay with the plane."

"Leave the pretty little thing too and I'll make sure she is safe."

"The pretty little thing has a name," Ranae said calmly. "And claws. If you refer to me like a piece of meat again, I'll feed you your balls, *capiche*?"

The Hudson River wolf began to grin. "I knew I liked you."

"If you would like me to hold him down," Diesel offered, glancing at her. "I'd be happy to assist."

Pleased that Diesel at least spoke to her again,

she gave him a wide grin. "Thank you."

"Luc, shut up." Julian seemed as thrilled about their companions as Diesel. "What happens after we cross the border?"

"We have a friend meeting us with papers and transport. Our destination is a city called Lebeninsk in the Krasnoyarsk region. It's a two-day drive, and we're better traveling on two feet rather than four."

"Something special about the town?" It was one of the first time Trask joined in the discussion.

"It's a closed city, has been for fifteen years." Diesel rubbed a hand against his jaw. A hint of stubble decorated the hard cut of it, and it tempted her to test the roughness against her own palm.

"What do you mean closed?" Her Russian geography was nil. If it was anywhere near a certain failed nuclear power plant, she wanted to be prepared.

"It's an old cold war era trick, a city can be declared closed to all foreigners," Diesel slanted her a look. "The government liked to do that when it wanted to protect security secrets or special installations. They limit the populace and keep them contained."

Trask looked troubled. "So we're going into a top secret government city?" Skepticism rose amongst the testosterone infused atmosphere.

"No," Diesel said, then canted his head to meet her gaze. "We're going to a wolf controlled city."

"Wolf controlled? Wolves control an entire city in Russia? And the government closed it?" Even the calm Etienne appeared startled.

"You'd be surprised by what the wolves control, and what the government will do to keep them appeased." Diesel's gaze remained on hers. "It's a dangerous place for foreigners, which is why they are forbidden as much to protect their secrets as to keep other wolves out."

"How much of a problem are we going to have getting in? Wolf cities will have wolf guards." Julian kept his focus on their preparations.

"Like I said," Diesel said. "We're meeting a friend."

After that, no amount of questioning lured Diesel into a response. When the lights dimmed on the plane as it prepared to land in the night shrouded land she braced herself for the panic attack. In such close quarters, she had to keep it under control.

A hot hand covered hers, and the anxiety ebbed immediately. Someday, maybe she would grow out of the ridiculous reaction. Once they taxied to a parking spot and the lights came up, Diesel rose and tugged her from the chair.

"Give me a moment," he ordered the others, then guided her to the exit door. He opened it and stepped out onto the tarmac.

Three wolves awaited them, two males and one female. Ranae did her damndest not to stare at the Asian wolves. Their scent was wholly unfamiliar, but then so was the air around her. A thrill skated through her and she had to lock down the wholly inappropriate flare of excitement.

Diesel squeezed her hand, then greeted each of the men in their language and bowed with such precision, she knew without a doubt he'd been there before. The men said something to him in short statements, then walked away leaving only the woman—who was definitely not Asian.

"Hello, Diesel," the woman said, her gaze flicking to Ranae once then to him again. Her accent was perfectly American. Oddly, the woman seemed familiar. Ranae couldn't place her, though. Tall, lean and athletic, she had a pixie cut of black hair with red streaks. "Your documents."

"Thank you." He accepted the envelope. "I appreciate your help on this matter."

"I owed you." She gave a brief smile, then glanced at the plane. "Well, this should be fun...does he know?"

"What the fuck is she doing here?" Julian's harsh voice cut through the night.

After brooding for three days on how expertly his Dove had gone around him to make sure she was part of his journey, Diesel discovered her presence actually delighted him, even with all the danger they faced. Instead of being driven away by his foul temper on the subject, she'd endured.

His cousin Julian's reaction to their guide, no matter how amusing, proved a larger threat. Dallas Dalton was a rogue and the white whale Julian had hunted for decades. One moment Julian stood at the steps to the plane, the next he loomed over Dallas.

"Good morning to you, too, Julian." The female rose to the inherent challenge and tension spiked the air.

Fortunately, his cousin's loss of temper occurred after he stepped foot onto foreign soil. "Julian," Diesel kept his tone modulated, and even. "Dallas is our guide. Do not make more of this than it is."

His cousin didn't look away from the wolf before him. A quiet kind of rage simmered below his controlled surface. The other wolves had followed him, but wisely kept their distance.

"We don't have time to negotiate or deal with egos," he continued, aware of the way Dove positioned herself at his back, freeing him to deal with his cousin if necessary but also shielding him. The positioning so effortless it reinforced the quiet promise she'd made to him three days before. She hadn't accepted...yet.

With absolute icy control, Julian said, "A word." Then he strode into the darkness. To follow his cousin meant leaving Dove alone with the others. Etienne, Diesel could accept. He was a brother through marriage. Luc, however, might piss his mate off enough to cause a fight.

"I will be a moment. Are you all right?" he said to his Dove. It wasn't pitch black, but it was far from light.

"Yes," she kept her reply sub vocal. "I can see."

Satisfied, he gave her hand a squeeze. "Try not to kill anyone while I'm gone." Her snort of amusement soothed his concerns.

"Aww," Dallas said after Julian left them. "No hello kiss?"

To the rogue, he settled for giving her a baleful look. "Don't incite him."

"But it's been such a long time since I got to prick...the prick." Still, she spread her hands in a gesture of false innocence. At his quelling look, she sighed. "Fine. I'll leave him alone." Then, all business, she added, "Get a move on. We want to be over the border before dawn."

Diesel found Julian studying the darkened landscape. The cloudless skies and crescent moon afford a small measure of light, once they'd shut off the private runway.

"You knew she'd be here." It wasn't a question. Julian's attention riveted on the rogue despite the distance.

"Yes." No point in dissembling.

"Which means you have a way to contact her." Also not a question.

"Be angry, but be quick." Diesel sliced a palm through the air. "We are not in North America. She is not free for you to capture nor do you have the right to act here. In the matter at hand, she is an ally and a guide. We will move more swiftly with her assistance. The moment you stepped foot on land you fell under my purview. You agreed to follow me. Have you changed your mind?"

The weight of Julian's glare slammed into him, his dominance rising, and Diesel lifted his chin and met like with like. They were too well-matched for either to overwhelm the other. "No." With that, the aggression abated.

Clapping a hand to Julian's shoulder, Diesel lowered his voice to near sub-vocal. "Can you handle her presence?"

"I have no choice."

"Don't try to take her here." It was his only request and he didn't make it an order.

Julian sighed. "Let us get this over with."

Since he hadn't invited his cousin on the

mission, he didn't apologize to him. Together, they returned to the group where Luc scooped Dallas into a hug, and the wolf laughed softly at something she said. Watching the pair, Julian remained expressionless. Diesel handed them their papers, leaving his Dove's till last. She glanced at them. They were in Russian and she didn't speak the language nor read it, so she wouldn't see what Diesel had already noted.

Dallas had listed Dove as his. The choice pleased him, and eased the fist on his heart. With only light gear, they set off from the plane and loaded into a truck. From the moment he'd taken off in Prudhoe Bay, an internal timer ticked away within his soul.

Two days he'd been away from his pack. Two days to reach Lebeninsk. No more than twenty-four hours to locate any Volchitsa within the wolf controlled city, then to leave again. His pack could hold a week without him, the distance already wearing on his psyche. Dove's presence buoyed him, but like his wolf, they remained watchful and wary.

Dallas knew the lay of the land, and it was her contacts Diesel utilized to make arrangements for smuggling them into Russia. Luc road in the front with Dallas while Diesel, Dove, and the rest took the back of the truck. It served two purposes—to separate Julian and his prey as well as putting Luc's annoying presence elsewhere. Long before she'd gone Lone Wolf, Dallas Dalton had been a part of Hudson River. Rumor had it that Brett offered her a place to return which she'd declined so far.

Dove sat next to him, her thigh pressing into his and her head resting on his shoulder. The darkness in the back of the truck was profound, but she trusted him and that trust gave him strength. "Once we arrive, we will be going to one of the bars Dallas knows," he filled in the group. "Lebeninsk is a wolf city, and it is controlled by one faction; however, it is a neutral city amongst the Russian packs."

"What are the local rules of engagement?" Trask's martial interest reminded Diesel of the losses Sutter Butte had sustained.

"Straight combat, one-on-one only and it has to be through direct challenge." He focused on the other wolf. "I know the losses your pack sustained. Do not seek to resolve that debt in blood."

"What is your goal, then?" Etienne braced himself as they bounced along a particularly unpleasant track of road.

"We want to find the Volchitsa presence within the city," he told them after a long moment. His initial plan had included tracking the Volchitsa, then making the bastard tell him where their pack wintered. If he had to fight his way through Russia, he could— though the time involved threatened to be too costly. "Identifying the element is only a portion of the plan. A wolf named Alexandrovich rules Moscow. He and I have…a history of sorts." If Dove wanted to know the details, he would tell her. The rest didn't need to know. "He has contacts and wolves throughout the country, of all the packs in Russia—Moscow's is the one no one tangles with."

He had their undivided attention. By now, his packages of Yury's organs had been delivered along with the message to leave the Yukon alone. The last package, the one containing the lieutenant's tattoos, would be in Alexandrovich's hands before they reached Lebeninsk.

"Russian pack law is very much survival of the fittest," he said with a glance at Trask. "Like their history, it can be bloody and tragic. Their packs, however, can be driven from one territory to another. Our targets may have few allies. When we leave, they will have none."

"The enemy of my enemy is my friend." Etienne closed his eyes. "It is a gamble."

Julian said nothing, the Chief Enforcer's focus locked on the wall of the truck separating them from the driver's seat as though he possessed the vision to laser through it to where Dallas sent.

"The enemy of my enemy is a useful ally and nothing more." He slid an arm around Dove and she curved into him. "Sleep if you can. Once we're in Lebeninsk, we will move as swiftly as possible." A surgical strike, get a face to face with one of Alexandrovich's people, then hunt the Volchitsa and set the dogs loose on them. Dallas knew a guy.

She knew a lot of them. Her network of contacts far more extensive than his cousin could imagine. The debt she owed him was one of her own choosing. He would never call in such a marker, and had only contacted her for a favor. He suspected, debt or not, she would have done it. Her child was a part of the packs. She would not allow anything to threaten her.

Ranae hadn't expected to sleep even after Diesel advised it. Between the choking darkness and the aggravated Enforcer, not to mention the presence of strangers, which had to agitate Diesel, she'd still fallen asleep with her head on his shoulder. A light touch of his hand on her thigh awoke her. The thin gray ribbon of light appearing in the crevice of the truck's back panels promised the darkness was no longer so deep or so absolute.

"We're taking a break," he told her, with a squeeze to her thigh.

Rubbing a hand over her face, she blinked and glanced around the truck bed. "How long was I out?"

"About ten hours," he said gently, then pressed a bottle of water into her hands.

Ten hours? Her neck ached then cracked as she straightened. The tepid water soothed her parched throat. The other wolves all appeared to be exactly where she'd left them. The truck ceased moving and the doors slammed shut as Dallas and Luc left the cab, a moment later the canvas pulled away to reveal Dallas.

"We're trading the truck here. We'll go overland for the next two hundred miles. It's a hard run, so pack your things tight and we'll shoulder them." She didn't wait for their response and turned heel to walk away. Julian abandoned them immediately…though from the way he leapt from the truck, Ranae didn't think it had anything to do with her or the other wolves company.

Neither Trask nor Etienne seemed in any great hurry to follow, either.

"Cowards," Diesel said to them, though the insult lacked any heat and carried an element of humor. He rose, then extended his hand to her. "Let's go shield them from the battling wolves."

Ranae laughed, the teasing on Diesel's part welcome. They jumped down together. The truck was parked in a desolate little parking lot that was more a broken down cow pasture than actual lot. Some gravel remained visible through the winter dried grass, but if there had been a structure, it too had been reclaimed by the land.

Fingers twined with Diesel's, she studied the area. A road ribboned through the fields, winding up and down the hills to vanish over a rise. Beyond the yellow grass verge were woods, deep, thick and foreign.

Scents of moss, bear, and more touched her nose. Above, gray clouds hung low, muting the light. But at least there was light. Trask busied himself stripping and shoving his clothes into a body pack. Hunters all carried them when on patrol. In most territories they had clothing caches, places they could find fresh clothes should they find themselves without.

Deep in foreign, likely hostile, territory? No, they needed to have their clothes. Diesel guided her around the truck until they were away from the others. When he slid his hand to cup her cheek, she raised her gaze to meet his.

"Does this mean you've forgiven me?" The worry slipped out, but she didn't regret the honesty.

"Yes," he said, pressing his forehead to hers. "I won't ever like you going into danger."

"Right back atcha." Frankly, the last place she wanted him to be was thousands of miles from his pack in the middle of a territory she half-believed populated by real boogeymen, brutal wolves without conscience or remorse.

The corners of his mouth curved. "I also appreciate a fine tactic when played well. Involving the other Alphas meant you came at me sideways, and you didn't need my permission to do it." A generous helping of pleasure removed any sting from the comment. It damn near sounded like a compliment.

"I'm not sorry I did it," she admitted. "I'm only sorry that I didn't take the time to fight with you on the subject first, because let's face it, it would have been a fight."

"Absolutely." He stroked her cheek. On the other side of the truck, the other wolves shifted. The sounds rippled seeming to echo against the near silence of the woods. They could have been a million miles from anywhere. "But don't apologize for your success. Even furious with you, I want no one else."

The admission sent her belly fluttering again. Kissing his palm lightly, she gripped his hand then rose to press her lips to his. They didn't have time for more than a quick, fierce kiss, yet she reveled in the contact. "When we're done, and we return to the states. I have to go to Willow Bend."

His eyes darkened.

"I have to go first. I can't do what Linc did." Although his brother hadn't meant to offend Mason, she suspected—even though the Alpha couldn't punish the authority challenging action—he'd offended him anyway. "When he mated Sera, it ripped him out of our pack." It had hurt, and it had left an ache. Joy soon filled in the crevice created, but for those few moments... "I can't do that to my family or Mason. I won't." Swallowing once, she searched her soul, but didn't have to look far. Her wolf rubbed against the inside of her skin in agreement. "I need to declare to them in person, to seek Mason's permission."

"You don't need his approval." Diesel's tone solidified. "He can't deny a mating. No wolf—not even an Alpha—will stand between a mated pair."

"I know I don't *need* it. I know I could mate you right this moment. You would pull me from Willow Bend, and I would be yours—as mate, as pack…as everything." Shifting on her feet, she found herself almost wanting to drop her gaze but fought the inherent shyness in it. The way Diesel watched her, the vibrant love burning in his eyes, seemed to encompass the whole of her. "But I *want* his approval. I failed him when I lost control, when I attacked a packmate—when that attack ended up with Alexis bleeding because I cut her. I failed my family. I have worked so hard to make up for it, to prove my capabilities and my strengths not just to them…"

"…but to yourself." Understanding dawned, and he pulled her into a tight embrace. "Dove, you are worth everything to me. You are a fiery blade in the night, a breath of summer sunshine in darkest winter…you have my heart and my pledge." Releasing her, he pressed another kiss to her forehead. "If you need to go to Willow Bend, then you shall go, but when you come home, it will be to me."

The emotion clogged her, threatened to pull her under with the wealth of sweetness and depth. No one had ever looked at her the way he did. "Or you'll come get me?"

"Never doubt it."

"I have your word?"

"If you need to hear me say it, then I swear. I will come for you if you do not return to me."

Pleasure speared her belly, and her wolf released a deep sigh of profound relief. "That means you absolutely have to come home from this journey. You just gave me your word."

Delight bubbling through her, she retreated from him to strip out of her clothes and get them stowed. Diesel stared at her until she stood naked in front of him. Desire seemed to be a torch adding to his already incandescent gaze, and it left no room for the chilly air to touch her flesh.

"Dove? You may just be the cleverest wolf I've ever met."

"Maybe," she was already reaching for her wolf, but she couldn't help tweaking him once more. "Remember, it's no fun if I don't cause a little trouble."

As her fur sprouted and her body twisted, his laughter chased her through the change. It took him bare moments to strip, pack his clothes then follow her. They both stepped through their body duffels, then trotted around the truck to find the others.

With a sharp bark, Diesel gained their attention then shifted his toward the only other female with them. Dallas let out a small yip of acknowledgement, then pivoted and took off like a streak.

Like missiles fired from a weapon, their motley crew of wolves—one from each pack, an enforcer and a rogue lone wolf—shot after her into the dark and forbidding forest.

There's a sitcom in here somewhere…or a Joss Whedon series.

Snow Wolf

Chapter Sixteen

The trek through the forest took them right to the edge of the Siberian plateau. They stopped only for brief breaks, long enough to drink, catch their breath and then ran again. Though Dallas set a grueling pace, Diesel had no trouble keeping up with her nor did Julian. His cousin probably reveled in having the source of his discontent within his sights.

When Dallas called the last halt, they were still deep in the woods but the air carried to them scents of the city. Night draped their forest, leaving dense pockets of shadows around the bases of the tree. Overhead, the moon had near reached its zenith. Working toward full, its light shimmered through openings in the canopy. Dove flopped down, sides heaving.

She was not alone. The other wolves dropped in a loose circle. Everyone taking a much needed rest. Diesel flicked his ears, listening. The intensity of the night and lack of wind aided them in their stealth run. Two hundred miles in what was just under five hours had been a killer pace.

When Dallas began her shift. Julian rose and took position at her flank. Still panting by the time she reached her feet, Dallas opened her pack and began to shrug into her clothes. Her breath fogged in the much cooler air. Considering the heat rolling off Diesel in waves, he hadn't taken much notice of the external temperature. It was still warmer than his tundra.

Dressed, Dallas took a moment to pull out a water bottle, then she drained it. A minute later, she was pulling open a power bar. She ate it swiftly, not talking, then ate a second. Finally she drank another bottle of water, before she looked to Diesel. "I'm going in to find him for you."

Dove lifted her head, flicking her ears toward Dallas. Though the rest of their group showed similar signs of exhaustion, they focused on their rogue guide.

"It could take a couple of hours. The town is three miles to the west." She gave a jerk of her thumb. "If he is willing to leave the city to meet you here, we'll be back by dawn. If one hour past dawn and I'm not here, come ahead. Use your papers to enter." The rogue raked her fingers through her short, dark hair almost spiking it. "Word of advice? Don't enter as a group…stream in ones and twos. Absolutely no more than three. None of you smell like pack…well, almost none of you." She flicked a look to Dove then back to him.

Diesel opened his mouth and let his tongue loll in a bit of a wolf grin. Yes, he'd more than noticed his scent on his Dove. It was another reason he had stayed close to her.

"Once you're inside the city, head to the Krasnyy sector. It's just outside their inner ring. It's filled with clubs. You'll want to go to the Fioletovyy Luna." While she spoke, Julian shifted, as did Trask and Luc. Like Diesel and his Dove, Etienne was in no hurry. "Find the club, but don't bother to go in till evening. They don't open till the sun is down."

"Is it safe to build a fire?" Trask looked their

rogue guide, and seemed to be taking his cues from Diesel. Cassius had done well in sending the brutish, deadly seeming man. He understood his orders and obeyed then, he also seemed to accept Dallas' expertise.

"Yes," she told him as she tied her boots. "This close to the city, it's not unusual for some of the wolves to go for a roam or sleep rough. But…if military or others challenge you, and you don't speak Russian, just don't. Play the badass, go all silent and pissy, stare them down. There are two roaming volka tribes that come and go from Lebeninsk. They do not talk to outsiders, and they are known as vicious fighters when crossed. Since no one makes friends with them, if they think you are…they will avoid you."

"Good to know." Trask dressed as he spoke, using an economy of motion. "I'll gather some wood." He glanced at Etienne. "Up for a quick hunt? I can cook." Delta Crescent's second rose with a nod, and then the two vanished into the wood.

"And I suppose you speak fluent Russian." They were the first words Diesel had heard Julian utter in her direction since their unexpected reunion.

Dallas slid on jacket, sparing the Enforcer an unreadable look. "*YA ne mogu dazhe smotret' na vas bez slez.*"

Julian had dressed while she did. "You're not going alone."

"Oh, yes, I am." She rounded on him. "You're too annoying to go unnoticed, and I fit in here. You don't."

"If you think I'll allow it…"

Julian didn't get to complete the sentence. Dallas had knelt to stow her duffle then rose, a loose log in hand, and clocked Julian across the face. One moment the Enforcer was up, the next he hit the ground.

Luc surged to his feet, mouth open and his ears pinning as he looked from Dallas to the downed Enforcer and back again. Dove might have done the same, but Diesel covered her paw with his and she gave him a wide-eyed look before resuming her flop.

Though more than capable, Dove was smaller than the rest of them and had taken extra strides to keep up. He wanted her to rest before they walked into what could one long fight night.

Blowing out a breath, Dallas looked at the downed wolf at her feet and tossed the log away. "Sorry, I don't have time to debate this in committee." With a glance at Diesel, she said, "If this is to work, you know I need to go alone."

He did. With a bob of his head, he told her to go. She clenched a fist, then without another word left their moon and shadow patch. Luc sniffed at the downed Enforcer cautiously, then shook. Shrugging off his body duffel, Diesel shifted.

Dove tracked his movements with a flick of her ear, but she continued to rest, her panting becoming less pronounced. On his feet, Diesel crossed to his cousin and checked the goose egg beginning to form at his hairline. Testing the skull, he didn't find any sign of bone malformation.

"He'll heal," he said more for Dove's benefit than Luc's. "When he wakes, let me deal with him."

Neither Dove nor Luc seemed to have any

objection. He adjusted his position so he could keep watch over all of them. It would be a long night. Etienne and Trask returned within the hour, several decent sized rabbits and firewood in hand. It wasn't long before they had the meat spitted and cooking.

Luc shifted only when the food was ready, an easy grin on his face as he declared their efforts passable. Yet, he also took care with all the remnants of their meal, carrying it out to bury it. Like Diesel, none of the men ate until Dove had taken her fair portion and they saved another portion for the Enforcer. When he woke, he would need it.

Dove didn't shift, and Diesel didn't have to ask why. She listened to the forest around them, relying on her sharp senses to alert them to any potential threats…and if she stood naked in front of the rest, it would create another layer of tension. They were close, she'd all but said yes to him, but he didn't *know* these other wolves and one smart ass comment more from their Hudson River contingent and Brett would be minus a wolf.

They kept the fire low, and through unspoken agreement, Trask rose to take first watch with Luc keeping him company. Etienne checked the Enforcer, who still slept off his concussion, then they pulled a light insulated blanket over him so he could stay warm. The Delta Crescent second settled against his own thermal cover on the far side of the fire leaving Diesel sitting nearer to it and the Enforcer with his Dove sleeping against his thigh.

The warmth of her bracketed him, and though he could call none of the wolves with him his, he found himself admiring—albeit reluctantly—the choices the other Alphas had made. They worked well enough together. Diesel glanced at his cousin, then shook his head. Julian would be furious when he woke.

A movement against his thigh snagged his attention and he glanced at Dove to find her watching him. Her ear flicked toward Julian, then to him.

"He's still fine," Diesel told her in a sub-vocal tone, stroking a hand over her fur. He had the right to touch her, a right she'd given him. As he petted her, he removed bits of bark, dust, and other detritus she'd accumulated during the run. "He'll have a headache when he gets up, but it's just another in a long list of headaches he's had since he met her."

Curiosity rolled off Dove in waves, and Diesel swallowed a chuckle. With only the faint crackling of the wood and the steady sounds of breathing around them, he still listened for other movement in the woods, tested the air whenever a hint of a breeze stirred and maintained his vigilance. He could continue at this pace for another three days, then he would have to sleep.

Three days was enough to get in, then get out and get Dove away. In the meanwhile, her rest kept her fresh and combat ready.

"You want to know what she said to him?" He rubbed the line between her eyes and felt her relax further against him. To be alone with her anywhere but hostile territory bracketed by allied wolves he barely knew. "She said, I weep every time I look at you."

Dove whined, a low, soft sound.

"It's an insult and a curse," he told her. "I

would guess very much a truth for those two."
Shaking his head, he dismissed worry for Julian and
Dallas. They were very much adults and very set in
their ways. "Sleep my Dove. We have much to do
tomorrow."

The first step in ending foreign aggression so
they could go home and he could claim his mate.

Finally.

Lebeninsk was a far cry from the ugly city
she'd been expecting. Though, truth be told, Ranae
had no idea why she thought it would be dark and
decrepit. The roads into and out of the city were
monitored, and industrial warehouses sat on the
outskirts. Walking in didn't earn them any special
attention. They'd followed Dallas' direction when
sunrise came and went without her appearance.

They broke into three groups, with Etienne
electing to stay behind with Julian. The wolf hadn't
woken. Cold cocked he might have been, but the
Chief Enforcer would have a hard time living down
that story. To that end, Diesel commanded the word
of the wolves present to never share the tale—even
with their Alphas.

She and Diesel walked in hand in hand, just two
lovers returning from a long hunt. No one gave them
a second look. The guards on the road challenged
them, and Diesel didn't speak though his stare had the
two men gripping their guns a little tighter even as
they gave them more space. When they'd backed
down, Diesel handed them their papers. The men
barely looked at them before waving them inward.

Something to be said about Alphas, humans

didn't want to mess with one even if they had no idea who or what they were. The military presence ended a mile outside of the city, though they seemingly covered all the access points. Vehicles trickled in, a couple of motorbikes, but the majority of those entering arrived as she and Diesel did—on foot with no luggage.

The town itself mingled old and new worlds effortlessly from paved streets giving way to cobblestone to ancient buildings with their red facings to two new sprawling condominium complexes. Apartments stacked over shops, and though it was early and the air held the promise of snow, wolves by the hundreds began the process of opening their doors for business.

Diesel didn't seem to choose any one particular direction. They meandered through the town, as though in no great hurry to arrive at their destination. In fact, at one small coffee house, he guided her to a table and left her to sit with her back to a wall. It gave her a premium view of all on approach. The doors to the shop had been left open, and rich scents of dark roasted coffees, brewed tea, and even grilling sausage teased her senses.

It had been a long time since they'd eaten the rabbit. She'd also burned more than her fare share of calories on the run. Diesel approached the counter and ordered, in fluent Russian, his voice blending into the symphony of foreign sounds around her—a deep bass which could not be ignored.

When he returned, he carried two large mugs of hot tea laced with sugar and lemon, as well as an oversized plate with bread layered by slabs of sausage and cheese. Her stomach growled at the scent and she grinned at him. He scanned the area, moving his chair until he sat immediately next to her and his back was also to the wall of the shop.

Saying nothing, they tucked into the food, each devouring two of the breakfast breads. The sausage had a spice to it she couldn't identify, and left a pleasant burn on her tongue. She washed away the last bite with a deep drink of the tea. It retained its heat, the strength a welcome respite with its hint of sweetness from the sugar lifted by the sharp tart of the lemon.

Diesel nodded to a street on their right, then pressed his lips close to her ear. "We're near the Krasnyy sector, the club she told us to go to is two streets over. It's closed at this time of day." He must have obtained directions inside.

Did he plan on waiting for it to be open? Before she could ask, a figure striding toward them from the direction he'd indicated arrested her attention. Most of the wolves coming and going, crossing the street, were just that. Wolves going about their business, but the one heading toward them seemed much more. Power radiated from him, and the wolves in his path cleared away like water breaking for a stone.

Placing her hand on Diesel's thigh, she gave him a light squeeze of warning. She needn't have bothered, he'd already noticed and despite the need to keep a low profile, he locked gazes with the other.

Energy sizzled over her senses, rising aggression as power collided with power. Whoever their visitor was, he was an Alpha. Diesel rose, unfolding from his chair with a predatory grace as the man crossed the street. As tall as Diesel, and dark where Diesel was blond, the wolf didn't give her a second glance. All of his attention locked on the Alpha at her side.

Torn between rising to defend her mate, and understanding she had no place in the wordless communication passing between the two Alphas, she did her best to stay still but aware. Transferring her gaze from the drama playing out between them, she studied their surroundings. What wolves had been in the area had all vacated it. Even those in the shop behind her had gone quiet.

No one wanted the Alphas to notice them.

The man spoke first, his voice a low rumbling growl as though he didn't waste more energy on speaking than absolutely necessary. Diesel responded in kind. *Oh, why the hell didn't I study Russian at school?* She'd taken Spanish and paid exactly enough attention to get a passing grade, doing the bare minimum necessary and then promptly forgetting it all.

Another long, drawn out silence left her wanting to claw something when a smile suddenly split across the local Alpha's grim expression. He offered a hand and Diesel accepted it. They shook, hugged once then clapped each other on the shoulder.

The two men sat at the same time, the foreigner taking a chair that put his back to the road. A woman exited the shop and delivered more hot tea without looking at any of them, then cleared away their plates and vanishing back inside.

"Dove," Diesel said. "This ugly bastard is Leonid Petrov."

"Ugly?" Leonid said with a booming bear laugh. "Who are you calling ugly you thin pasty-skinned shank?"

Since Diesel only grinned at the remark, Ranae let herself relax a fraction.

Leonid spared her a brief look. "What he does not tell you is that we are cousins, and he has sent a devilish woman to heckle me from my bed for this meeting."

So that was where Dallas had gone.

"No, I suppose he didn't mention it." It was the best she could come up with. One hard and fast lesson she'd learned over the years—when dealing with dominants, especially those more dominant than her, was don't play the game unless aware of all the rules.

"Cagey. I like her," Leonid said, then took a long swallow of his tea. His friendly demeanor waxed to a fiercer one. "How much would you take for her?"

"You can't afford it," Diesel's tone remained mild.

"I don't know Maxim, I have much money and many land deals. Lebeninsk is very profitable for family. How much?"

"Your head and your balls. Are you willing to part with them?" A very real promise of violence lurked in those words. Ranae had little use for being bartered about, but she had to admit, Diesel's cutthroat attitude really did it for her.

Instead of being offended, Leonid appeared to mull the idea and rubbed his chin. Then with another glance at her, he offered an apologetic smile. "I'm sorry, pretty wolf, but you are not worth stealing away for my balls."

"Not a problem," she replied in the same levity. "It wouldn't have ended well for you, anyway."

Leonid let out another boom of laughter and slapped his hand to the table. Their drinks jumped, but even Diesel's proprietary smile held elements of humor.

"And enough foreplay because you are in a hurry. Your gifts were received, Maxim, and not all were so amused by your thoughtful reminder that you've already claimed North America."

It took real effort for her not to gape at the statement, but Diesel merely shrugged. "Apparently they were also not paying attention."

"Eh, what can you do? Some wolves, they need a firm hand and others, they need their brains bashed in. These wolves harassing you…Alexandrovich has placed a bounty on them in Moscow. The word is already being spread. The Volchitsa will be hunted in Russia. This may not be so good for you."

"No," Diesel agreed, stretching his legs in front of him. He settled a hand on her thigh, and she relaxed further at the contact. If he wasn't worried, then she would still be watchful but not paranoid.

The street around them remained far too quiet for her peace of mind. Maybe it was the presence of two Alphas or perhaps it was simply a normal occurrence. Either way, it put her teeth on edge.

"If they are hunted here, it will drive them into other territories. We know this and I think Alexandrovich is annoyed that you did not contact him privately. Then again, perhaps he simply wanted an excuse to get rid of the riff raff. He does not talk to me of these things."

"Are they in your city?" Nothing friendly lived in Diesel's inquiry.

"If I were to answer you, cousin, you would feel compelled to hunt them and spill their blood. My public works budget is limited, so I would prefer to not scare the people with gory stains on the stone." Leonid took a sip of his tea. "To that end, I must advise you to leave as quietly as you arrived."

"If I don't?"

"Maxim, Maxim, Maxim." Was that Diesel's name before he'd taken Diesel? "You are not in your North America here. This is my city...my rules. I have given you the courtesy of asking you nicely. It is what one does for family. Do not make me ask you not so nicely."

Diesel's response came in Russian, but she didn't need to know the words to read the other man's irritation at it. He answered, then began a rapid fire exchange she couldn't follow, but the aggression which swept through them earlier amped higher.

Her wolf raked claws along the inside of her skin. It wanted out. More it wanted to shift positions so she could shield Diesel's exposed side. Something pulled at her attention and she jerked her head around to gaze at the surrounding buildings. She'd noticed something, a movement? A flash of light?

Ignoring the debate between the two men, she studied the area. What the hell had she noticed? Another flash, and she saw the extended barrel just peeking over the edge of a building.

Instinct kicked in even as the first pop exploded the glass behind her. She hit Diesel sideways and took the table with them. They rolled onto the pavement as more bullets sprayed the area. Stone chipped and flew. More glass shattered. A thunk slammed into the ground right next to her head then rebounded and a streak sliced across her cheek.

Hot blood seemed to scald her cool cheeks, then she was on her feet. Diesel hauled her around the building with him and Leonid.

"So, maybe I help you find the bastards and gut them in the square," Leonid said, then a scream ended the rain of bullets and a crash ended with a sickening splat. Diesel braced her with one hand as he glanced back, then she followed him around the corner.

A wolf lay in the street, the contortions of his body promising he was already dead. Above on the rooftop, Trask leaned against the stone, his expression grim. A few feet away on another rooftop, Etienne pointed two fingers at his eyes, then east.

"We will collect your other female on our way," Leonid pulled a phone from one pocket and a handkerchief from another. When he offered the second to her, she raised her eyebrows. "You're bleeding, *milaya devushka.*"

Diesel took it, then pressed the cloth to her cheek. "A scratch," he told her. "Excellent reaction time."

Not excellent enough. She should have located the threat before he fired. Still, Diesel's compliment warned her.

"Come," Leonid said, the phone still to his ear. "I've called a healer to check on those in the shop. Let us be quick about this." He jerked his head to the side and Diesel touched a hand to her lower back so she would precede him. They left the body in the street. So used to having Diesel take her hand, she almost paused to reach for his. It would have to wait; they weren't on a casual stroll anymore.

No, they were hunting.

Snow Wolf

Chapter Seventeen

Sending Dallas ahead to roust Leonid proved an excellent plan. His cousin could be unpredictable. A hothead with a big heart and a vicious temper he could turn on a dime and he hated to owe anyone anything. Less, he hated to be asked to do a favor. His presence at the scene of an attack, however, earned the Volchitsa one more enemy.

In this case, the enemy of his enemy made a damn fine ally who knew the city and its inhabitants. The cut on Dove's cheek angered him, but her swift, fierce response pleased him. Even now, she strode ahead of him, a warrior on her way to battle. She had no idea where they were going, nor what awaited them, yet she took him at his word and followed his instructions. The sway of her hips drew his gaze to her ass, and what a fine ass she possessed. Muscled and athletic, she radiated confidence and sensuality. Both attracted him. Yet it was the way she worked around him, tried to think through it all

To be done with everything so he could claim her once and for all. He wanted her returned to Tikaani, her training continued with Grinder and where he could spend his nights learning her every curve, and every day showing her his pack and the wonders of his land.

"If the goal is to drive me crazy," she murmured over her shoulder. "You're succeeding."

"Good." It hadn't been his intention, but he appreciated knowing he affected her every bit as much as she affected him. They reached the Krasnyy sector easily enough. More wolves appeared, and they were not mere bystanders but guards, or at least some of them were.

"Pathetic." Leonid laughed at the men, as he passed more than one sitting or leaning disheveled and bloody.

Above Trask and Etienne tracked them, but they didn't join them at ground level. Each wolf had a part to play and theirs was simply to provide backup and support should he require it.

Killing the sniper proved he'd required it.

At the entryway to the club, Dove halted and shot him a glance. He read the question in her eyes and nodded. He appreciated the gesture, but he wanted her inside with him. They fought better together than apart.

The interior featured standard lighting, and harbored no shadows for possible attacks to lunge at them. Inside, Leonid stripped off his coat as he walked toward a table where Dallas rested with her feet up and a glass in her hands. In addition to her bloody and barked knuckles, she had a swelling black eye, bloody nostrils and a split lip.

"Diesel, the next time you ask me for a favor, I'm going to remember this." She grinned, then tossed back the drink. "Leo, your men suck."

"So I see." If the Alpha was upset, he didn't act it. Instead he rolled up his sleeves and gestured to the far wall. "Bring me the Volchitsa scum." The last he delivered in Russian.

Grabbing a chair from one of the other tables, Diesel swung it over so his Dove could sit. Though

Dallas wasn't his to protect, she had come to his assistance at personal risk to herself. "Do you require anything?"

"Nope," she said, pouring herself another drink. "I beat the shit out of all of them myself."

Leo scowled. "And now you drink my best vodka."

"You're lucky I didn't bust all your bottles of good vodka, Leo." Then her grim expression cooled to something friendlier. "But we've known each other a long time, so I decided to drink it instead."

"We shall all drink vodka," Leo stated, then clapped his hands together when his wolves returned with four prisoners, all in chains, and all looking not the worse for wear.

"They're children," Diesel said, disgust curling for through him.

"They are Volchitsa," Leo growled. "They come here for their pack. They steal, they take it away. Sometimes they come to fly other places. Like this one…" He pointed to the tallest of the four. "He was taken at airport with ticket for Australia. Russian wolves do not go to Australia. Most likely, he take another flight."

Dove leaned forward, staring at the captives. None of them tried to meet their eyes, or growled—or showed any real signs of resistance. They looked…defeated.

"How long have you held them?"

"Since you send me such a lovely tongue kept cold in a box."

Good to know the express shipping option worked. Diesel folded his arms and stared at the teens. If any of them were a day over eighteen, he'd eat his shirt. Their age troubled his Dove. Kids should never be in the middle of a war, yet inevitably it seemed to be where they always ended up.

"Have you questioned them?"

Leo spared him a dour look, then in Russian asked, "What do you want to know from them?"

"What do they know about the wolves sent to the U.S.—their destination and their goals?"

One of the boys in the middle jerked a little at the question, somewhere in his midteens if Diesel were to judge, the kid fidgeted.

"So, I think maybe that one wants to answer your question." Leonid used a sub vocal tone, one too low to carry to the prisoners. With a wave of his hand, and a slight increase in his voice, he ordered, "Bring us that one."

The kid struggled as soon as they dragged him forward. Dallas for all her causal posed, ceased drinking and Dove curled her hands into fists.

"If you tell us a lie, I will kill one of your friends," Leonid's tone made the statement a fact not a threat. "If you refuse to answer, I will kill one of your friends. Do you understand?"

Wide eyed, the kid nodded jerkily.

"Good. Who sent you to Lebeninsk?"

Though he'd much rather handle the interrogation, he was still a guest of Leo's and their very thin blood relationship only gained him so much leeway.

"Dominik." The boy answered, pointing to the older of the four. The wolf in question snarled at him.

"So, he sent you here, why is he here?" To give

Leo credit, he honed right in on a way to ask the kid for more information which condemned only one of his associates.

"To make deals, to buy information, sell information…" The kid shrugged. "I am just a runner. I take packages, I pick up packages. That is all. I promise." Not one ounce of lie clung to him. Terrified, the kid seemed determined to cooperate.

Leo nodded, approaching the kid. "Who is your Alpha?"

The youth licked his lips and swallowed once before saying, "We are Volchitsa. We are not allowed an Alpha."

With a swift strike, Leonid backhanded the boy. Dove shot out of her chair, but Diesel clamped a hand on her shoulder and pulled her back against him rather than let her complete the lunge. Dallas' feet were no longer on the table, but she still held the bottle in her hand.

"Shh," Diesel said against her ear. "Their pack, their city, their rules." He disliked it intensely. Beating children served no purpose. He also didn't have a city of several thousand to deal with either.

"Not a lie," Leo said, his voice calm as though he hadn't struck the child. "But also not the answer to my question."

"Forgive me, sir." The boy's lower lip trembled. "If I answer you honestly, I tell you all Volchitsa have broken the law. If I tell you a lie, you will kill my friends. I have no answer I can give you."

Though they all spoke in Russian, his Dove didn't seem to have any trouble empathizing with the child's emotions. Even seeing the necessity of distance didn't assist Diesel in the matter.

"True…so I give it to you to decide, but you must choose." With his hands spread wide, Leonid eyed the boy. "You must choose now."

"Volchitsa," the youth said, his quavering voice gaining in strength and tempo. It was like watching the moment when a youth achieved adulthood. "Do not have an Alpha."

Leo nodded, and Diesel had to bite his tongue to keep from warning Dove to look away. The youngest of the four hit the floor, neck snapped. At least it was a merciful death.

Twice more Leonid asked the same question. Each time, the boy answered the same way. When all of his companions lay dead, he kept his chin high and his over bright eyes narrowed. Bravery—or foolhardiness—Diesel couldn't determine which held more sway.

"Leonid—whatever you are asking him, please don't ask it again." Dove said, her tense frame so rigid in Diesel's arms he worried she might snap in two.

The Lebeninsk Alpha paused to look at her. "You are right he will probably give me the same answer."

"Then would you mind asking him if he wants to live?"

Shrugging, Leo looked at the youth and said, "The very beautiful American wolf worries for you. Your lies make her heart weep. She wishes to know if you want to live."

For the first time since he'd been dragged forward, the boy looked at Dove briefly. He didn't disguise the naked curiosity in his expression. "Tell the American female to save her tears. I do not want them or need them. She should cry for her own, because the Volchitsa will have a home, even if we have to take it in blood." With a crack of his teeth, he spit something. Swinging Dove out of the way, some of the liquid spattered on his jacketed arm. It sizzled, but even as Diesel stripped off the jacket—Leo let out a roar.

Acid.

Dallas grabbed a pitcher off the table and sloshed it in Leo's face. The other wolves scrambled when she barked an order for more water. The boy didn't make it another step, his mouth burning and his face becoming a rictus of pain before he to, fell over and collapsed.

His heart ceased beating a moment later.

A wolf hurried over to Leo as Dallas poured more water onto his face. Diesel checked his Dove over but so no evidence that the acid touched her. Dropping his jacket on the floor, he hurried over to help brace the Alpha. He roared, his pain adding to his power.

Behind him, his Dove whispered, "What the fuck was that?"

The journey from Lebeninsk was far more sober than their venture inside. They also left knowing even less about their enemies than when they'd arrived, except whomever lead those wolves held such sway, that children would rather die than betray him. More horrified than she could begin to describe, Ranae walked hand in hand with Diesel. As when they'd entered the city, they left in ones or twos, though they gathered together once they hit the edge of the woods.

Dallas' injuries looked pretty bad but she waved off any concern. They'd filled Trask and Etienne in on what transpired inside the club. Four dead youths, an acid burned Alpha, and only a pain-filled oath that the Volchitsa would pay.

"I don't get it," Ranae said finally into the quiet. They'd walked for over an hour and no one shadowed their trail. Both Etienne and Trask had shifted, retraced their path and returned. They ranged around them, making sure nothing surprised them in the rapidly descending dark. "What the hell kind of pack believes in sacrificing kids?"

"A pack with nothing to lose," Dallas answered though Diesel squeezed Ranae's hand as though to offer comfort in the situation. "Volchitsa aren't a pack like at home or even like here in Lebeninsk. They're outsiders, roamers, they have no territory. They travel throughout, taking jobs and resources where they can until the locals run them off again. Occasionally they strike out for Europe or south to Asia, and now, to America."

"Why not merge with another pack here?" She still couldn't wrap her mind around the idea. Even when Toman hadn't let them go to A.J., he'd never have done the same to a child, had he? It truly baffled her.

"Because, they aren't wanted," Diesel told her, then touched a finger to her cheek. "We will clean this again and bandage it at the plane if it is not healed." The fact they would all have to shift and run back hadn't been lost on her either.

"They're children…"

"Sometimes they are children and sometimes they are far more mature than you realize, Dove. That young man in there made a choice, as did all the wolves with him. They knew Leo was capable of executing them, yet none gave him the information he requested."

She sighed, weary as hell. "That's fucked up."

"Yes it is," Dallas said. "When you run alone, and you don't have much, what alliances you do have are far more valuable. You never betray them."

"You sound like you admire what the kid did." Sure the lady was a lone wolf, but she'd not been born that way. She knew what a pack was like, what was important. Right?

"I admire his will and commitment. I think there were better ways out, but then my goal wasn't killing the Alpha of Lebeninsk." She shrugged. "They knew we were there and they didn't care about us. They were destabilizing the city, that was their plan or maybe it was simply their backup if they were caught. Either way, it's not our problem anymore."

With that, she increased her speed and strode ahead.

"I think she means that," Ranae said.

"She has a right to. I asked her for a favor, repayment on a very old debt. She did what I asked. Now we go home."

"Where Julian is probably going to try and kill her as soon as we're on the ground in Seattle." Ranae grimaced, and while she once believed strongly the law was the law, she was starting to get the feeling that nothing was ever what it appeared. Everything had mitigating shades of gray.

"Don't worry about Dallas, Dove." Diesel raised her hand to his lips and brushed a kiss to it. "She is quite skilled in looking after herself."

Eager to talk about anything that might wipe the images of dead and dying teens out of her mind, she stole a glance up at him. "Maxim?"

The Yukon Alpha gave her a faint smile. "The name my mother gave me when I was born. It is how Leonid knew me. Our fathers were cousins. We met for the first time when we were boys when my parents took me to Russia to meet some of my father's extended family. They were not rulers of Lebeninsk yet, nor was it entirely a wolf controlled city—close, but not fully. We stayed there a month one summer, then the following for four years, I spent a month every summer with them. My father insisted. He wanted me to know where I'd come from, how strong my blood was." An air of poignant melancholy clung to him. For his parents? His childhood? It didn't matter other than it made him sad.

"And you learned Russian." She wanted to ease the burden of his unhappiness, earn a smile from him.

"*Da*," he said with another of those small, very genuine smiles. "I did."

They found Luc and a now very awake, and very pissed off Julian at the camp. Dallas faced off against the much larger enforcer, her expression almost sanguine. Luc sauntered over to them.

"Please tell me to go ahead and run on back, hell, I'll swim, just don't leave me alone with those two anymore." The wolf shook his head. "Dallas is…just *damn.*"

"I heard that," she said, not looking away from Julian.

Diesel chuckled. "Cousin, leave her be. You couldn't go with her and you would have insisted."

Julian finally looked from Dallas to Diesel. His expression so frigid, it seemed a frown had permanently frozen to his features. Ranae covered her mouth, trying to smother the laughter bubbling up.

"She's a *rogue* and you let her just wander off and get…beaten up…while I was unconscious?"

Dallas released a snort of disgust. "Beaten up. I've had worse bruises after going cliff diving. Trust me, I don't need any of you to *save* me." Not content to leave the discussion there, Dallas sliced a hand through the air. "It will be night soon and the moon's already risen. If we shift and run now, it will be hard, but we can get back to the truck before dawn. If the Volchitsa are really making a play for Lebeninsk, we don't need to linger here."

"Agreed," Julian said, giving Ranae a start. "We go." Then he took Dallas by the arm and hauled her with him away from the rest. If he said anything further, it was far too quiet for Ranae to hear.

She was exhausted even if making a run for it sounded good.

"Eat," Diesel told her, pressing something into her hand. A napkin had been folded over a thick, sweet bar of baklava. It smelled terrible and wonderful all at once. Not arguing, she took several bites. Luc had shifted, and he joined Trask and Etienne on their perimeter. While she ate, Diesel cleared away the signs of their makeshift camp, then pulled out his bag and hers to stow their clothes.

"If you were Maxim when you were a boy…when did you become Diesel?"

He stripped off his shirt, then looked at his arm. A faint red dot appeared on his flesh where the acid had hit the fabric. It had burned through quick enough to do a little damage. "After Amara faded, and roamed to join the wild packs, I made a point of looking after them. A fuel company decided they were going to build a pipeline through our lands, and drill. They had no approval, they were working…under the table…as it were. I made sure they found the work too hazardous for their health or their profits. The others began to call me Diesel, for the fuel." He shrugged. "It was a good enough name and it helped for a time to become that person, the one who had not lost his mate."

A dense, well of sympathy opened within her. She ached for him. "I'm sorry you lost her."

"As am I." He didn't hide his emotions or the cost. "I have been alone a long time, Dove. I never thought I would find another."

Until her. He didn't have to say it.

"Are you done?" He pointed to the food when she didn't reply immediately.

"Yeah, I am."

"Then shift. We have a long run."

Even after she slipped into her wolf form and had her duffel snug to her body, she couldn't stop thinking of all the years he'd served as Alpha without his mate, all the years he'd taken care of his people and yet he'd been alone. Who took care of him?

His pack. Her wolf didn't hesitate in the

answer. They'd done everything for him they could, loved him, held him to them, and needed him. They'd given him purpose.

We can give him joy.

The absolute certainty within her wolf bolstered her own faith and her speed. Even when she wanted a break all she had to do was brush up against Diesel to remind herself exactly what and who she ran for. Tapping into a fresh reserve, she increased her speed.

By the time they reached the truck, she was dragging and didn't even pretend to try and shift as the others took stretched, then gradually regained their human form. Instead, she guarded Diesel until he stood.

Weariness didn't loosen its hold on her. Diesel spared her a look as he pulled on his jeans. Dressed, he reached for her and pulled her into his arms. With one leap he climbed into the truck. Someone pulled down a blanket, then another and he made a pallet for her. When Diesel set her in it, she lowered her head to her front paws.

Resting his hand on her head, he murmured. "I have you. You're safe," and that was all it took. She slept.

She woke to Diesel carrying her, her head tucked against his shoulder. Thankfully, she was dressed, but irritation stretched her along her nerves until she spied the plane in the distance.

"You didn't sleep, did you?" she demanded of him.

The cool look he gave her had her almost regretting the snapped words. Almost. "Not yet."

He hadn't on the plane ride, during the ride in

the truck, and barely at all in the woods. In fact, she couldn't recall him sleeping since they left the Yukon. The man needed sleep, too.

"Shh, Dove," he kissed her forehead as he approached the plane steps. The small airport was quiet and the Asian wolves who'd greeted them on arrival, stood waiting for them once more.

"Put me down a minute before we get on board," she amended her tone. She'd never been a morning person, much less any kind of person before coffee. Her whole body ached, and she must have been deeply asleep if she reverted while out. For certain it had been Diesel who dressed her because he wouldn't have allowed anyone else.

"Of course." He paused to set her on her feet. With one hand, he touched two fingers to her cheek. "It's healed mostly, a little pink. More food and rest, and another shift and it will be gone all together."

"It was just a ricochet." It stung when it happened, and had been messy, nothing more.

"Good."

Dallas cleared her throat, and like Diesel, she looked weary as hell. Her bruises only looked nominally better since her shift. "Job is done."

He inclined his head. "The job is done. Thank you."

She nodded, then flicked a look toward Julian who stood like a stone statue at the plane door. "He's really pissed."

"He'll get over it." Diesel shrugged. "Or he won't…"

"…yeah, but now I feel bad so I'm going to throw the dog a bone." She raised her hand, palm forward. "I'll be in Kansas City in three weeks to go to a comic book convention. Tag, you're it."

Then she was gone. The speed with which she moved startled Ranae and she jerked her head right, then left and scanned the area. "Holy shit…"

"She's quick," Diesel grinned, but his gaze rested on Julian and the smile didn't quite reach his eyes.

"Quick? I didn't know we could move that fast." And she knew how fast wolves were, it was as though Dallas could move between the blinks. "I feel bad about leaving her."

"Don't," he said, cupping her elbow and turning her toward the plane. "Dallas can take care of herself."

At the plane entrance, Julian met Diesel's gaze and shook his head, then climbed aboard.

"And that is a very unhappy man." She pursed her lips. The one upside to the plane was it was comfortable versus the tin can she'd flown up to Alaska in. The downside, the Enforcer released a lot of aggression in a small space. "Are you sure we have to fly back with him?"

"We'll be fine. We're all tired, and a little cranky."

"Speak for yourself," she patted his arm before beginning the short climb up the steps. "I'm a lot cranky."

The scent of fresh coffee, orange juice, danishes, bacon, and eggs met her inside the cabin. The other wolves had already dropped into their seats and dug into the food. They'd left a wider sofa in the back open, so she headed toward it with Diesel right behind her.

No sooner had they taken their seats than the crew brought them food. Like the others, she and Diesel ate without saying anything. Her abdomen actually ached, and her stomach felt hollow.

Soon as the first meals cleared away, the pilot announced they would be taking off. The lights in the cabin dimmed, plunging them into a gray darkness. Diesel closed his hand over hers and she settled her head against his shoulder. Oddly, the panic she'd come to expect didn't put on an appearance.

Maybe she was just too damn tired to be scared.

Or maybe watching a child choose death rather than reveal anything about his pack... There were more monsters in the world than just what existed in the dark.

One by one the other wolves dropped off. Too tired to worry about what each other was doing, the low snores filled the dark. Next to her, Diesel didn't sleep. He was thinking, she could practically feel it. The tense energy licked over her skin.

Sliding her hand along his arm, she teased her nails along his nape. Light, gentle pets until she felt the muscles in his neck begin to unlock. When he continued to relax, she reached for his seatbelt and unclicked it, then patted her lap. "Lie down a bit."

"I'm fine, Dove."

"I know you are, but I need to take care of you for a change." The request did what no amount of coaxing or orders would manage. He relented, then shifted his weight until he could sprawl on the sofa, his feet propped on the end. With his head in her lap, she began to massage his temples then stroke her fingers through his hair. She alternated the slow and smooth movements until the last of the wildness batting against her ceased and his soft breathing drifted up to her ears.

She doubted he would sleep deeply or for long, but whatever minutes she could give him. She would.

Almost eleven hours later, she had lost all the feeling in her legs and her fingers were numb, but the look of surprise then pleasure in his eyes when he woke to see her looking down at him made it all worth it.

He looked almost embarrassed, then even more pleased. When he slipped his hand around her nape and pulled her down for a kiss, she savored the sensuous taste of him and to hell with their audience.

The last hour of the flight they went over the trip, what they'd learned and what needed to go back to the other Alphas. Julian said nothing. His attention somewhere else.

Maybe on someone else.

It wasn't until Etienne offered to give her a ride back to Willow Bend after they landed that it struck her. It was time to say goodbye.

Everything in her system resisted the idea. When the others trickled out while Etienne went to deal with issues for refueling the plane and prepping it for further travel, she was left alone with Diesel.

"How will you get back to the Yukon?" Somehow, she suspected Julian would not be flying him.

"I'll manage," he traced the line of her cheek. "You'll know where I am."

A part of her wanted to say, *Wait, I'll come*

with you. We'll go together. At the same time, she kept those words to herself. "I'm going to miss you."

"We'll work on your aim." It took a moment, then she laughed even as tears flooded her eyes.

"You made a funny."

"I did." Then he kissed her tenderly, a gentle brush of his lips to hers. "Fly home, my Dove, then come to me."

She was still trying to wring the tears out of her heart, when he exited the plane then he was gone. Torn between heartbroken and heartsick, she sank back onto the sofa.

In truth, she didn't *have* to go to Willow Bend. Intellectually, she knew that. She understood everything, but it didn't matter. She needed to go. She needed to tell Mason, face to face and her parents. It would be hard to say goodbye in person, but it would be better for all of them if she did it the right way.

She dug her phone out of her bag and stared at it. Less than ten days since she departed Seattle for the Yukon. *Ten days?*

It had been an eternity.

Chapter Eighteen

All through her uneventful flight home, she texted Mason, filled him in on the events in Russia. She edited some of the information—only those parts which were personal and private to Diesel. Two more skirmishes had happened...one in Delta Crescent and a second in Sutter Butte. Cassius had routed a pocket which had set up on his southern border.

Your brothers are both fine. The Delta Crescent attack was sloppy. They went after the Omega that's no longer there and ended up getting one really pissed off Hound. Ty and Claire were with Cassius, but neither were hurt.

Relief flooded her. So now all the packs had faced some type of attack, all except Willow Bend and maybe Three Rivers.

What about us? Have we seen anyone in Willow Bend?

Not yet. The addition of the word yet added a fresh layer of worry and guilt stabbed at her. She was a relatively young Hunter in the scheme of things, and losing her wouldn't hamper the pack's defenses much. Still, she was planning to leave them and it ate away at her. Was she being selfish? Hadn't that been why she'd been so angry with Claire? She'd chosen herself over pack?

Or she chose herself over Ty...is it the same thing to choose pack over mate? The whole idea made her sick. Etienne didn't disembark from the plane, the wolf needed to return home and she understood the desire. He promised to punch her brother for her when she gave him a kiss on the cheek.

Collin waited for her with a vehicle. He gave her a quick hug, dropped the keys into her hands and a bag of take out burgers before telling her to go home and don't report for duty for at least a week.

She was halfway back to town before she realized she wouldn't be reporting for duty at all. Everywhere she looked, she saw a place she had a memory. Trees she'd climbed, fields she'd run through, a dock where she'd had her first kiss. A bridge where she'd shoved the same wolf who'd kissed her off and into the water cause he'd gotten handsy.

Willow Bend was her home, her heart should be singing to return and it wasn't. She still loved it, the cozy shops where she was always likely to find a familiar face or Sexton's Grocery where the family who ran it knew her as well as her own.

Wiping a hand over her face, she brushed away the tears. Maybe her exhaustion ran deeper than she'd believed. She was getting all maudlin over whether Willow Bend felt like home or not. Turning onto her parents' street, she had to laugh. Her mother stood in the middle of it, with a giant sign in her hands. A banner stretched across the front of the house.

They all said welcome home. Wolves were all over the yard, and on the porch. Family. Friends. She parked the car and climbed out, well aware she stank of travel, and woods, dirt and blood. Then she was in her mother's arms. Claudia Buckley gripped her tight.

"You're nothing but skin and bones. Let's get

you fed." But she hugged her again, then Ranae's father had her, hugging her tight to him. Pride shone in his eyes when he stepped back.

Ranae pivoted a step, then A.J. swooped into her watery vision. He scooped her up and gave her a whirl of a hug. Then another. "You get three," he told her. "Since Ty and Linc aren't here to claim theirs."

"Put me down, you brute." But despite her words, she hugged him tighter.

"Hey," A.J. murmured against her ear. "You okay?"

"Yeah," she sniffed once. "Not going to ruin a party they're throwing for me."

"Oh, you think this party is for you?" A.J. leaned away. "They just found the banners to put up for Ty—ow." Ranae punched him in the shoulder, but he laughed, then hooked his arm around her neck and rubbed a hand to her head. It was so much like he would do to their brothers that she laughed alongside him. "Speaking of homecomings, brat…you made it just in time."

"For…" Before she could even finish the question, she heard the sharp cry of an infant and her heart did a little somersault. Then a second one joined the first. "Oh my God, they're here…twins?" She whirled on her brother.

A.J.'s grin couldn't be contained. "One boy, and one girl. Twins."

Squealing, she threw her duffel at him and raced up the stairs. The other wolves laughed and she waved to everyone on her way by. A.J. followed her, smugness rolling off him in waves. In his old bedroom, she found Vivian settled on the bed with a babe in her arms.

"Oh," Ranae whispered, captivated by the sight of her nursing her little one. She pressed two fingers to her lips. "How long?"

"Come in," Vivian gave her a tired smile, but one full of maternal delight. "A couple of days ago. It was really quick, I thought A.J. would have a heart attack."

Ranae crept deeper into the room and paused to look down at the baby sound asleep in the little crib. They were perfect.

"Don't talk about me like that, I was very diligent in handling everything—even your grip when you had to push." He rolled up his sleeves to show off the deep, but well on their way to healed claw marks on his forearms. With absolute care, he settled on the side of the bed and put his hand on the baby's head.

The mated couple locked gazes, lost in adoring each other and their babies. Ranae wanted to hold them, to stroke their tiny little heads. But she was so filthy.

"I'm going to go take a shower, then I'll come back and snuggle my niece and nephew." She crept out as quietly as she'd crept in, then walked down the hallway to the bedroom that had been hers her whole life. Nothing in the room had changed. It still had the big bed in the corner, the book shelves, a stack of mail waiting for her on the desk and an unopened package—probably a movie or a game she'd ordered. The quilt on the bed was one her mother had made her when she was still a teen.

Nothing in the room had changed, it was exactly the way she'd left it, yet it seemed so much smaller.

"You know it's okay, right?" A.J.'s quiet voice behind her pulled her around.

"What is?"

"Feeling out of place here, not really seeing it as your home anymore. It's okay."

"A.J. you were gone a lot longer than ten days, I don't get why…"

"…because when you know your mate, your world turns upside down and your priorities shift. You changed. Not the room, not the home and not us. You." He caught a lock of her hair and brushed it away from her forehead. "You've been growing up on us for years, I saw it more than they did. When you left here to go on this mission, you were an impetuous, determined Hunter trying to make her mark. The woman who came home? You know who you are now. You know what you want…and I think you know where you want to go."

"I thought it would be harder."

"Coming home? Or leaving?"

"Leaving. I'm sad. You and Vivian made those two perfect babies and I want to be here. I want to see them grow up and I won't be…and that's sad."

"You'll see my kids, don't you worry. They need to know their Aunty Ranae."

Everything in her vision shimmered, then she was in his arms, gripping him as fiercely as he held her. "I want that," she told him. "I feel like you came home and now we're all leaving."

"It's the way it's meant to be, squirt. We grow up. We find out mates. We build our lives and, whether it's here or somewhere else, we don't stop being family." Leaning back, he studied her and she could almost feel his approval radiating through him. "You did good kid, you've really owned it. Just do me one favor, okay?"

"Anything."

"Make sure they have internal plumbing before we visit."

Laughter burst through her tears, and she punched him again, but they were still laughing.

An hour later, after she'd showered, dressed in fresh clothes and cuddled her new niece and nephew, she descended the stairs to find the party had reached the coming and going portion.

Though there had been snow on the ground when she left, they were having an unexpectedly mild day with the sun shining down. Most of the wolves had taken advantage of the weather. Her father grilled, her mother tutted about moving from group to group. Kids ran and played, romping.

So many people, just hanging out, laughing, sharing stories—like so many other days when she'd been growing up. She found the coolers with the beers, and tugged one out. A part of her wanted to go crash for about thirty hours, then pack to head north. Before then, she needed to spend time with her pack, to let her parents then Mason know. Twisting off the cap of her bottle, she tipped it up for a drink then stopped. A distinct scent of snow on fur touched her nose.

She'd know that scent anywhere. Pivoting, she searched the gathering and caught sight of A.J. leaning against the porch with a shit-eating grin on his face. Not two feet away from him stood

Mason…and Diesel.

Mason whistled, and the chattering crowd quieted, everyone turning to face him. Diesel's beautiful blue eyes seemed to glow even at the distance she stood.

"Ranae Buckley," he called across the open yard. "My Dove, I told you I would come. I'm here to declare before your Alpha, your family, and your pack…you are my mate. I want you to be mine, forever and always…what say you?"

Pure, unfettered joy burst through her. "What are you doing here? I thought you were going home."

The entire gathering remained silent, though she heard more than one snicker at her questions.

"First off, *you* are my home." Diesel told her as he began to close the distance. "And someone once told me it's no fun if I don't cause a little trouble."

Relief and happiness twined together when he stopped in front of her. He was there. God, it hadn't been a whole day and she'd missed him horribly. "You know, I've heard that before."

"Good, and you cause a lot of trouble for me. Trouble I've enjoyed."

"I can be demanding."

"Your brother warned me." Diesel managed that with a straight face and she leaned sideways to glare at the brother in question. "No, Dove, not that one." He turned her around and she stared at Linc and Ty crossing over the yard from Claire's house. Laughter rippled through her and whoops went up all around. Giving A.J. another look because he'd been in on it, she glanced at Diesel again. "Family is important," he told her. "You needed to see all of them, you needed to know they were okay. I needed to make that happen for you."

"I love you," she announced, the words barely encompassing the depth of emotion she felt.

"Good. Now will you have me, my little Dove?"

"I—crap. Mason?" Had he taken care of that wrinkle, too?

"It's all good Ranae," her Alpha told her, his smile encouraging. "Not thrilled about losing you, but I am happy for you. You will always have a home with us and you have my blessing."

"And mine," A.J. called.

"And ours," her parents added.

"Mine, too, kiddo," Ty said as he reached them.

"Not mine." Linc threw in and she pinned a look on her brother. "Hey," he held up his hands. "Do you have any idea how long the flight is up there?" Then he gave her a faux punch with the light touch of his knuckles to her chin. "Of course you have our blessing, as long as that yahoo can make you happy and takes care of you."

"Oh, he will." Ty said, unequivocally. "We already had that discussion."

"Yes," Diesel seemed in agreement. "I told them if I hurt you I would let them beat me senseless."

"See, it's a good deal." Ty clapped Diesel on the shoulder, then kissed her cheek. "Put the man out of his misery, Ranae."

Sliding a sidelong look at Diesel, she shook her head but couldn't contain her grin. "You didn't fight this one fair."

"No," he said. "I learned from the cleverest wolf I know—Get everyone important on my side then present the plan."

"Wow...who says an old dog can't learn new tricks?"

"That sassy mouth of yours." He said the last sub vocal and she stepped right up to him, wrapped her arms around his neck and smiled slowly.

"You love it."

"I do, and I love you."

Gripping him tightly she rose on her tiptoes and surrendered to the pull she'd felt from him nearly from the beginning. "Yes."

His mouth closed over hers, fierce and possessive. Beyond them, she knew her family and the pack cheered, but she only had eyes for Diesel.

Mine. Hours after the party and festivities ended, Diesel swept Ranae away to the house Mason had him occupy during the council. He and Ranae barely made it in the door before they stripped each other out of their clothes. The first coupling was fast and fierce, on the stairs. The second they made it to the landing. By the third, he tumbled her into bed and as he thrust into her, he closed his teeth on the point where her shoulder and neck met.

The world shifted sideways. She locked her legs around him and sank her teeth into his shoulder. Their blood mingled, and their bodies twined as their souls danced. Radiance seemed to flood him, his Dove occupying all the shadowy places of loneliness.

Never alone.

Never again.

More, he felt the surge of pack and the welcome of his wolves calling down the ties that bound him to them together. His mate. His pack. His.

Sprawling together, he cuddled her to his chest and she traced a line across his pecs. "I still can't believe you came so fast. I thought…"

"That I would go home and wait patiently until I couldn't stand it anymore?" Even being with her over the last several days, he'd miss simply holding her, talking to her and teasing.

"Does it sound awful that I thought you would?"

"No, foolish maybe, but not awful." When she pinched him for his remark, he chuckled. "Dove, I told you that first night in the Yukon, you were mine."

"This is true," she scraped her teeth over his shoulder lightly. "You were all caveman, my woman, thud, mine."

Snorting, he smacked her on the ass. "I did not thud or go caveman."

"Yeah, you didn't see you." Not that she sounded like she minded. Sobering, she rolled onto her belly, sprawling atop him and gazing down. "How is Demon? Chowder? Have you been able to check with them at all?"

"They are fine," he said, rubbing his palm over the part of her ass he'd smacked. "I did talk to them. The fevers have broken and the infections are all clear. I also told them when I returned, my mate was coming with me if it took me a day, a week or a month to persuade you."

"You can't stay away from them that long," she

sounded positively scandalized.

"I know, it was my secret weapon if you wanted to make me work harder to win you." And one he'd been prepared to gamble, but she'd all but committed to him in Russia. Her need to declare her intentions, to own her actions before her pack, he'd also understood.

"I'm not going to get mad about that. I can't." Satisfaction rolled off her. "I almost got off the plane in Seattle, then wanted to turn around and leave as soon as we landed here. The farther away from you I thought I was, the worse it seemed."

"Never again," he promised.

"Never, though I admit I'm not sure I am keen on the idea of running wolf for months on end. I know it's how you've always done things…"

"So is change," he assured her. "We can change anything, Dove. We can change where we live, how we live, even our rituals and order. What I will never change is loving you."

"Good," she snuggled against him again. "I'm very possessive, and I never give up what's mine."

"Then we're perfect for each other." They quieted, drifting together. The next day would come soon enough, and he would meet with Mason and the other Alphas. They would settle on their course of action, then he would take his Dove home.

"Diesel?" Dove half-mumbled, her yawning whisper betraying her sleepy status.

"Yes, Dove?"

"What did you have to give Mason? Serafina gave him Tennessee for Linc. What did you give him for me?"

Diesel chuckled.

She opened her eyes, then lifted her head to study him. "What was it?"

The last thing he wanted to give anyone. "My phone number." When her eyes rounded, he chuckled again. "And my promise to always answer it when he called."

His Dove was worth far more than ignoring the rest of the world. For her—for their pack—yes, even he could change.

About the Author

National bestselling author, Heather Long, likes long walks in the park, science fiction, superheroes, Marines, and men who aren't douche bags. Her books are filled with heroes and heroines tangled in romance as hot as Texas summertime. From paranormal historical westerns to contemporary military romance, Heather might switch genres, but one thing is true in all of her stories—her characters drive the books. When she's not wrangling her menagerie of animals, she devotes her time to family and friends she considers family. She believes if you like your heroes so real you could lick the grit off their chest, and your heroines so likable, you're sure you've been friends with women just like them, you'll enjoy her worlds as much as she does.

www.heatherlong.net

Also by Heather Long

Always a Marine
Once Her Man, Always Her Man
Retreat Hell! She Just Got Here
Tell It to the Marine
Proud to Serve Her
Her Marine
No Regrets, No Surrender
The Marine Cowboy
The Two and the Proud
A Marine and a Gentleman
Combat Barbie
Whiskey Tango Foxtrot
What Part of Marine Don't You Understand?
A Marine Affair
Marine Ever After
Marine in the Wind
Marine with Benefits
A Marine of Plenty
A Candle for a Marine
Marine under the Mistletoe
Have Yourself a Marine Christmas
Lest Old Marines Be Forgot
Her Marine Bodyguard

Elite Metal

Pure Copper
Target: Tungsten

Fevered Hearts

Marshal of Hel Dorado
Brave are the Lonely
Micah & Mrs. Miller
A Fistful of Dreams
Raising Kane
Wanted: Fevered or Alive
Wild and Fevered
The Quick & The Fevered

Going Royal
Some Like It Royal

Some Like It Scandalous
Some Like It Deadly
Some Like it Secret

Mongrels
Mongrels, Mischief & Mayhem

Soulgirls
Into the Spotlight
Taking the Stage
Waiting in the Wings
Playing Against Type
Behind the Curtain

Wolves of Willow Bend
Wolf at Law
Wolf Bite
Caged Wolf
Wolf Claim
Wolf Next Door
Rogue Wolf
Bayou Wolf
Untamed Wolf
Wolf with Benefits
River Wolf
Single Wicked Wolf
Desert Wolf